EYES
TIGHT
SHUT

BOOKS BY D.K. HOOD

Where Hidden Souls Lie

A Song for the Dead

D.K. HOOD

EYES TIGHT SHUT

Bookouture

Published by Bookouture in 2024

An imprint of Storyfire Ltd.
Carmelite House
50 Victoria Embankment
London EC4Y 0DZ

www.bookouture.com

ISBN: 978-1-83525-283-3
eBook ISBN: 978-1-83525-282-6

To Charlotte Hession, a ray of sunshine, who always makes me smile.

PROLOGUE
THURSDAY

I'm going to kill her. The need burns, twitching my fingers and racing my heart, and it's taking all my patience to just enjoy the moment—that special time between the buildup and the kill. A twilight time much like that floating feeling before going to sleep or waking up snug in your bed. That's how it feels in the seconds before I kill. I'm relaxed and not crazed like some would imagine. I'm patient, like a wild animal hunting its prey. The right moment will come and when it does, I'll strike and someone will die.

It hadn't taken long to seduce her. Lonely women are easy to find. They work and go to an empty home each night, have few friends, and need to work long hours to pay the bills. There are some who've been through nasty divorces, some who don't trust men—until they meet me. You see, I'm a nice guy. I look good and know how to charm the skin off a snake. I've had practice. Charm comes naturally to me, so no one ever suspects I'm a threat.

I met Dakota Slade at the general store, working at the counter. A quiet woman, mid-twenties, with a face you'd forget in a second. My "confused guy looking for something" gets them every time. The moment I made contact I isolated her by taking her from behind the counter. I asked her advice, became more confused, and after leaving with a few purchases returned the next day, and referred to her by name as if we were old friends. I asked her advice about setting up a home in Black Rock Falls. Acting dumb sometimes works wonders, and rather than leave me all alone and confused, she accepted my invitation to lunch in the park to talk more, even though outside was freezing and snow was forecast. You see, the park is "safe" for women like Dakota. It's not a date but a "get to know you better" situation. It always works and now here I am standing on her front porch after accepting an invitation to watch my favorite show with her. She opens the door and I smile. "My, you look pretty enough to make a grown man cry."

"You say the nicest things." Dakota stands to one side, holding the door wide. "Come in out of the cold."

No smell of home-cooked food greets me as I check out the neat home. The furniture is dated. The cushions on the sofa yawn at the base. The thick brocade covering is damaged in places as if a cat had sharpened its claws there at one time. I don't smell a cat, but a hint of perfume lingers in the air. Maybe Dakota used an air freshener to remove the old-house smell. The rug in front of the fire is new and its bright colors make the rest of the decor appear dreary and tired. There's a flat screen in the family room and she urges me to sit on the sofa, but I shrug and just look at her. "I feel stupid coming here to ask you to watch a show. My stuff should arrive soon, but you know how it is when you have a favorite show. You can't wait to watch the next episode, right?"

"It's my favorite show too." Dakota smiles shyly at me. "I'll enjoy your company."

I don't want to touch anything, least of all sit on the filthy sofa. I meet her eyes. They are uncertain and she tries to avoid my gaze. "You've been so kind to me. How about I cook you a fine dinner when I get settled?" I give her my best smile and lower my lashes. They all fall for that one. It makes me look shy.

"That would be very nice, but I don't date." Her gaze moved over me and she tensed. Suddenly I was a threat. She looked at her hands. "Can we just be friends?"

Why did they always do that? I stare at her. Her refusal wakes me from my twilight slumber. The time is now. I can already see her dead. Her sightless eyes watching an endless stream of reruns. Will anyone even find her body? I try to keep the hunger to kill from my expression and nod. "I understand." I look past her and wave toward the door. "Mind if I use your bathroom?"

"Sure, it's the first door along the passageway." Dakota turns on the TV and looks at me over one shoulder. "Don't take long. The show is about to start."

As she turns her attention to the screen, I walk behind the sofa. The urge to kill shoots through my veins in an explosive jolt. My lips tug back into a smile as I step into my reality. My hand closes around the handle of my weapon. Silent but deadly. "Yeah, it sure is."

ONE

FRIDAY

It was hard to believe that Thanksgiving was just around the corner, and Jenna had already made a list of things that needed doing. The medical examiner, Dr. Shane Wolfe, and his family; agents Jo and Carter; and Deputy Rio and his brother and sister always came to Thanksgiving dinner at the ranch. This year, Tauri asked if Atohi Blackhawk could join them, and to Jenna's delight, Blackhawk had agreed. She peered out of the window, checking the gray sky for snow. The last couple of weeks had been quiet in the office and she welcomed a break after Halloween, although a past sting operation run by the Snake-skin Gully field office had dragged her husband and ex-special forces operative, Deputy David Kane, into a dangerous situation. His weapons expertise had made him the perfect choice to impersonate the spokesperson for a militant organization attempting to buy weapons from the cartel.

Under the FBI's watchful eye, six months previously Kane had agreed to Carter's plan and they'd flown to California. Being fluent in many languages, he easily passed all the tests the cartel had put him through to verify his identity. Unable to wear a wire, he had a tiny transmitter fitted inside his nose. After a successful arrest, he'd been required to pick out the members of the cartel in a lineup and be available to give evidence in court. His testimony would take down underworld kingpin Eduardo Souza and his henchman Mateo. The initial court case would be rushed forward to avoid the holidays, and Kane had received a summons to appear.

The problem of Kane testifying concerned her. They had a good life together, including a young adopted son, Tauri, and she hated the idea of Kane being involved in cartel business. She'd started her life as DEA Agent Avril Parker and ended up in Black Rock Falls in witness protection with a new face and name because she'd testified against a drug cartel. Kane's circumstances were much the same but far more serious. With an international bounty on his head, he'd undergone extensive facial reconstruction and a change of name before arriving in town, and he still remained on active duty. His work in Black Rock Falls as a deputy was only a respite. As a US asset, he could be called upon by POTUS to engage with the enemy at any time. She glanced up as Deputy Jake Rio walked into the office. "Is there a problem?"

"Maybe." Rio's brow creased into a frown. "Dakota Slade, one of the salespeople at the general store didn't show for work. This never happens, so the owner called her and got no response. He called 911 while I was on patrol and Maggie asked me to drop by for a welfare check. I stopped by her home and got no reply. I looked through the window and she's just sitting in front of the TV." He gave a helpless shrug. "No amount of knocking or yelling got her attention. Rowley's out at the ski resort on a complaint. I didn't want to break in without due cause."

"I'll go with you. Duke needs a walk." Kane rubbed his bloodhound's ears and then looked at Rio from across his desk. "No sign of a break-in? No blood?"

"Nope. She's just sitting there watching TV." Rio rubbed a

hand down his face. "Maybe she just died, but she's only in her twenties."

Concerned, Jenna stood and gathered her things. "We'll follow you. I've got nothing to do here and Maggie can handle the office."

As they went down the stairs to the counter, Jenna informed their receptionist, Maggie Brewster, of their destination. "If we're not back soon, tell Rowley to stay and mind the store."

"Not a problem." Maggie pushed a lock of black curls under her woolen hat and smiled. "Mind you bundle up. It's looking like snow."

Jenna gave her a wave and followed Kane to his tricked-out bombproof black truck, affectionately known as the Beast, and climbed inside. She waited for Kane to adjust Duke's coat and attach his harness to the seatbelt. "We don't need a case right now. Not with you heading off soon to LA to give evidence."

"It will only take a few days and I'll have Wolfe to watch my back. He's checked out the arrangements and it's all good." Kane shrugged and followed Rio along Main. "My identity has been suppressed, so I won't get any kickback. I know you're worried, but the idea is to take down criminals, right?"

Biting her bottom lip, she looked at him. "My identity was supposed to be suppressed too, but the press was everywhere when I left court and I was threatened by Victor Carlos right in front of the judge." She shook her head. "They probably already know who you are and where you live. What happens if your secret identity is exposed? We'll have bounty hunters world-wide trying to get a piece of you."

"That can never happen. My file is sealed and anyone remotely involved from my time before I came here believes I'm dead." Kane touched her cheek. "I went into the meeting in disguise, wearing a beard and mustache, and my skin was darkened. I speak many languages like a native and this makes it easy for me to fool people, Jenna. Stop worrying." Kane snorted. "Do you honestly believe anyone could take me down?"

Shaking her head, Jenna couldn't shake the underlying anxiety. "Then it was just you, Dave. Now we're married and we have Tauri. This madness puts both of us at risk and we could be used as leverage against you."

"You're safe at home and at the office." Kane glanced at her. "Tauri is under protection. That kindergarten has been approved safe, so has Nanny Raya's home. She's a capable operative as well as a super nanny. Nothing is going to happen. Once we have the main man behind bars, the dominos will topple. During the raid conducted during the event, the FBI seized information from every part of the syndicate. There won't be anyone left once they have a conviction." He smiled at her. "Do you honestly believe they'll discover my true identity, Jenna? Heck, you don't even know who I am, and you're my wife."

Annoyed, Jenna stared at him. "Carter isn't giving evidence, is he? He's just taking his vacation. Although what he finds so alluring about holing up in his cabin for weeks in this weather defies imagination."

"He doesn't want to be alone in Snakeskin Gully, I guess." Kane blew out a sigh. "He likes fishing and women. Whatever he's doing is none of our concern." He slowed the Beast as Rio turned into a driveway and followed his truck. "Let's just hope this woman is fine and we can get back to the office and plan Thanksgiving."

Climbing from the Beast, Jenna pulled down her black woolen cap and zipped up her jacket. The wind cut through her clothes in an icy chill, raising goosebumps on her flesh. The ranch-style house sat at the end of a long driveway. No garden beds or lawn. It was as if the forest had crept up to surround the house. She followed Kane, Rio, and Duke to the front door. Kane walked around to the family room window and, cupping his hands around his eyes, peered inside. Jenna looked at him. "What do you see?"

"It looks like a dead body to me." Kane turned to Rio. "The lips are blue." He took lockpicks from his pocket and walked to the front door. "I'll have this open in a second." He looked at Duke. "Go walkies." The dog wandered off toward the trees.

Jenna pulled on examination gloves and a face mask. She waited for the others to do the same. As the door opened, the smell of death and burning wafted toward them. The house was warm, the heating turned up higher than comfortable. She raised her voice. "Sheriff's department. We're coming in to do a welfare check. Is anyone here?"

Nothing.

She nodded to her deputies. "Clear the house."

Standing in the passageway to apprehend anyone who planned to slip out of the door, Jenna waited for the calls of "clear" to come from all over the house. She looked at Kane as he came down the stairs. "Any sign of anyone being here?"

"Nope." Kane frowned. "One cup on the kitchen table, takeout-for-one wrapper in the garbage. She lived alone. No men's clothes in the closets."

"I found nothing of interest either. The back door is secure and everything is as neat as a pin." Rio shrugged. "I guess we check out the family room."

Wrinkling her nose, Jenna walked into the room with Kane at her side. Her heart raced at the sight of the woman, and bile rushed up the back of her throat. The victim's blackened eyes bulged and her mouth hung open. "Oh my, what caused that?"

"Electrocution." Rio moved closer. "It wasn't something close by, like a lamp or anything she touched. There are no contact marks on her hands."

"It wasn't anything inside the house. The surge would have tripped the circuit breaker." Kane walked around the back of the woman and moved her hair to one side. "Hmm, two distinct contact points. It looks like the marks from a stun gun, but the amperage in a stun gun isn't high enough to kill. Hence the name, *stun gun*. I guess Wolfe will be able to work out what exactly happened here."

Jenna pulled out her phone and called Dr. Shane Wolfe. "Hi, Shane. It's Jenna. We have a potential homicide."

TWO

Special Agent Ty Carter took his time selecting groceries at the local market. He liked that this store had a delicious deli and he could taste the various cheeses and charcuteries on offer. This place had expanded over the years to accommodate the influx of people into Black Rock Falls from all walks of life. It had adjusted the selection of goods to please everyone. Sausage from all over the world hung in rows above the counter. The cheese range was extensive, and with a bakery incorporated into the store, a hot food bar could supply a fresh bun filled with anything his heart desired. A selection of cute women served the food, all dressed the same, in jeans and tops with the store's logo printed on front. He flirted with the server at the deli, tasting various cheeses and cold meats before making his selection.

His cart was already full. He'd purchased enough food to keep him happy for weeks, but he did love coming into town and spending time over a steak at Antlers or at the Cattleman's Hotel. He loved people but he liked his solitude as well and had spent some time fishing or just hiking through the forest. Not that solitude meant being alone. He always had his Doberman, Zorro, by his side. Although right this minute, his dog was asleep in the rental.

Carter smiled at the server. "You've been so kind. I never knew there was such a selection of fine foods in this store." He took his packages and dropped them into his cart before heading to the hot food bar.

He gave his order and pushed his cart to a nearby table and sat down. He'd been flirting with one of the servers the previous day and she came over with a pot of coffee. "Well, good morning, Jennifer." He smiled as she filled his cup, leaning back casually in his chair.

"Good morning, Ty. You've dropped by three days in a row." Jennifer placed the fixings on the table. "We must have made a good impression on you. Are you staying long in town or just passing through?"

Carter removed his hat and ran a hand through his hair. "I have a cabin in the woods and often stop by to do some fishing or just relax."

A bell rang on the counter and Jennifer turned and hurried to collect his order. She placed it on the table before him with a smile. He met her gaze. "Is there a good stylist in town? I prefer not to get my hair cut by a barber."

"Yeah, the beauty parlor is at the other end of Main opposite the pizzeria." She eyed him critically. "Hmm, I wish I had blond hair. Bleaching it is always a problem. Do you mind if I ask if the blond highlights are natural?"

Carter nodded, knowing the untidy shaggy look he preferred, which went just over his collar, attracted women. His hair was naturally blond and so were the highlights. The layers were from the stylist, and as it was getting a little long, he needed a trim. "Yeah, this is my natural color. You wouldn't believe how many people ask the same thing." He chuckled. "I was born lucky, I guess." He smiled. "You have very pretty hair. Don't change it. I love brunettes with blue eyes."

"Oh, well, that's very kind of you." Jennifer blushed to the roots of her hair and smiled. "I'd better get back to work. Just wave if you need anything else." She turned and hurried back to the counter.

Carter ate his bun and emptied his coffee cup. He liked Jennifer. She was a friendly girl. Once he had paid for his purchases, he gathered up the bags and headed outside. Bracing himself against a blast of icy wind, he walked along the sidewalk, dumped his groceries in the back of the rental, and then climbed behind the wheel. After giving Zorro a pat on the head, he headed for the beauty parlor. Yeah, he could go to a barber, no doubt they'd cut his hair just fine, but he liked the service offered in a beauty parlor. The stylists were always friendly and happy to chat about their lives. In the time it took them to wash and cut his hair, he just about knew what they ate for breakfast each day. He never made an appointment. He just walked inside and smiled. "Morning. Would one of you beautiful talented ladies have time to cut my hair?"

"Yeah sure." One of the stylists waved him to a chair before a basin. "My name is Donna, and if you don't mind waiting a few minutes, I'll be free. Come and sit here and I'll wash your hair." She placed towels around his neck and pushed him back against the basin. "You just relax and I'll be right there." She removed his Stetson and handed it to him.

Carter rested one cowboy boot on his knee and leaned back with his head resting on the basin. He inhaled the perfumes in the beauty parlor and let out a long sigh. This was living. He could hear giggles and lifted his head to grin at the women staring at him. He loved the attention. Being an FBI agent had its drawbacks. Dating was one of them. The badge frightened many women away and he just wanted the chance to be a regular guy for a week or two. The chance of meeting someone special was always possible, but for now he'd just enjoy being a single male. He inhaled the fresh air and then tossed a toothpick into his mouth. The cabin in the forest had been a great idea for some alone time. He loved being on vacation.

THREE

Checking the time and making a note of it on her phone, Jenna followed Kane and Rio out of the house. "Okay, grab what you need from the forensic kit in the back of the Beast. Rio, go around back, check for footprints and any signs of forced entry on any of the windows or back door. Look for an exterior opening to the cellar and check that as well. Use your fingerprint scanner and collect prints along the way."

"Yes, ma'am." Rio headed toward the truck. "Do you want me to call Rowley?"

Jenna shook her head. "No, with Wolfe on scene soon, we won't need him." She turned to Kane. "Someone murdered that woman. He must have left a trace."

"First up, we get her prints and run them against anything we find inside the house." Kane pulled a fingerprint scanner from his pocket. "I'll need to move her hands. So we'll need photographs of her in situ."

Nodding, Jenna scanned the front yard and walked slowly across the driveway. "It's impossible to see if anyone parked a vehicle here. I guess we start with her phone. I'll look for that and her purse. We need to positively ID her, although I believe she is Dakota Slade. It's the right address and Rio ran her plates. The vehicle here belongs to her. I recall reading a death notice for a Wilma Slade, who was the grandmother of Dakota, so I'm guessing the house belongs to her as well."

"If she's lived here all her life, there will be dental records as well." Kane frowned at her and pulled his hat down over his ears. "Why would someone want to murder her? Did she have any relatives? Anyone who might want a cut of the house and any inheritance?"

Raising both eyebrows, Jenna stared at him. "Looking at the house, I doubt anyone left her a huge amount of money. The place needs work and the furniture must be fifty years old at least. I'm sure if she lived here with her grandma, she'd at least splash out and make one room comfortable. I didn't see much apart from the new rug."

"There is a new TV." Kane led the way inside the house. "I didn't see any closets filled with clothes either. I figure she cleaned out her grandma's things. Apart from one room, which was obviously hers, the bedrooms upstairs are stripped bare. Empty, apart from beds, closets, and nightstands."

Jenna followed him inside, pulling out her phone. "The house is clean. Maybe grandma was a hoarder? She'd likely been wanting to clean it for years." She walked into the family room and took photographs. "How did her killer get inside the house?"

"She must have invited him." Kane waited for her to finish and bent to scan the victim's fingerprints. "We'll need to check out her movements before her death. She must have had a boyfriend or at least met someone. Single women don't just open the door to strangers."

"Hmm... unless he was masquerading as someone else." Kane straightened. "Someone checking for a gas leak, for instance, or delivering a parcel?" He shrugged. "Not that there's a parcel anywhere. Although, he could have taken it with him. It seems to me he walked in and murdered her."

Nodding, Jenna looked at the victim. "She looks so relaxed. Not posed. I figure she knew her killer."

"Yeah." Kane moved around the room, scanning for finger-prints. He bent over the doorknob and shook his head. "All her prints so far. This guy is a ghost."

Searching for a purse or phone, Jenna moved a cushion beside the victim. "I've found her phone. I'll check out the kitchen for her purse."

"No need." Kane turned to her and pointed into the passageway. "It's on the table beside the front door, with a bunch of keys."

As Jenna walked into the passageway, Rio came through the front door. "No signs of a break-in anywhere. The back door and all accessible windows are fine. No footprints, tire tracks... zip." He turned as a vehicle came along the driveway. "Wolfe has arrived." He smiled. "Ah good, Em is with him."

The slow-burning relationship between Rio and Emily Wolfe was on hold while she completed her studies to become a medical examiner, but they did spend their downtime together. Jenna smiled as Rio turned on his heel to go and greet her. She photographed the keys and purse and then dropped them into separate evidence bags. She added the phone to the pile at the front door and went to greet Wolfe. He'd arrived with Colt Webber, his assistant and badge-holding deputy. Wolfe stood over six feet with white-blond hair and piercing gray eyes, a true professional on the job but with a heart of gold. "Morning. Dave figures the victim was hit with a powerful stun gun at the base of the skull. We haven't found any prints other than the victim's. We presume her name is Dakota Slade. Her vehicle checks out and so does her general description."

"A powerful stun gun?" Wolfe's expression darkened and he pulled on mask and gloves. "They are made to stun not kill.

If this is so, someone tampered with the device to increase the amperage. That's the only way to make one lethal. It would mean a complete rebuild. They don't have the capacity to create enough amps to kill."

Hearing Kane's explanation echoing in her head, she walked behind him into the house. "Kane said the same thing. The body is in the family room on the left." She followed him inside. "No signs of forced entry. No signs of anyone else in the house but Dakota."

"It's warm in here." Wolfe turned to Emily. "Check the temperature and hunt down the setting on the thermostat." He looked at Rio. "Go with her and check the thermostat and all around for prints." He looked at Jenna. "I'll need to know when she was last seen. The high temperature in here will give a false reading on her time of death, so you'll need to find as narrow a window as possible."

"I'll call the general store. It was the manager who called 911 this morning when he couldn't reach her." Kane walked to the door pulling out his phone.

"You mentioned sweeping for prints." Wolfe walked around the sofa frowning. "Did you move the body?"

Jenna handed him her phone. "Yeah, but only her fingers. Kane used his scanner to get her prints for elimination purposes. These images were taken prior. I've uploaded all the shots we took to the server."

"Kane's correct. The burn marks on the back of the neck would suggest a stun gun." Wolfe indicated the marks at the base of the skull. "They are typical of contact wounds. The hair here is singed as well, but y'all know this might not have been the cause of death. There's always an entry and exit wound, and although y'all believe the charge came out through the eye sockets, you'd be incorrect." He bent and lifted up the victim's feet, one at a time. "See here?" He pointed to burn marks on the base of each shoe. "Electric charge grounds itself through the body. If she'd been wearing rubber-soled shoes, the outcome may have been different."

Confused, Jenna stared at the black holes where the eyes should have been and swallowed hard. "Hit by a surge of electricity that burned out her eyes must have fried her brain."

"Not always." Wolfe shrugged. "People get hit by lightning, and because they're wearing rubber-soled shoes they survive. It's the grounding that kills." He bent to take instruments from his forensic kit. "An electrical charge that caused that much damage to the eyes could cause a brain stem dysfunction or a cardiac arrest, then we need to consider respiratory paralysis, not to mention multiorgan failure. All are caused by the passage of electric current through the body when it grounds. An autopsy will determine the correct cause of death." He smiled at Jenna. "This is all part of the mystery, Jenna. The obvious is often the last thing we expect to find."

She looked up as Kane walked into the room. "Did you get any info?"

"Yeah, heaps. She left work at the usual time. So if she came home without stopping by the store or anywhere else, she would have been here by six-thirty." Kane scratched his cheek. "She's never missed a day since starting work, is always on time. Lives alone here since her grandma died. Doesn't have a boyfriend, but the manager noticed a guy hanging around the general store. He came by three times in a row and she helped him. He said they became quite friendly." He looked at Jenna. "I figure we need to speak to the manager and get more information. He was shocked by the news of her death, and I tried to ask more questions but he's alone in the store until lunchtime and was too busy to talk."

"What time did Rio drop by?" Wolfe straightened from examining the body.

Jenna checked her files. "He dropped by at nine. She

usually shows for work at eight sharp. So last seen at six leaving work and nine this morning."

"Okay." Wolfe blew out a long sigh. "That's your time of death. No amount of science will make it any closer, but from the livor mortis in her arms and feet, I'd say she wasn't moved and died here. The time of death in my estimation would unofficially be before midnight. It takes some time for the blood to pool in the extremities."

The thought that a lonely woman had been tricked into allowing a stranger into her home saddened Jenna. She looked at Wolfe. "Do you need us for anything else? I'd like to catch the manager at the general store while all this is fresh in his mind. I'll leave Rio to assist you."

"Sure." Wolfe nodded. "We'll remove the body and complete a forensic sweep just in case the killer left anything behind. I'll leave the autopsy until tomorrow morning, make it eleven. I promised to take Anna into town for ice cream. She had a dentist appointment and came out with an all clear." He stared at the body. "This is a strange one, isn't it? What motive could he have? I can't see the thrill in killing someone this way. It seems almost hygienic."

Biting her bottom lip, Jenna met his gaze. "This is the problem. Some of them don't need a reason. They just like killing people."

FOUR

Kane pulled the Beast into a parking spot outside Aunt Betty's Café and glanced at his watch. "We haven't given the manager of the general store time to get his staff sorted yet. Do you want to go and grab a coffee and a bite to eat?"

"Yeah, that crime scene was nasty." Jenna climbed out of the Beast and waited for him on the sidewalk. "We need a plan of action."

Scanning Main, Kane looked at the gray sky and back along the sidewalk. Remnants of Halloween hung from dumpsters in the alleyways, and one lone jack-o'-lantern hung from a street-light, tipping to one side, grinning and slightly battered from the hail storm the previous evening. He let Duke out of the back seat and followed Jenna into Aunt Betty's Café. At the counter, manager Susie Hartwig greeted them with her usual smile. "Peach pie and coffee for me." He glanced at Jenna.

"I'll have the same." Jenna glanced at Kane. "Ah, just a minute. I've changed my mind. I'll have hot chocolate with extra marshmallows with my pie. It's freezing outside right now."

"Coming right up." Susie looked pointedly at Kane. "Only one slice of pie? We have savory turnovers just out of the oven."

Laughing, Kane winked at her. "You sure know my weakness. Yeah, I'd love one, but I'll have the pie as well."

They headed for their reserved table at the back of the room and Kane turned to see Duke still sitting at the counter staring at Susie. As a patrol dog, he was allowed entry into any establishment. When he barked, Kane went back to the counter. "What has he ordered today?"

"Oh, I figure it must be the beef sausage we had left over from yesterday." Susie leaned over the counter and smiled at Duke. "Okay, Duke. It's on its way." She giggled and headed out back.

"Honestly, you spoil him." Jenna shook her head. "You confuse me, Dave. We agreed we'd never spoil Tauri, but I know you will. You already have."

Shocked, Kane stared at her. "Duke's a dog who works hard for us and deserves a few treats. Tauri is our son and we both decided that he needs a stable homelife. Yeah, we'll spoil him. That's what birthdays and Christmas are for. Unless you mean the bicycle? I figure every boy needs a bicycle. We give Tauri love and attention. We make him feel safe, but I'm afraid nothing we do will ever make up for his early upbringing." He took both her hands. "He knows we love him, and you can't spoil a kid with love, can you?"

"No." Jenna squeezed his hands. "Being a mom takes a lot of getting used to. Not having any brothers or sisters, I have only my mom to use as a role model. She was always a little distant with me and I don't want that with Tauri. I'm worried I might make a mistake. After seeing how many serial killers come from being bounced around the system, I want to make things perfect for him."

Smiling, Kane glanced up as Susie came with the drinks.

He waited for her to leave and looked at Jenna. "You're a great mom. I had a great mom but she made mistakes sometimes. We're human, we make mistakes, but we're smart enough to recognize them and fix them. Tauri is very smart. It's unlikely he'll get into trouble." He frowned. "When he's old enough to understand, we'll tell him about our previous lives. Not for a long time, though, so he fully understands the ramifications about speaking to anyone."

"That's one day I'm not looking forward to." Jenna pulled her hands from his as Susie came with the food and placed a plate on the floor for Duke. "Okay, enough about that. We need a plan of action."

Biting into the savory turnover, with crumbly pastry and a filling that made his taste buds dance with delight, he nodded. "You must try one of these. Do you figure they'll freeze okay? We should take some home with us."

"If I say yes, am I spoiling you?" Jenna snorted a laugh. "Sure, take some home, but first we need a plan of action. We'll speak to the manager of the general store and see what he can give us on the man Dakota spoke to. A description will give us some idea of who she came into contact with, and maybe they'll have CCTV footage we can look at as well."

Finishing the turnover in a few delicious mouthfuls, Kane sipped his coffee, turning his thoughts to the positions of the local CCTV cameras around town. "She'd come into contact with many people working in the general store and we're only assuming her killer is a man. We have no indication either way. I figure we look into her background. If her grandma died recently, Dakota could be in line for a sum of money. She must have been given the house but probate takes time. What if someone else was mentioned in the last will and testament? This could be a relative left out of the will and the cheapest way to contest a will is to remove the first in line."

"Oh, that's terrible." Jenna looked at him, eyes wide. "We've had so many serial killers I automatically assume we have another in town but the idea a relative killed her for money never entered my mind." She sat with a forkful of pie hovering in midair. "Okay, so we need to know who her grandma used as an estate attorney. I know Samuel J. Cross handles just about everything in town and he took over from at least three deceased lawyers that I know of. I'd assume he'd be the first one to speak to." She ate her pie and then pulled out her phone. "I'll call him and see if we can stop by this afternoon." She made the call.

Eating slowly, Kane ran other scenarios through his mind. The victim was a single woman, mid-twenties, not very social, who didn't own a pet and her only life appeared to be going to work. Why would anyone target her? Most murders sat in their own categories. They usually concerned money, hate, a love triangle, obsession, or were to hide a secret. He couldn't see Dakota being involved in a love triangle, nor being murdered for hate or obsession. He pushed his plate away and sipped his coffee. "If it's not a serial killer with his own agenda, there's another thing we should consider. She might have information on someone. Perhaps a secret they don't want coming out that might affect their career or something."

"Like the manager of the general store cooking the books or laundering money?" Jenna sipped the hot beverage and sighed. "I figure the money idea makes more sense. She appeared to live a quiet life—unless she was hiding from someone?"

Kane finished his coffee. "Ready? We need more information. Let's hope the manager of the general store is forthcoming." He stood. "I'll ask Susie to box up a pile of pastries and we'll drop by and grab them after we've been to the general store."

They walked to the store. The wind had picked up again

and cut through every seam in Kane's clothes. He pulled his black woolen cap down over his ears and shoved his Stetson over the top. Keeping the metal plate in his head warm was more important than how he looked. Headaches crippled him in winter and he avoided them at all costs. He followed Jenna into the general store and walked through the range of goods to the counter. Two women worked behind the counter and Kane smiled at them. "We need to speak to the manager."

"He's expecting you." A woman with the name tag SUE PLANT indicated to the other woman. "Mandy will show you where to go." She turned away to serve a customer.

Kane nodded, reading the woman's name tag. "Thanks, Ms. White. I appreciate it."

"No problem at all." Mandy led the way through the store to a door marked MANAGER. "There you go." She turned and walked away.

After knocking on the door, Kane looked at Jenna and raised an eyebrow. In his mind everyone who came into contact with Dakota was a suspect, including the manager. When the door opened, a middle-aged man waved them inside. He looked tired and pale. "Thanks for seeing us. I didn't catch your name?"

"Pete Daybrook." He waved them to chairs before his desk and dropped slowly into an office chair. On the table was a sandwich and a cup of coffee. "What happened to Dakota?"

"We don't have a cause of death, Mr. Daybrook." Jenna took out a notebook and pen and placed them on the desk. "She was found dead in her home. Do you know if she had any health issues?"

"Not that I'm aware." Daybrook shook his head slowly. "She never took a personal day in the time she worked here. This is why I called to check on her. I was concerned. Living alone in this town can be dangerous for a young woman."

"Indeed." Jenna looked at him. "You mentioned to Deputy

Kane that, out of all her customers, one man in particular dropped by a few times. Can you describe him?"

"He could be any one of many men around town. Stetson, cowboy boots, Levi's. He wore a sheepskin jacket. I could tell by the collar." He stared into space for a few seconds. "Snakeskin boots. They clicked when he walked, as if he wore spurs. That's what drew my attention. It would be strange for a guy to be wearing spurs around town without a horse tied up outside, and there was no horse. I looked."

Kane raised one eyebrow. He'd never use spurs on a horse. "Okay, do you recall what hair color he had? Did he have a beard or moustache? How tall?"

"Oh, six feet, maybe more. Hard to tell with a Stetson. Clean shaven, blond hair over his collar. Shaggy like."

Glancing at Jenna, Kane narrowed his gaze. He'd just described FBI Agent Ty Carter, right down to his snakeskin boots with metal tips. "Okay. Did he pay by card and would you have a record of his purchases?"

"I already thought of that and went through the credit card receipts." Daybrook shook his head. "I recall he purchased cleaning supplies and needed some assistance on what to buy. The next time he was asking about toasters. He paid in cash."

"How about CCTV footage?" Jenna made a few notes and then looked up at him. "I see you have a camera watching the store."

"Yeah, but it deletes every twenty-four hours. So was wiped clean at eight this morning." Daybrook ran a hand through his hair. "I didn't expect anything like this to happen. Do you think this man was involved?"

"We don't know." Jenna folded her notebook. "Could you pick him out in a lineup?"

"The thing is, I was busy with customers and I didn't get a good look at him." Daybrook rubbed both hands down his face.

"I'm so sorry. I should have taken more notice. If he comes by again, I'll call you without delay."

Kane stood and handed him his card. "Yeah, that will help. Thanks for your time." He turned to Jenna. "We'll split up and talk to the women behind the counter. They might know something."

"Sure." Jenna followed him out of the office door.

"Do you have a minute?" Sue Plant came toward them and dropped her voice to just above a whisper. "Is this about the man who came by three times to speak to Dakota? I saw the man, chatting to her after work on Wednesday last." She frowned at Jenna. "If something happened to Dakota and I can identify the man she spoke to, I'm in danger... right?"

"If it's who we think, no, you're not. If you see him again, call us." Jenna handed her a card.

Kane moved closer. "We're just trying to find anyone who came in contact with Dakota. Mainly to discover if she mentioned anything about her plans for Thursday night." He straightened. "So this guy, could you pick him out in a lineup?"

"No, I can't say I got a good look at his face." Sue narrowed her gaze. "He was tall, with blond untidy hair. He first came by Tuesday last. That's the day I worked with Dakota. When he came inside, he headed for the appliance display, removed his Stetson and shook the rain off it, but was turned away from me. I recognized him more by his clothes and build." She scrutinized Kane. "Not as tall or broad in the shoulders as you, but one size down maybe."

"Does Ms. White work alongside Dakota?" Jenna glanced toward the woman serving a mother with a screaming baby.

"Nope." Sue frowned. "She's here to replace her at the moment."

Kane nodded. "Okay, thanks for your help." He led the way out of the store and stopped on the sidewalk and looked at Jenna. "What do you make of that?"

"They described Carter and it just so happens he's in town." Jenna looked at him. "I guess he could be fixing up his cabin."

Kane shrugged. "Well, one thing's for darn sure, he's not killing women."

FIVE

Scanning Main both ways, Jennifer Kriss ran across the blacktop to her vehicle. The town from Halloween to Thanksgiving and right through the holidays was filled with people. The town where she'd spent her childhood was vastly different from the Black Rock Falls of today. Most times she wouldn't worry about vehicles following her, but over the last week she had the distinct feeling someone was following her home. Living some ways out of town had been a fun idea when she'd purchased the house from a large sum of money her uncle had left her. The old home, built eighty years ago, had a large footprint with room to move. Five bedrooms, each with their own bathroom, made it perfect for her and her two college friends to move into. They'd had fun living together, but one by one they'd married and moved out, leaving her all on her lonesome. She didn't mind so much during the summer, but in fall and winter the sleeping trees and dead vegetation all around her made the house creepy.

The upkeep of the house was getting expensive. An old house needed constant repairs and she'd posted a flyer in the window of the market asking for housemates. Although it was some distance from the local college, the bus ran past the end of her road. She'd gladly live with up to three female students, but couldn't put that on her flyer—although, it might be useful having a strong young man around to help with the maintenance. She'd even reduce his rent for some assistance. Jennifer climbed behind the wheel of her old Nissan truck and headed along Main. She glanced in her rearview mirror and swallowed hard. A familiar white truck fell in behind her and her stomach clenched. Convinced it was the same truck that had followed her home and driven past her driveway for the last couple of days, she slowed and took a left, and drove to the end of the road. Sure enough, the white truck followed. Fear knotted her stomach. Should she drive to the sheriff's office and say she believed a white truck was following her? There would be hundreds of white trucks in town. Heck, her vehicle was a white truck.

The truck turned into a driveway, and relieved, she turned her Nissan around and headed back to Main. As Main turned into Stanton and the surrounding forest darkened the road, her heart raced at the sight of the white truck, following her again. Was it the same vehicle? It was way past the sheriff's office now and she'd already driven past the Triple Z Roadhouse. That was the last possibly safe place to stop. Panic gripped her and she accelerated, driving faster than comfortable. She always drove within her limits and overtaking slower-going delivery vans and fuel tankers wasn't her style. She bit down hard on her lip as the latter came into view. She moved out into the oncoming lane, and pressing the gas pedal hard to the floor, hoped her old vehicle would make it past before another eighteen-wheeler came hurtling along the highway. White-knuckling the steering wheel, she gasped in terror as the white truck merged in behind her. There was no doubt in her mind someone was following her. What could she do? She didn't have a fancy phone that connected to her radio and taking her hands off the wheel at this speed would be suicide. One more mile and her turn would come up. Could she make it along her road and into her driveway? If she made a fast turn, maybe he'd sail right on past and she could make it home and dash inside?

It was her only chance. She accelerated at high speed, passed a gray van, and then slammed on the brakes, leaving a trail of rubber across the blacktop as she slid into the road leading to her home. Tearing off at breakneck speed, she bounced into her driveway, the driver's-side door brushing against the gatepost with a sickening grind of metal. The back wheels spun, showering the tall blackened trees lining the driveway with gravel. Driving recklessly, she made it to the front porch, leapt from the truck, and dashed up the steps. With her hands trembling, she found the key and after four attempts managed to get it inside the lock. Panting, she fell inside the door and turned the deadbolt. She leaned against the front door, trying to suck air into her lungs. Petrified at the sound of a vehicle moving along the gravel driveway, she froze.

A door slammed and footsteps, unfaltering and determined, crunched toward the house. Too afraid to move, Jennifer pressed her back against the door. She needed help. Terrified, she plunged her hands into the pockets of her jacket and then realized in horror that she'd left her purse and phone on the front seat of the truck. There was no landline and now she had no way to call for help. Footsteps came on the stoop, making a loud tapping sound. Trembling all over, she waited. Where could she go? Dread paralyzed her. Had she locked the back door this morning? Unsure what to do next, she waited for a knock on the door, but nothing happened. At the sound of the tumblers falling, she jumped away from the door and gaped at the lock in disbelief. In her rush to get inside, she'd left the keys in the lock. The brass handle turned slowly and she tried to scream as the door swung open, but the sound was little more than a moan. Frozen with dread she stared at a smiling man standing in the doorway. Her gaze fixed on the muzzle of the gun in his hand. The gray round hole was pointed at her chest. She took a few steps back, unable to speak as fear gripped her by the throat.

"Hello, Jennifer."

SIX

The sky had darkened and Jenna checked her watch. It was a little after four and clouds had blocked the watery sunlight filtering in her office window. Winter in Black Rock Falls could be as spectacular as it was dangerous and this year the snow was late. By November they usually had a few feet, but this year sleet, rain, and high winds had made life uncomfortable. She had spent the afternoon, along with her deputies, searching for local men who fit the description of the man seen in the general store speaking with Dakota. They hadn't been able to contact Carter. When he said he was going dark, he meant pitch-black. Jenna had hunted down as much information about Dakota as possible, after thinking through Kane's ideas about possible others wanting her inheritance, or any information she might possibly have on someone. She hadn't found anything of interest at all. The visit to Sam Cross, the lawyer, didn't add any intrigue to the investigation. Dakota's inheritance had gone through unopposed. There was, to his knowledge, no one else entitled to inherit.

From what she discovered, Dakota had always been a homebody. She went to church, helped out in various charities, but apart from that, didn't seem to have a whole lot of friends of her age. She mixed more with the elderly, and Jenna figured after living with her grandma for so long, she must have preferred their company. Maybe it was safer. Although she hadn't discovered any mention of any love affairs, she guessed she'd need to question some of her school friends, if she had any, to find out that information.

She leaned back in her office chair and looked at Kane. "Find anyone fitting the description?"

"Most guys in town have dark hair or red hair. Not many are coming up on the databases that have blond hair. I'm running a search for men between five-ten and six-two and see what it spits out." Kane yawned explosively and rolled his shoulders. "I miss having Bobby Kalo on hand. I'm getting used to having an FBI computer whiz kid on the end of the phone to do this work. He loves it but I find it as boring as watching paint dry."

Standing, Jenna went to the counter and refilled the coffee machine. "They'll be back soon. It's a five-day trip to Disneyland, so probably a week away with traveling. Jo deserves time with her daughter, and Jaime was so excited to be going. Kalo was as well. He's still a kid at heart." She leaned against the counter. "Do you want cookies with your coffee?"

"You have to ask?" Kane grinned at her. "Did you find anything interesting?"

Jenna took down two cups and the cookie jar. "Nothing. She was a very quiet woman. I can't see any reason for someone to kill her. The method of murder seems so strange too."

"How so?" Kane stood and went to the counter. He opened the cookie jar and poured cookies onto a plate.

"It was what Wolfe said." Jenna bent to take the creamer from the refrigerator. "How it was a clean kill. Sure, we know women usually use poison but this one has me thinking. Male killers usually like to mess women up. Where is the thrill in electrocution? It looked like he or she sneaked up behind her and zapped her."

"I see what you mean." Kane nibbled on a cookie, his gaze on the coffee dripping into the pot "If it was a thrill kill, where is the thrill? Although, it is a brutal way to die—visually, I mean. There's no blood, but the murder would be graphic in nature. The smell of burning flesh and hair, the body would jerk... and you saw her eyes. This might be the thrill for the killer. For him, it's clean. He can walk away without any trace evidence on him but the brutality is there."

Everything that Wolfe had said filtered through Jenna's mind. She filled the coffee cups and added the fixings. "I know I'm not allowed to ask you about your missions, but can you tell me a little about your training?" She noticed the nerve ticking in his cheek but ignored it. "I'm guessing you would've been trained similar to the SEALs."

"What are you getting at, Jenna?" Kane took a cup of coffee and sat in front of her desk. "Specifically."

Leaning back on the counter, Jenna looked at him. "Would Carter be capable of changing the amperage on a stun gun?"

"Probably. We were both trained in skills to get the job done." He lifted one shoulder in a half shrug. "It's not all about shooting and muscle. A good deal of planning goes into it as well. Meeting unusual situations head-on and acting accordingly to survive is essential. Many skills are involved." He shook his head slowly. "I can see your mind working. You think Carter is involved, don't you?"

Taking her coffee and sitting at the desk, Jenna stared at him. "I've never believed that Carter is unstable. The thing is that many people have been fooled by psychopaths, and we know that Carter was alone in the forest for a long time."

"Ah, come on, Jenna." Kane barked a laugh. "Do you have any idea how many tests he would have endured to get back into the FBI? In all the time I've known him, I've never seen him slip up once. In my opinion, he is as solid as a rock."

Sipping her coffee slowly, she eyed him over the rim of the cup. "Do you ever recall reading accounts of the crimes of Ted Bundy? The notorious serial killer? He was out there, killing people for years, and still managed a relationship with a woman who would refuse to believe he was a murderer. Then we have the Iceman. He was married with children, a loving father, and his wife never suspected he was a vicious serial killer." She sighed. "The problem is the people closest to them don't recognize them for who they are. We shouldn't discount him as a possible suspect until we know for sure he's innocent."

"The problem with that conclusion, Jenna, is that we've known Carter for years and he hasn't killed anyone. He cares about people." Kane turned his coffee cup around with the tips of his fingers. "If he was a serial killer, as you are assuming, wouldn't he have fallen off the rails by now?"

Placing her coffee cup on the table, Jenna smiled. "This is where I rely on your profiling skills, Dave." She pushed a strand of hair behind one ear. "I watched an interview with a serial killer who was married with kids, and the one thing he said he regretted the most was losing his family. So they might not show empathy for their victims, but they are capable of caring. This is what makes catching them so difficult."

"We know they hide behind a mask, but that idea is flawed too." Kane looked at her. "I don't figure it's just psychopaths that do that. Many people who move around us on a regular basis are living two lives. We are and we're not serial killers."

Stumped, Jenna pushed both hands through her hair. "So where do we go from here?"

"I believe you're on the right track." Kane gave her a long

look. "We do need to be looking for someone with the skills to change the stun gun into a killing machine. Once the results come through, we'll do background checks on the possible suspects and see if any of them are capable. It will take a long time. It could be tomorrow before the search comes up with anything. I'll just leave it running overnight and see what it has found in the morning."

After closing down her computer, Jenna stood, collected the cups, and washed them in the sink. "There's nothing left for us to do here today. I'll check in with Rio and Rowley and see if they've found anything." She collected her things from the desk and grabbed her coat on the way out the door.

Downstairs, she went to speak to her deputies. "Do you have anything for me?"

"Nope." Rio leaned back in his chair. "We've hunted down friends, and discovered she doesn't have any, apart from a few elderly women she knows from church. She goes to a quilting circle with them, but that's just about all we could find about her social life."

"I called Father Derry." Rowley raised both eyebrows. "He wasn't too happy about being asked questions about his parishioners, but when I explained, he said Dakota was always there for any fundraisers but was a solitary person who liked her own company."

Confused at why anyone wanted to murder Dakota, Jenna blew out a long sigh. "It's after five. Head on home. We have an autopsy tomorrow at eleven. If you could tend the office in the morning and we don't get a break in the case, you can take the rest of the weekend. We'll call you in if we discover anything of interest. Right now, we've got no suspects and no motive. Someone killed her, but it could have been any one of a dozen blond men in town. All we can do is wait for results to come in and then act."

She headed for the counter and smiled at Maggie. "We're all heading home. Lock up and we'll see you in the morning."

"I'll switch the 911 calls to my phone." Maggie looked from one to the other. "You go and spend some quality time with your boy."

Jenna gave her a wave. "We will." She headed for the door.

SEVEN

SATURDAY

Kane slipped out of bed, not wanting to wake Jenna, and hurried into the barn to do his chores. He loved the smell of the stables. Horses, leather, hay, and feed has its own special blend of fragrances. The air inside was warm and Warrior, his black stallion, and Seagull, Jenna's white Arab mare, greeted him with nods and grunts. Anna's pony always nodded and tossed her head. It was wonderful to be appreciated. The radio was always on to keep the horses calm and happy, and as he groomed them and mucked out the stalls, he sang along to a few tunes until Duke decided to howl along with him. He looked at him. "Are you joining in or is my voice so bad you're howling in pain?"

When Duke came to him and leaned against his leg, he bent down to rub his ears. "You know, you could have stayed inside in the warm."

The sky was clear this morning, with the distinct smell of winter. The frosty air and pine fragrance made him yearn for a day on the slopes. Skiing was something they both enjoyed. But although it was a freezing-cold day, he had a date with his Harley. Saturday mornings he went for a ride, tearing along the backroads around the ranch to clear his head and just enjoy being alive. He loved speed and his motorcycle fed that need. The urge to be out on the road riding fast made him complete his chores in record time. He emptied the wheelbarrow filled with horse dung and hurried back to the house, steam pouring from his nostrils. He fed Duke and then headed for the shower in one of the spare rooms rather than disturb Jenna.

He'd dressed, eaten four Pop-Tarts, and was halfway through his coffee before Jenna called his name. He filled a cup with coffee, added the fixings, and headed to the bedroom. "Morning." He set the cups on the bedside table, sat on the bed, and bent to kiss her. "I'll finish my coffee and then head out. I'll be back to fix breakfast. I'm not going far. It's bitterly cold this morning. I should be back in half an hour."

"There's no rush." Jenna sipped her coffee. "Rio and Rowley can handle the office and we don't need to be at Wolfe's until eleven. If there's not a break in the case, we'll have more time with Tauri this weekend."

Smiling, Kane moved his gaze over her. He loved the way she looked first thing in the morning, all tousled and sleepy. She'd always be the sheriff, but in the mornings she was just his Jenna. "Stay in bed and relax. It's early and Tauri won't wake for ages. I'll be back by then." He finished his coffee and bent to kiss her again. "Get some rest while you can. This case might blow up at any moment." He went to the closet, pulled out a thick sweater and his leather jacket.

Pulling the thick gloves out of the pockets, he took his helmet from the shelf and, carrying it, headed for the front door. He set the security system and walked to the garage. Underfoot, the grass crackled, the leaves stiff with a white coating of frost. He pulled on his helmet and, using his palm print to open the garage, stood for a few seconds to admire his motorcycles. The Harley he'd built from a pile of pieces now sat glistening under the lights. Beside it, his work in progress, an old Indian Chief. Finding parts had been difficult but he'd been determined to restore it to its former glory. He only needed a little more time and it would be complete. He climbed onto the Harley and kicked it over, hearing the satisfying rumble of the powerful engine. Helmet secured and gloves on, he drove out of the garage and along the driveway. The garage door closed behind him and the main gates to the ranch slid open as he approached.

Wind blasted him as he flew along the blacktop. All around, the lowlands were covered in a coating of frost. The rising sun sat low on the horizon. Its long golden fingers spread out across the white landscape as it climbed slowly to wake the earth for another day. The backroads around the ranch followed the river along the border of Jenna's property. He drove past the snow-plow guy's house and then the old Mitchum Ranch, the latter known for its myths and ghosts. It was a favorite for the local kids at Halloween, even after a series of grisly murders. He took his usual route through the small forest area. The narrow strip of blacktop was part of their ranch and rarely used. Seeing the way ahead clear, he accelerated.

Trees flashed past in a sea of brown trunks, and exhilaration filled him. The roar of the engine and the sheer joy of riding made him smile. He increased his speed, moving under the canopy of trees in a flash. The next moment, something hard struck him across the chest. Air rushed out of his lungs as a massive force lifted him from the Harley. Airborne, he tumbled backward, flew through the air, and crashed onto the blacktop, sliding and spinning head over heels. The forest spun around him and he heard the sound of a powerful engine close by. A millisecond later he slammed into a tree and everything went black.

EIGHT

Jenna woke to the sound of Tauri's voice. She blinked, not realizing that she had fallen asleep. "Good morning, sweetheart." She gathered up the little boy and kissed his cheeks. "You're up early."

"Where's Daddy?" Tauri climbed onto the bed and frowned. "I can't find him and when I asked Duke, he just went and sat in his basket."

Jenna sat up and smiled at him. "You know he likes to ride his motorcycle on Saturdays if we're not working. He'll be back soon." She glanced at the bedside clock and blinked. It was five after eight. "Oh, it's later than I thought. Why don't you go and get dressed. I'll take a shower, and if Daddy's not back, I'll cook your breakfast."

When Tauri scampered off, Jenna frowned. Kane had been gone for two hours. He never stayed out that long. Calling him would be a waste of time because he'd never hear the phone on his motorcycle. She took a quick shower and dressed. Not wanting to show her anxiety to Tauri, she made eggs and toast for both of them. She ate her meal and smiled at Tauri. "He might be in the garage working on his Indian. You finish your breakfast and I'll go see."

Dragging on her coat, she hurried outside and made her way to the garage. The door was locked, but she opened it using her palm print. Everything was as it should be. The Beast sat where he'd left it the night before and his project motorcycle hadn't been touched. Fear had her by the throat. What had happened to him? It was so unlikely he'd been in a wreck. He drove fast but was very experienced and wouldn't risk his life doing anything stupid. She glanced around the yard. Frost still glistened on the grass. Maybe he'd hit a patch of ice. She needed to go and look for him. He always took the same route. If something had happened, she'd find him. She looked at the Beast and her stomach cramped. Her cruiser was parked outside the sheriff's office. She'd have no choice but to take the tricked-out truck. The power of the Beast unnerved her. She couldn't do much to damage it, but as it was Kane's pride and joy, she rarely got behind the wheel. The truck was programmed with fail-safes and recognized her tracker ring, so she wouldn't need a key. She opened the door and climbed behind the wheel. The roar as she started the engine deafened her and, watching the camera array, she backed out of the garage and drove to the front door. Leaving the engine running, she ran up the front steps and back into the house.

Keeping a happy expression on her face, she waited for Tauri to finish his milk and then placed the plates into the dishwasher. "Let me get you bundled up and we'll go and see if we can find Daddy. Maybe his Harley has a flat tire and he's pushing it home."

"Okay." Tauri scampered off and she followed him into his bedroom. "If he's lost, Atohi will be able to find him."

Tauri was mentioning their good friend Atohi Blackhawk, a Native American tracker they'd known for a long time. He'd been Tauri's guardian prior to his adoption. Jenna smiled. "I'm sure he will but let's hope Daddy isn't lost. He knows his way around these parts. I'm sure he's fine." She helped Tauri into his coat and hat, pushed on his mittens, and took his hand and led him to the front door. "The Beast is outside. Wait there for a second. Come on, Duke." She put on Duke's coat, set the security, and hurried to the Beast.

Nerves in tatters, she aimed the truck along the driveway and headed along the glistening blacktop. She drove slowly, searching the sides of the road for any sign of Kane. "Look for Daddy. Tell me if you see him or his motorcycle in the grass."

"Okay." Tauri looked at Duke. "Bark if you see my daddy."

Fear mounting for Kane's safety, she turned the corner into the straightaway that went through a wooded area. This part of the road went along behind the ranches and at the end circled back to her ranch. The sunlight barely broke through the canopy of trees but by the time she'd driven halfway, a glint in the trees caught her attention. She pulled the Beast to the side of the road. "Stay here."

Jumping out, her heart missed a beat. The Harley lay on its side, and pieces had sheared off as it hit the trees, but it didn't seem to have been in a wreck. Both wheels looked fine. She looked around. "Dave, are you out here? Dave?"

Nothing.

From this point he could have walked through the trees and made it to the snowplow guy's ranch in ten minutes, unless he'd broken his leg. She bit hard on her bottom lip. If he was hurt, he'd have called her, but if he was injured and lying in the forest, his phone might be broken. She pulled out her phone and used it to locate the tracker in the belt she'd given him for Christmas. Only she and Wolfe knew of its existence. She gaped at the phone. There was no signal. She ran back along the road, searching each side for any sign of him. "Dave, Dave, call out. Wave. Do something. Dave."

Nothing.

Panic gripped her. She called Wolfe. "Shane, Dave's missing. There's no signal on his tracker. I found his Harley smashed on the side of the road near our ranch."

"*Call the hospital. If anyone was involved, they'd have called the paramedics.*" Wolfe sucked in a deep breath. "*Track his phone. I'm on my way.*"

After calling the hospital without luck and finding no response to the locator she had on her phone, Jenna went back to the Beast. *Think.* Knowing Kane, he'd have been riding fast. If he'd swerved to miss an animal, there would be evidence where the Harley left the blacktop. If he'd been knocked from the motorcycle, it could have traveled some ways on its own before coming to rest where she found it. She walked back to the Harley and searched all around. The soil was moist and impact marks where the vehicle had slid sideways evident. Although she found no signs of footprints or marks to indicate Kane was riding the Harley when it hit the trees. Fear mounting for Kane's safety, she walked slowly following the tire marks back to the blacktop, stopped and called again.

Nothing.

Refusing to fall to pieces in front of Tauri, she called Blackhawk. Whatever happened here, she needed expert eyes to scan the area. After explaining, she heaved a sigh of relief to discover Blackhawk was close by on the edge of town. "I'll wait here for you and keep searching."

"*I'm on my way. Tell Duke to search for him, Jenna. He'll find him if he's there.*" Blackhawk blew out a long sigh. "*Dave is very resourceful, if he can walk, he'll be heading home. Do you have spare phones at home?*"

Cold blasted through Jenna's clothes, sending chills over her flesh, but she kept walking along the blacktop, searching each side as she talked. "Yeah, satellite phones and spares. If he's there, he'll call. He'll know I've taken the Beast to go look for him." She turned and ran back to the Beast to get Duke. Not wanting to leave Tauri alone, she'd left Duke with him. "I'll go and get Duke. He's with Tauri in the truck."

"I'm turning off the highway now. I'll see you very soon." Blackhawk disconnected.

Jenna unclipped Duke's harness and helped him down from the truck. She looked at Tauri. "We need to hunt for Daddy in case he's hurt." She unclipped Tauri from his car seat and lifted him down. Taking him with her might be a problem if something bad had happened to Kane. She took his hand and, pulling Kane's woolen cap from between the front seats, held it out to Duke. "Seek, Duke. Where's Dave?"

Duke moved along the highway, crossing from one side to the other with his nose to the ground and tail out straight like a rudder. They'd walked at least fifty yards before Duke barked and turned in circles looking at her. She picked up Tauri and ran to the dog. Heart racing, she stared all around. Setting Tauri on his feet, she smiled at him. "Stand here on the grass and don't move. Uncle Shane and Atohi will be along soon, and I don't want you on the road, okay?"

"I'll wait right here." Tauri stepped away from the road and stood with one hand resting on the trunk of a tree.

Trembling, Jenna patted Duke and held Kane's hat in front of his nose again. "Show me."

Duke moved off slowly, nose to the ground. He walked another ten yards and barked. Jenna ran to him and searched the blacktop. Panic gripped her at the sight of blood. The next moment, Duke walked off again heading for the trees. Keeping close behind him, Jenna noticed the crushed vegetation and then to her horror, Kane's helmet in the bushes. One side was dented and her stomach cramped. Frantic, she turned searching all around. "Duke, seek. Where is he?" She cupped her mouth, "Dave, Dave where are you?"

Nothing.

When Duke walked back to the road, barked, and sat down,

everything fell horribly into place. She swallowed hard and pushed her trembling fingers into her pockets. This had the markings of a setup. The only way to take down Kane would be to render him unconscious. He never left the house unarmed and she'd seen him take down six men with his bare hands. Teeth chattering, she pulled out her phone and called Wolfe. "This looks like a setup. Dave's been kidnapped."

"No one could take him alive, Jenna." Wolfe sounded serious. *"He must be around somewhere. Have you tracked him with Duke?"*

Shivering as the cold seeped into her clothes, she nodded. "Yeah, Duke tracked him. We found his helmet, but he just vanishes in the middle of the road. His helmet is damaged, Shane, and there's blood on the blacktop. He must be hurt bad." She sucked in a deep, freezing breath. "He's gone."

NINE

Shane Wolfe followed Blackhawk's truck along the backroad and parked behind him at the sight of Jenna waving frantically on the side of the road. If Kane had been kidnapped, it was a serious issue and would mean his cover as Dave Kane had been compromised. It had been over five years since Kane had arrived in Black Rock Falls and all had been well. Even with the media blasting his face all over, neither Kane nor Jenna would be recognized by anyone from their pasts, so the idea that anyone had kidnapped Kane for the bounty on his head seemed remote. He'd hold off before notifying POTUS but he could bring in Carter, not by giving him any of Kane's secrets, but for a simple kidnapping for whatever other reason someone might have for taking Kane, Carter would be a great help.

He climbed from his van and went to Jenna. "Let Blackhawk take a look around. He'll see things we can't."

"What happened?" Blackhawk walked toward them and stared at the helmet in Jenna's hand. "Did he wreck his Harley?"

"It's not that simple." Jenna's face had drained of color and she was shivering. "There's blood on the road and Duke can't find him."

"I'll go and see." Blackhawk turned to Tauri and held out his hand. "Come with me. We'll go and look for signs."

As Blackhawk moved out of earshot, Wolfe bent to speak to Jenna. "If there was any noise mentioning Kane, I'd have heard something. If anyone had kidnapped him for the bounty, they'd be crowing all over the media. I'll need to be sure this isn't a local incident before I call in the big guns, and once we do that, your life here is over. If Kane is rescued, he'll be shipped out and you'll never see him again. They'll give him a new handler and nothing I say or do will prevent this from happening. POTUS will protect his asset no matter the cost."

"What the hell do you plan to do? Nothing?" Jenna let out a sob. "I can't just carry on as if nothing has happened. Dave could be dying or being tortured. I'm not sitting around and hoping he'll be able to get himself out of the situation."

Wolfe took her by the arms and gave her a little shake. "Right now, you have no choice. If I report it, all they'll do is wait and listen to the scuttlebutt. They'll never admit he is one of ours. Dave knows this and is prepared for the outcome. There might be a demand for his release, as in money or an exchange of political prisoners. In the meantime, if the bad guys have him, y'all know Dave will be tortured. He's taken down more sadistic regime leaders than I can risk telling you about. Many people want a piece of him. You must prepare yourself for the worst-case scenario." He stared into her tear-filled eyes. "God willing, this is a local matter and someone from his past here in Black Rock Falls is seeking revenge. If it is, then they'll soon discover messing with him is a big mistake."

"If he's badly injured, he won't be able to escape or fight them, Shane." Jenna stared at the helmet. "Look at this, he's hit his head on the same side as the metal plate. It must be killing him. We must find him." She looked over one shoulder as Black-hawk came out of the forest leading Tauri by the hand.

"There's something here you need to see." Blackhawk pointed to a tree.

Wolfe squeezed Jenna's arm and they went to peer at the trunk of a thick pine. "What have you found?"

"A metal cable was tied around this tree and the one oppo-site. It broke." He pointed to the shredded wire. "Someone knew Kane rode here at this time and stretched it across the road. When Kane drove by at high speed, the cable would have lifted him off his motorcycle. I'd say the blood is where he hit the road, maybe he rolled a few times before hitting a tree. I found evidence that his helmet struck a tree. There's paint on the trunk and wood scraping."

"If he was alive, he wouldn't have removed his helmet." Jenna stared at Wolfe and then examined the helmet. "The strap is fine and it's not damaged inside. He'd have kept it on to keep his head warm. He never goes out in cold weather without covering the plate in his head."

"Duke, as you said, stopped searching in the middle of the road." Blackhawk walked along the blacktop and stopped. He pointed at a chalk mark circle." This is where Duke stopped and there is a drop of blood here. So Dave isn't bleeding heavily."

Wolfe bent to examine the spot and straightened. He looked at Jenna. "There's no evidence Dave braked hard or swerved to avoid a collision before the wire and there's no trail of him past this point. Someone lifted him into a vehicle, which means he's been abducted." He looked at Blackhawk. "Can we push the Harley onto the back of your truck? You have ramps, right?"

"Yes, but we'll need to collect the parts as well." Blackhawk frowned. "Do you have an evidence bag I can put them in?"

Wolfe returned to his truck and handed the bags to Jenna, along with a few swab kits. "I'll help Atohi move the Harley. Take a sample of the blood on the blacktop and collect any parts you can find. When Dave comes back, he'll want to see if he can salvage anything." He leaned closer. "Right now, we play this as a local matter. You'll need to get into the office and hunt down any cases where he was involved and the perpetrator is due for parole or release. I figure this is payback."

"Shane." Jenna's grip on his arm was so tight he winced. "I'm not convinced. I'd rather never see him again than have him tortured by terrorists. We must do something now."

Shaking his head, Wolfe looked at her. "You have no idea what you married, have you? Even after all this time and what you've seen with your own eyes, you still don't understand what he is capable of doing. He is a weapon, so highly prized by POTUS he is protected as an asset. If this is a local group of thugs or anyone else we've discussed, Kane will drop into combat mode and use all his skills to escape. Even if it means taking down every last one of them. He'll be in full control unless they try to harm you or Tauri, then without me in his ear issuing orders, he'll kill them all." He rubbed the back of his neck. "Find out who might have done this and we'll hunt them down before this happens. Some things I can't clean up, Jenna. In this town, he's just a deputy."

"I'll need help and Kalo is on vacation." Jenna blew out a sigh. "He'd find a connection in seconds. I'll get Rio and Rowley to search the database as well. I can access Dave's case files but as far as I know, we were both involved in just about all of them. If he's been abducted, he could be anywhere. We'll need help. I can only search to the county line."

Taking in her ashen face, Wolfe nodded. "Why don't you head back to the ranch? I'll see if I can locate Carter. If not, I'll call the Rattlesnake Creek field office and ask Dax Styles to assist on your behalf. We need a military man to help out, one that works well under fire and I know Styles is like Carter—bombproof."

"Don't call in someone I don't know just yet." Jenna shook her head. "I need to check out a few things first."

TEN

Hugging her chest to stop trembling, Jenna watched as Wolfe and Blackhawk loaded Kane's Harley onto the back of Blackhawk's truck. She dropped one hand and went to Tauri, who seemed more inquisitive than concerned. She looked down at him. "We'll head back to the ranch. Daddy might have walked home by now."

"Atohi said Duke would find him if he walked anywhere." Tauri wrinkled his nose and shook his head. "Daddy told me about how Duke barks and wags his tail when he finds something and sits down when there's no scent to follow." He pointed to the road. "Atohi said Daddy got into a vehicle." He frowned. "Why did he do that? It's bad to get into a vehicle with strangers."

Always amazed by Tauri's retention of information, Jenna forced her lips into a smile. She needed to reassure him right now. If anything bad happened, she'd deal with it at the time. "That's right, but Daddy can take care of himself and he was carrying a weapon. He'll be safe. Don't worry, we'll find him."

Legs like Jell-O, Jenna led Tauri back to the truck and placed him in his car seat. She clipped in Duke and climbed behind the wheel. Nothing was making a whole lot of sense right now. All their trackers worked the same as a satellite phone. To disable them, someone would need to know about them in the first place, which was impossible. They could switch off Kane's phone but not his belt. Using a signal jammer or holding Kane deep underground would likely interrupt the signal. Stomach clenching as images of Kane trapped somewhere underground danced across her mind, she swallowed hard. Driving slowly, she continued the circuit around her ranch. She recalled the time it had taken to clear this old road. They'd worked side-by-side discovering the once hidden backroad, mapping it, and then getting in a crew to clear it. Now she wished it didn't exist. Someone had laid a trap for Kane, which meant they had been watching their movements for weeks. With their high security, the only possible explanation is that they used a drone. She'd need to talk to Kalo when he got back and see if there was any way they could detect drone activity around their home.

She left the Beast outside the ranch house and headed inside when her phone buzzed. She grabbed it and stared at the caller ID. It was Rowley.

"Morning, Jenna. We just got a call from Brian Lock, he's a local carpenter. He had a job out at Rosemount Drive for a Ms. Jennifer Kriss. The owner's truck is there but she's not answering and there's a bad smell. He said the woman was insistent he come by today at this time as she works." He sucked in a sigh. *"Do you want us to go and check it out? Lock is on scene now."*

After giving him a quick rundown on Kane's disappearance, she gathered her wits. They had a murder to solve and this might be another. As sheriff, she must try and work on both problems at the same time. She had no choice. "Yeah, check it out and call me if there's anything suspicious. If not, get back to the office ASAP. I'm going to need everyone on duty this weekend."

"Not a problem. I don't believe anyone is capable of kidnapping Kane." Rowley's footsteps sounded on the tiled floor. "Rio just walked in. I'll bring him up to speed. We're heading out now."

Jenna nodded. "Copy that. If I don't hear from you, I'll meet you at the office. If not, send me the address." She disconnected and called Nanny Raya. Having a nanny with high military clearance was a priority.

After explaining the situation, she went into Tauri's bedroom and packed his things into a backpack. Nanny Raya had changes of clothes and everything else he needed, but Jenna liked to make sure Tauri had his special toys with him, especially when the time she'd be away from home was uncertain. She smiled at him. "I'm sorry but I have to go to work, but I must try and find Daddy. Nanny Raya is making cookies today. Maybe you can help her cut them out?"

"She has dinosaur cookie cutters." Tauri giggled. "Dinosaurs with chocolate spots."

Grinning, Jenna hugged him close. "That sounds like fun. I'll be home as soon as I can."

"I don't mind." Tauri hugged her back. "Daddy would be sad if you didn't look for him. I'll have fun with Nanny Raya. She lets me watch TV but not all the time."

Jenna nodded. "Okay, I have your things. Is there anything else you want to take with you?"

"Duke." Tauri scampered out of the bedroom. "Come on, Duke. Walkies."

Debating if it was a good idea to leave Duke with Nanny Raya, Jenna collected her things. She strapped on her utility belt and holstered her weapon. Finding Kane was her priority, but she couldn't leave Rio and Rowley to handle the murder case. She chewed on her bottom lip. *What would Dave do?*

Indecision pulled her in all directions. As sheriff, the homicide was her responsibility, but so was finding Kane. She straightened. One step at a time had always been her motto—their motto—from a relationship, to adopting Tauri, to solving cases. She'd been in tighter corners and could handle anything with the right mindset. She'd gather her team around her and do her job. Pushing down all doubts and fears, she held her head high and headed for the Beast. "You can have Duke with you for company. I have food and spare bowls for him in the back. If I need him to track Daddy, I'll come and get him."

"You'll find him." Tauri yawned and leaned back in his seat. "He's just resting right now."

Her chest squeezed as she looked over one shoulder at him. Her little boy seemed to have a sixth sense about things. Blackhawk said he was an old soul. What kept her going was the fact that he wasn't overly worried about Kane going missing even though he'd seen his Harley in pieces. That sight alone had shaken her to the core. As she headed for Nanny Raya's house, she allowed Wolfe's words to percolate through her mind. He'd never discuss Kane's missions, but he'd know what situations he was capable of handling and how he'd cope under extreme circumstances. She hoped he was right.

ELEVEN

Even on the coldest mornings, Johanna Worth ran in the forest. Appreciating the solitude after working at the pizzeria until late, with the noise and extremes of heat, plus being on her feet all day. The forest rejuvenated her, and although exhausted by the time she arrived home, running each morning was a different kind of exertion. She had many things on her mind. A handsome cowboy had come by a few times and been very attentive. He'd laughed and joked with her, leaving a huge tip each time he dropped by. No one like him had ever shown interest in her. Her disastrous marriage had lasted a little over two years when her husband had come clean and told her he'd only married her to get permanent residence and a green card. His lies had destroyed her faith in men, but the cowboy was a citizen. She'd joked with him and gotten the conversation around to where he was born and raised.

She left the trail in the forest and a gust of freezing wind hit her the moment she crossed Stanton and headed along Pine. She turned into Craggy Rock and, breathing heavily, gave an extra burst of speed before reaching her front door. She opened up and went inside, quickly putting in the code for the home security. She'd made her home safe using gadgets all around. She loved technology and was considering a device that allowed her to talk to a pet during the day when she was at work. Soon she'd visit the animal shelter and find herself a nice little dog. Her ex-husband had been allergic to pets, but she could do whatever she liked and even the cowboy had mentioned he loved dogs. She smiled. It was going to be a good day and she didn't need to show for work until six.

Startled by a sound as she walked into the mudroom to kick off her shoes, she turned slowly. Heart pounding, she peered around the door into the passageway leading to the family room and past the stairs to the kitchen. A chair scraped across the kitchen tile and panic gripped her. How had someone gotten inside her home? She had the latest in security systems, and living in Black Rock Falls, she'd taken every precaution to stay safe. She'd saved long and hard to get the best possible for her budget. She tried to listen, but her breathing came so hard it blocked any noise coming from the house. Looking around, she searched for a weapon and bit her lip in dismay. The only thing she could use was a plastic coat hanger. She snatched it up and edged slowly out of the mudroom and, keeping her back to the wall, moved slowly. The gun safe was in the family room beside the bookcase she'd purchased from a yard sale. If she made it inside the room, she'd be armed and safe from any intruder.

Moving like a cat, she stepped with caution, trying to miss the creaky floorboards. The sound came again and a bumping noise came from the kitchen. She froze mid-step as something moved and then laughed as her robot vacuum cleaner bumped its way out of the kitchen and headed along the passageway. She sidestepped it and ran up the stairs. Once in her bedroom, she took a quick shower. Hungry after her run, she ran through in her mind the food she had in the refrigerator, deciding on something nice to eat. She dried her hair and pulled on sweats. After pushing her feet into her old comfortable slippers, she headed back downstairs and into the kitchen. She opened the refrigerator door and decided on toast and coffee. She had purchased a jar of strawberry preserves from one of the stalls in town over Halloween and couldn't wait a second longer to try some. Carrying her coffee and toast back along the passageway, she hummed a tune. She'd sit in front of the TV, watch the early news, and relax.

She turned on the TV and sat down, placing her coffee on the table. A movement out of the corner of her eye startled her. She turned and stared into the grinning face of the cowboy from the pizzeria. "How did you get in here?"

"What, no 'hello, great to see you again'?" He stared at her, one hand wrapped around a Glock. "I know you like me, so I dropped by. I don't know what's wrong with women. They act all nice when I meet them, but the moment I get them alone they turn ugly."

Johanna's gaze flicked to the gun locker. It was only a few feet away, but she'd never make it. The cowboy looked bigger than before and she was five-five and small. She placed the toast on the table and swallowed the rising fear. Screaming would get her nowhere. Her house was too far from the next property for anyone to hear her. "Hello. It's good to see you again, but why are you in my house? What do you want?"

"Nothing." He shrugged but the gun was pointed at her chest. "I like to see a woman's reaction to seeing me. First they're all sugar and spice, and then it's 'why are you here?' They treat me like trash."

Trying hard not to show he'd terrified her, Johanna nodded. "I'm sorry to hear that, but I'd still like to know how you got inside my house without triggering the alarm."

"No one is safe, Johanna." He folded his arms and leaned against the wall, but the gun remained pointed at her. "All your gadgets, the motion-sensing cameras, the one on the door, the robot vacuum cleaner, and all the smart things you have in your home—the coffee pot, the refrigerator that tells you when food is low—all have cameras. I've been watching you, everything you do. In the shower, getting dressed, pulling on the pink floral panties. I see everything. I know the code to your security system. I can turn them off and on just by using my phone. Right now, all your cameras are switched off. No one saw me walk into the house, nobody knows I'm here." He smiled. "No one can see what happens here. It's just you and me, Johanna."

Trembling with terror, she bit down hard on her bottom lip. Why was he here? Did he just intend to frighten her? He wasn't acting violent, but he'd been watching her and her skin crawled at the thought. She stared at him in disbelief. "How did you do that?"

"Don't you know appliances with Wi-Fi are the easiest to hack? Security cameras, nanny cams, those stupid robotic vacuums that go all around a house once a day. They are the best for seeing if anyone is at home or not. Most people program them for when they're away. It makes it so easy to break into a house. The motion-detecting sensor over your front door gave me the code for your security system. Do you know how many people have a robot vacuum cleaner for upstairs and downstairs and how easily anyone with a small knowledge of hacking can control them? I can move them around and watch your every move. It's better than any reality show on TV and mine is uncensored." He chuckled. "Oh, yeah. I see everything up close and personal."

Panic rising, Johanna tried to breathe. "I think you should leave now."

"I'm not going anywhere." He straightened and came to stand between her and the TV. "I came here to ask you to become my girl. You being here all the time on your lonesome, I figured you'd appreciate someone like me. I know about the other guy." He waved a finger at her. "You do put some interesting things on your computer. You planning on writing a book? I almost blushed when I read about me, but I needed to delete that part."

Startled by his request, Johanna shook her head. Suddenly the handsome cowboy had become a terrifying Peeping Tom. "If you like me, why are you holding a gun on me?"

"To keep you in line." He shrugged. "I didn't want you attacking me or running screaming from the house. The thing is guns are too messy. If I wanted to hurt you real bad, I'd probably strangle you. It takes a long time and is painful, but that's not my style." He leaned in closer. "You didn't answer my question. Do you want to be my girl?"

Gripping her hands together to prevent him seeing her terror, she shook her head. "No. Now can you please leave?"

"Sure." The cowboy shrugged. "That's your choice, just don't move until I leave. Don't touch your phone. Place it on the floor and kick it over toward the TV. Don't think about calling anyone, because you can't prove I was here and I'll come by at any time I want. Just remember that... any time. I'm like a ghost and I will come back. You'll never know when I'm watching you." He stared at her until she complied. "There's a good girl. I'll have my gun aimed at your head." He walked out of her sight.

Shaking all over, Johanna listened over the sound of the TV for his footsteps. A whiff of men's cologne drifted toward her. She could sense him close behind her and shuddered with apprehension. Too afraid to move, she stared straight ahead. Hot breath brushed her ear and she shivered as a finger moved the hair from the back of her neck. She clenched her jaw. "I thought you said you were leaving?"

"I am." Something cold touched the back of her neck. "So long, Johanna, it was fun while it lasted."

TWELVE

The wind howling down from the mountain buffeted Jake Rowley as he climbed inside his sheriff's department truck. As they headed for Rosemount Drive, he gave his partner, Deputy Zac Rio, a rundown on the Jennifer Kriss problem and then the mystery of Kane's disappearance. "I figure we'd be hunting down Kane if it wasn't for the 911 call." He flicked him a glance. "Jenna must be losing her mind with worry."

"We should be out looking for him." Rio shook his head slowly. "He wouldn't be sitting on his hands if one of us was in trouble, would he?"

Worry for Kane was knotting Rowley's stomach. "He'd risk his life for anyone, that's who he is." He shot a glance at Rio as they headed along Stanton. "Jenna and Wolfe are trying to get a fix on his phone. Blackhawk is still out in the forest hunting for any clues. They've come up empty. If anyone had a direction he went in, we'd all be out looking."

"What is Jenna doing to locate him?" Rio's mouth flattened into a thin line. "If he was abducted, who would take him and why? If we discover what's behind it, we might be able to locate him."

Rowley turned into Pine and followed the winding tree-lined blacktop before turning into Rosemount Drive. "I'd say Jenna is doing that as we speak."

"Then let's hope she has some leads we can follow by the time we get into the office." Rio ran a hand down his face. "We've gone as far as we're able with the Dakota Slade homicide. I hope Wolfe finds something." Rio shrugged. "The more I looked into her background, the less I found. She hasn't done anything in her life to make her a victim." He waved a hand. "I've come to the conclusion, apart from kids, peoples' lives bring them into contact with a variety of people. When we consider a serial killer' s victims, the most likely to be murdered are high-risk victims, like vagrants and sex workers. Next are women who live alone."

Rowley nodded. "Let's just hope this isn't another homicide. If it is, we're going to need help."

He turned into a driveway and followed it in a half circle to the front door of a ranch house. A man was leaning against his truck, with his arms folded across his chest. "That will be Brian Lock. He's a local carpenter." He stopped beside the carpenter's truck and climbed out. "Have you had any luck contacting Ms. Kriss?"

"Nope. I've called her phone and I can hear it ringing inside." Lock shrugged. "I figured if she's been in the shower, she'd have been through by now and then there's a smell. I walked around back and the door is wide open. The smell is coming from inside."

"Did you go inside or touch anything?" Rio frowned at the man. "You didn't mention the open back door when you called."

"I went round back in case she was in the yard." Lock straightened. "I knocked hard on the back door, so like the front door I used my knuckles but I'm wearing gloves." He looked from one to the other. "Then I came back here and called 911. This is Black Rock Falls. I'm not walking into a murder scene."

Rowley frowned. This man appeared to be calm and very controlled for the first on scene of a possible murder. "It doesn't concern you that this might be a crime scene?"

"Nope." Lock opened his jacket to reveal a shoulder holster. "I served ten years in the military. I can take care of myself. I figured staying here until you arrived was the correct procedure."

"Stay here." Rio glanced at Rowley and exchanged a meaningful stare. "Better still, get into your vehicle and lock the doors. If anyone is lurking about, it will be safer."

"I'm fine right here with a three-sixty view of everything." Lock shrugged. "You go and do your thing and I'll watch your backs."

Concerned about being shot in the back by a potential suspect. Rowley moved back to his truck. He tossed Rio a liquid Kevlar vest and, keeping the truck between them and Lock, removed their jackets and fitted them. He lowered his voice to just above a whisper. "Jenna mentioned some killers enjoy getting involved at crime scenes. We need to be aware Lock might be a problem."

"You read my mind." Rio pulled out his phone and messaged Jenna. When a reply came back, he looked at Rowley. "Proceed with caution. Check in ASAP." He shrugged into his jacket and pulled his weapon. "You go first and I'll cover you. Move fast, find a position, and then cover me."

Nodding, Rowley took off and, using the trees around the side of the house as cover, dashed into the backyard. He took a position on the corner of the house and waved to Rio. Nothing happened. Lock hadn't moved from his place beside his truck. As described, the door hung wide open, it creaked as the wind moved it back and forth. The smell of death leaked out and he holstered his weapon and reached into his pocket for a face mask. "That doesn't smell good." He pulled his weapon again. "Mask up and we'll take a look inside." He paused at the door. "Sheriff's department. We're coming inside."

"After you." Rio waved him ahead and they cleared the kitchen and moved slowly along the passageway. "The smell is getting worse. I'll watch the stairs, you go inside."

Swallowing the bile rising up his throat, Rowley edged inside the family room. The TV was on and a woman was sitting on the sofa staring straight ahead. An untouched cup of coffee and a plate of food sat on a coffee table. He moved closer and peered around the chair. His stomach heaved. Black empty eye sockets stared into nothing and the woman's mouth hung open in a horrific silent scream. He backed away and went out into the passageway. "One female deceased. Electrocuted, the same as Dakota Slade."

"We'll clear the house and then call it in." Rio headed along the passageway, checked the mudroom. "Clear."

Rowley nodded. "Okay, head upstairs but I doubt the killer is here waiting for us to arrest him. I'm not so sure about Lock, although why would he call it in?"

"This is the problem. The people who murder don't think like we do." Rio ducked into the bedroom and then back out. "This is why they're so hard to catch. They're never predictable." He led the way downstairs. "Call Jenna. I'll contact Wolfe. If he brings his team out here, we might be able to concentrate on finding Kane while he's processing the scene."

After making the call, Rowley headed out the back door. "Jenna's on her way. She said to get a statement from Lock and then send him on his way. She doesn't need any more complications, but she does agree with you. Wolfe can process the scene with Colt Webber and we can get back to the office and concentrate on finding Kane for a time."

THIRTEEN

Fighting her instincts to hunt down Kane and forget about everything else, Jenna ran the current murder cases through her mind. There must be a clue to the person who took him. It was impossible that a terrorist faction had discovered his where-abouts. Her mind went to his recent mission. He hadn't mentioned why he'd been reactivated and she hadn't pressed him for information, but if there'd been the slightest chance of him being compromised, Wolfe would know. She had to put her trust in him, and trust was all she had at the moment. Trust in Wolfe's judgment and her deep conviction that Kane had the experience to get himself out of trouble—but he was just a man and men could be shot dead. That thought alone gripped her chest so hard it hurt. Fighting for each breath and trying desper-ately to remain calm, Jenna parked beside Rowley's truck outside the victim's house and walked up to her deputies. "What have you got for me?"

"Same MO as before." Rio moved to her side. "Only differ-ence is that the back door is open. No sign of forced entry, no sign of anything. Nothing is disturbed. We looked around the house but didn't touch anything, apart from opening the front door. It stinks in there." He wiped at the tip of his nose. "Real bad and it was overbearingly hot."

"The victim has the same two burn marks on the back of her neck. Same with the eyes. It's a replica of the other murder." Rowley's face was sheet white. "The TV was blaring, so I turned it off using the remote. I was wearing gloves."

Dragging her professionalism from the depths of despair and pulling it around her in a protective shield, she thought of Kane. How many times had he used his combat mode to block out emotion? She'd try and do the same. Two poor innocent women had become the targets of a deranged predator with a modified stun gun and the only person who stood between him and the next victim was her. She pulled on a mask and examination gloves, lifted her chin, and walked into the house. "You've called Wolfe?" She glanced at Rio, who directed her along a passageway and into a family room.

"Yeah, he should be here shortly." Rio walked into the room and stood to one side.

The smell of death seeped through Jenna's face mask, but she took her time to scan the room. The body was upright and the victim's long brown hair swept to one side to display two distinct burn marks. She'd seen stun gun marks and cattle prod burns and these were similar. She understood the entry and exit wounds for electric shock and moved slowly around the body readying herself for the gruesome sight. It was the same as before but this woman's mouth hung open in almost a surprised expression. She bent and lifted one of her feet, the burn mark had traveled through the victim's body to exit through the moccasin-style slipper to ground. As Rio had said, it was the same MO.

A crunch of gravel announced the arrival of Wolfe's team, and Jenna led the way from the house to greet him. She walked to his side, glad to see Emily Wolfe with him. She had become a close friend and right now she needed a shoulder to lean on. For a young woman, Wolfe's daughter was worldly beyond her years, and Jenna welcomed the comforting hug from her. "Thanks for coming."

"Don't worry about a thing." Emily's face filled with concern. "We'll process the scene."

"Yeah, why don't you head back to the office and concentrate on finding who might have a beef with Dave?" Wolfe pulled out his forensic kit and looked at her. "I can't find Carter. I sent him a 911 message, told him about the abduction, but he's gone dark. Jo and Kalo won't be back for a week." He straightened. "Blackhawk has been out searching the forest. There's not so much as a footprint out there. He found a spot where he believes Kane slid across the road and hit a tree. There's nothing to indicate he stood and walked away unless he went along the blacktop. If that had been the case, Duke would have picked up his scent. As you said before, he wouldn't remove his helmet. Whoever took him removed it and threw it into the bushes." He shook his head. "And now two homicides." He gave her a long look. "Leave the autopsies to me and Webber. You'll need all your time. I'll give you a report as soon as I'm done."

Biting her bottom lip, Jenna nodded. "I'll need all the time I can get with two homicide investigations and Dave's kidnapping. I have no evidence in any of the cases and with Carter MIA, I have only Rio and Rowley with me to work them. Dave could be in mortal danger for all we know and the clock is ticking. This killer is escalating, if he's killed twice already."

"Y'all don't have a choice, Jenna. Kane is law enforcement and we need assistance to locate him." Wolfe met her gaze. "You must call in Agent Dax Styles from Rattlesnake Creek. His partner, if you recall, was with cybercrime. She'll be able to do everything Kalo could do. Styles will be able to access a wide spectrum of information and might be able to narrow down the field in Kane's disappearance." He gave her a long look. "He was a highly decorated MP before settling in Rattlesnake Creek. He has the experience you need right now."

Swallowing the lump in her throat, Jenna nodded. "Who I need is Carter. He's part of our family. He understands how we work." She rubbed both hands down her face trying to focus. "This Agent Styles, is there anything he needs to know about Dave?"

"Absolutely not for the reasons I've already given you." Wolfe squeezed her shoulder. "Leave the dead to me, Jenna, and I'll see if I can find answers. Use your resources and delegate the work the same as always. You're strong and resourceful. I have faith you'll solve these cases."

A tremble went through her, but she nodded. "Okay. Call me if you have anything and I'll do the same."

"If you discover where Kane is, I'll come with you. You'll need extra backup." Wolfe gave her a long look. "He's like a brother to me, Jenna."

Nodding, Jenna headed for the Beast. Heartache dragged at her, but as the engine roared into life, she could almost feel Kane surrounding her. He was alive, she could feel him inside her heart, but where the heck was he?

Once Jenna arrived at the office, she called Rio and Rowley upstairs. "Rio, I want you to run a background check on the latest victim. We believe her name is Jennifer Kriss. Do the usual checks and see if she has any next of kin. Problem boyfriends, estranged family members, you know the deal. Who would do this to her? Rowley, you keep on checking out the first victim, Dakota Slade, and see if you can find anything at all that might link these victims." She sucked in a deep breath. "If we can't find Carter, I'll call in a local FBI agent by the name of Dax Styles to assist me with finding Dave. His partner is in cybercrime and will be working from their office if we need her. For now I'll be scanning the case files to hunt down anyone who might have had a reason to kidnap Dave." She looked from one to the other. "It might be payback and he could be in danger, but we have nothing else to go on. There was nothing on scene to indicate another vehicle was involved but we found a wire cable tied across the road. Wolfe has it and will check it for any evidence. From what we can estimate, the cable knocked him from his Harley at chest height. The force would have thrown him backward. At some time he was injured, as we found a drop of blood on the blacktop."

"I've seen someone hit a tree branch and come off a motor-cycle. They are thrown back and tumble before sliding to a stop. If he was knocked unconscious, he could have been abducted without a fight. There's no way Kane would go easy and he's never unarmed, is he?" Rio raised both eyebrows. "It would be an easy way to incapacitate him. The worst-case scenario would be he landed on his head and broke his neck." He held up a hand. "That's not what happened, Jenna. Kidnapping a corpse would be worthless. So he must be alive."

Nausea gripped Jenna and she stood to grab a bottle of water from the refrigerator. She leaned against the counter and took long deep breaths. "Thanks for the visual. No, he wouldn't go easy. He can handle six guys and more likely he'd shoot them. Incapacitate them, not kill them, to find out what the heck they wanted." She swallowed hard. "We haven't got Kalo to help out with the searches, so we do the grunt work until Styles arrives." She looked from one to the other. "There must be someone who joins the two murders. I want the names and whereabouts of anyone you figure is suspicious." Running a hand down her face, she looked at them. "We'll run both cases at the same time."

"Why Agent Styles and not Carter? He must be around town somewhere." Rio frowned. "We know nothing about this other guy."

"Carter told me his phone would be switched off for the entire week." Rowley met her gaze. "I figure the only chance of finding him is to go to his cabin. If he's not around, we'll leave a note on the door. He and Kane are close. He'll want to be out hunting him down."

Jenna reached for her phone. "Good idea. I'll call Black-hawk. He goes close by Carter's cabin on his way home and he was out at the ranch assisting me when this happened." She made the call. When she disconnected, she looked from one to the other. "Get to work. We need to find this killer before he strikes again."

"We'll find him, Jenna." Rowley touched his hat and headed for the door.

Jenna stared after them and then dropped into her chair. Who had a grudge against Kane? So many cases over the years it could be any one of them. Fighting back tears, she pressed her face in her hands. She needed to be strong and trust in her team. Lifting her head, she turned to her computer and accessed the files. A mental list formed in her mind. Recently released, due for parole, and a list of relatives of anyone they'd killed in the line of duty. Sometimes people waited a long time, planned and schemed to get revenge. Kane's abduction had been well planned and whoever had taken him wasn't alone. Just lifting him unconscious would be difficult for two men. She ran the cases through her mind, trying to recall the trials and who was there to support the defendant. Without any other choice, she'd start there and, taking out a pen and notebook, made a list of names.

FOURTEEN

The last thing Kane remembered was flying through the air and hitting the road—hard. He'd fought to remain conscious and recalled voices and running footfalls. Confused by the memory, he didn't move a muscle. No vehicles were on the blacktop or parked alongside the ranch's private road. Instinct called on his years of training to assess his situation before opening his eyes. He inhaled with caution, smelling damp. A solid wall pressed against his back and cold seeped through his jeans, so not a hospital bed. Pain niggled at his shoulders because his arms were extended but not hanging in midair. A band of discomfort encircled his head. The image of a tree coming straight for him made sense now. The collision had knocked him out cold even wearing a helmet. He hadn't been sedated. He had none of the usual hangover from a hit of drugs enough to render him unconscious. Someone had abducted him for whatever reason. Making them believe he hadn't regained consciousness would give him time to assess his situation. He checked his body, tightening muscles and assessing the damage. No broken bones, that pain he knew only too well. Bruising, well that happened after being propelled from a Harley going eighty miles per hour.

He'd call himself lucky to survive but he hadn't hit anything... unless someone had rigged up a trap.

Kane opened one eye and peered from under his lashes. He'd been chained to a wall using metal manacles, but the bolts had been hammered into the old red bricks. No telltale ring of mortar circled the chain. Green moss covered parts of the wall, so maybe the room wasn't underground. He listened intently, hearing nothing. Was anyone in the room with him or did they rely on a CCTV camera? People breathed, moved around, scratched themselves, and there was always some noise or sense of them being there, and he didn't feel anyone in the room with him.

Why had they taken him? Convinced this wasn't an old enemy, because he'd been captured and interrogated more than once during his missions. It had started from the second they'd caught him and had been relentless with endless days of torture, no sleep or food. They'd been good but careless, and only he remained to tell the tale of what had happened the day he escaped. These people, whoever they were, had missed a crucial advantage. Attacking when a person was vulnerable and weak was usual practice and they'd left him to recover. He was wearing his leather jacket and gloves, but the weight of his M18 pistol was missing from his shoulder holster. The thought of him being used as a bargaining chip seemed ludicrous—so why? He ran cases through his mind and came up empty. Most if not all the killers they'd convicted were locked away for life or had died.

He rolled his head to the other side, slowly scanning the small room. Old boards covered a window and on a chair against the wall sat a lamp. No cameras. Needing to assess his physical condition, he pushed himself up into a standing position. He flexed his arms and bent his legs. Bloody knees poked through the rips in his jeans, along with a long scrape and black bruising down his right hip. His leather jacket was damaged but had protected him well. His neck was a little sore, so he'd hit the tree head-on. It made sense. He could remember everything, which was a positive. The metal plate in his head hadn't been damaged and the headache was slowly dissipating. The hard smack in the chest had thrown him from the seat but he'd seen nothing and had made a point of removing any low branches from that road to prevent any accidents.

Escaping his priority, he pulled at the chains. They allowed some movement, but punching would be a problem. Wrapping one of the chains around his hand, he tugged and small fragments of brick spilled from around the attachment to the wall. It might take time, but he'd be able to loosen the bolt. A long chain would make a lethal weapon. Jenna's concerned face brushed his mind and he pushed all thoughts of her away. His duty was to get back to her and not worry about her or Tauri. She would be safe and they'd discussed plans to put into action if anything like this happened. Jenna understood she must secure herself and Tauri. By now she'd have contacted Wolfe. She'd place herself in the company of Rio and Rowley and hopefully Carter. She knew the drill. He tugged again at the chain and then spun it around, the motion loosening the bolt. Footsteps sounded outside. They came from a distance, more than one man wearing boots that clattered on a hard floor. Kane dropped into the zone. He had endured torture by experts and survived. Whatever these clowns wanted, he doubted they were military trained. They'd already made mistakes and likely didn't know the true identity of the man behind the deputy badge. He spread the dust from beneath the loosened bolt with the toe of his boot—his steel-capped boots he always wore when riding his Harley—and smiled to himself. They might have taken away his weapon and his arms, but he could sure do a ton of damage with his legs.

FIFTEEN

The phone buzzing startled Jenna out of her thoughts and she grabbed it up and stared at the caller ID. "Shane, do you have anything for me?"

"First up, I've scanned all the usual channels to see if there's any scuttlebutt about organizations acting in Montana or anywhere else. It's something I do routinely, so it won't cause any problems. I found nothing that could possibly involve Dave. From what I know, and this is positive, the mission we completed was attributed to the Secret Service, which is just about as anonymous as you can get, so no foul there." Wolfe cleared his throat. "That's a positive because if anyone else took him, likely he'd be out of the country by now and up for sale to the highest bidder. I'm not sugarcoating the seriousness of this, Jenna. I'll keep my channels open as inconspicuously as possible because by now POTUS would know and he'd contact me. Have you discovered anyone locally who might have a reason to abduct him? Honestly, I was hoping he'd show by now."

Relieved but on edge, Jenna pushed a hand through her hair and stared at her computer screen. "I've hunted down anyone and everyone who is in jail and recently released on parole and you know as well as I do the dangerous ones are either dead or in maximum security. I've tried to scan their immediate families for any chance of a vendetta toward him. This is slow going but calling the prisons and asking about visitors and calls was my only option. Only a very few have anyone visiting them at all. The warden was a font of information. Most are women who believe a serial killer would make a good boyfriend. Most of the family members have never visited them and have changed their names to avoid any connection. I can't see why any of these would take Dave."

"What about the biker gang he messed up? The ones that took you at the Triple Z Roadhouse? It's been a time but they'd be out by now. They didn't do hard time as far as I'm aware." Wolfe's office chair creaked as he rolled it across the tile. *"Maybe look into them."*

Finding a trace of a biker gang would be difficult but it was a lead she couldn't ignore. "Okay. Have you found anything on our two homicide victims?"

"I've uploaded everything onto the server, but as I concluded on my initial examination, the cause of death was an electric shock from an upgraded or modified stun gun. The current, in fact, destroyed the brain stem in each victim and caused major damage to organs as it passed through the body and grounded out through the soles of their slippers. I've detailed everything in my report." Wolfe tapped away on his computer. *"Nothing of interest so far on the swabs we took from all over the house. No other fingerprints or so much as an indication that the homes were wiped clean. If I'd discovered a stun gun at the scene, I'd have considered the victims had killed themselves. I'm sorry, Jenna. I can't find a thing to point to anyone. Someone is murdering women, but whoever is doing this is on the next level of evil expertise. I can only imagine that this person has technical knowledge to be able to modify the amperage on the stun gun. The problem is so many ways to do things are available on the*

internet and more so on the dark web, it makes it difficult to track them down by profession."

Mind reeling at hitting another brick wall, Jenna leaned back in her chair and stared at the clock. It was almost five and she hadn't eaten since breakfast, and likely neither had her deputies. "I'll see if I can track down anything on the web. If not, we might be looking at someone who can access the dark web. That takes a special skill, doesn't it? Although criminals seem to gain access with ease, I've never been able to master it."

"You're being too hard on yourself, Jenna. It's a skill. For some, like writing code, it just slips into place like reading, but for others it's a mystery. It's not a place you really need to explore. There are things there that will live with you forever." Wolfe sucked in a breath. *"I gather y'all are chasing down anyone who came in contact with the victims?"*

Jenna stood and walked over to pour a cup of coffee from the machine. "Yeah, Rio and Rowley have been working all day. I hope they have a list by now, I haven't seen them since we arrived." She added the fixings and stirred. "I'll call Nanny Raya and tell her I'll be late. She is watching Tauri like a hawk, so he'll be safe."

"Maybe you should stay over with her tonight?"

Shaking her head, Jenna walked back to her desk. "No. I'm armed and driving the Beast. I won't take any risks. I'll use Nanny Raya's garage to move Tauri as usual and once inside the truck, no one can harm us. The ranch is secure. We'll be fine. I'd rather be at home, where I have a panic room."

"Okay, check out those bikers and call me if you need me." Wolfe blew out a long breath. *"I've sat waiting while Kane was captured. I can't say where or when or how many times, but it was a long time. He was alone, stripped naked, and subjected to mental and physical torture beyond belief, but he survived. If this is a biker gang, they don't stand a chance, but if we don't hear from him by morning, someone else has him. Expect a ransom or*

deal. If nothing happens and Carter is still missing, you'll need to contact Dax Styles. I know you don't want this but it's essential to get specialized assistance."

Jenna stared into space. "Okay, if we don't hear anything by the end of day, I'll call him." She sipped her coffee. "Thanks for all the info. I appreciate you."

"Stay strong, Jenna." Wolfe disconnected.

She made the call to Nanny Raya and then, feeling light-headed, headed downstairs to speak to her deputies. She looked from one to the other. "First up, have you eaten?"

"Nope, apart from energy bars and a gallon of coffee." Rowley shrugged.

Concerned, Jenna looked from one to the other. "We'll order a pizza for now. What do you have for me?"

"The main problem is that both women came into contact with a cowboy who has the same description." Rio leaned back in his chair, his expression grim. "If I said it was Carter, well it would be a close match and not just once. From all the people I called today, the same guy was mentioned each time." His gaze remained fixed on her face. "We've both been hunting down CCTV footage. Most has been deleted over a twenty-four-hour period, but we do have a few other places to check. I put out a media release for anyone with street CCTV footage over the times we know the movement of both victims to call the hotline. We might discover the name of the cowboy." He rolled his eyes. "It doesn't help that Carter is MIA. Not only do we need his help, but we need to eliminate him as a suspect. Right now, he is at the top of our list."

Astounded, Jenna stared at Rio. "Carter? A suspect?" She shook her head. "No way. We've worked beside him, spent time with him. He works alongside a behavioral analyst for heaven's sake. There's no way he's murdering women." She looked at Rowley. "Tell me you have someone else in mind?"

"We do have a couple of other people who the victims may

have come in contact with over the last two weeks." Rowley looked at his screen. "Dallas Strauss and Chase Holden. Both men have blond hair and fit the same approximate build. They were seen around town by locals, so we included them on the list." He turned to look at her. "That's all we have apart from a timeline for both women, and they followed the same routine like clockwork."

Jenna pulled her hair into a ponytail and tied it with a band from around her wrist. "Okay, we know about the guy in the general store. Hunt down CCTV footage from local stores. The bank is opposite and we have a few security cameras in the area." She looked at Rowley. "Who is the other guy and has he spoken to both women?"

"The guy fits the same description, as we mentioned, like Carter." Rio blew out an agitated breath. "I know it's hard to believe but that's what we have. He was in the market buying supplies and went to the hot food bar. He was seen speaking to Jennifer Kriss three days in a row. I spoke to her workmate, and she mentioned that the guy had asked about a hairstylist in town to get his hair cut." He snorted. "How many other blond cowboys do you know who get their hair cut at a beauty parlor?"

Nodding, Jenna considered the glaring evidence. "Carter is the only guy I know and he's been around town. He talks to women, so it might be a coincidence. If there's two or more men fitting the same description maybe one was him one day and one of the others speaking to Dakota?" She blew out a sigh. "Follow up with the beauty parlor and see if he went there." She glanced at her watch. "They'll be open."

The pizza delivery arrived and she handed them both a box. "Do what you can and we'll call it a day at six. I'll have the 911 calls transferred to my phone. I need to know what's happening." Jenna opened the pizza box and stared at the pie. Her stomach growled with hunger but she had no appetite. Emptiness surrounded her as her mind fixed on Kane. How could she explain his absence to Tauri? He would sense her worry. Her stomach clenched. Not knowing what had happened to her husband and being unable to do something—anything—to help him was driving her insane. What was happening to him and where was he? Without any other options, she opened up the database to hunt down the biker gang members' whereabouts. She hoped he hadn't fallen afoul of them. They were unpredictable and well hidden, and she figured they'd want more than revenge. They followed more of an eye-for-an-eye mentality and Kane might have roughed them up some, but he hadn't killed any of them. Without a clue, a ransom note, or even a threat, she was hog-tied to do anything but wait for someone to make a move. She pictured Kane's face and bit back a wave of fear for his safety. It wasn't easy doing nothing and a lump formed in her throat each time she looked at his empty chair. As Kane's voice drifted into her mind, reluctantly, she lifted a slice from the box and folded it over. "Yeah, yeah, I know. Eat when you can in a crisis because it might be a long time until you get the chance again."

SIXTEEN

The smell of sweat and garlic reached Kane before four armed men walked into the room. Keeping his expression neutral and relaxing to ready himself for any situation, he lifted his chin. He slid his gaze over the men and the reason he'd been abducted hit home like a punch to the gut. He recognized one of the men, introduced to him simply as Mateo, during the FBI undercover arms deal. He'd picked him out in a photographic lineup as the cartel's second in command. If he'd slipped through the net and not been arrested with the others, it meant only one thing: someone in Carter's team was dirty. This alone ramped up the danger of his situation. A dirty player meant protection for the bad guys, sensitive information passed around, and concealing evidence. Not Carter, Jo, nor Kalo—he'd trust them with his life. The organizing team came to him in a sea of names, random faces he'd never expected to meet again anytime soon. Any one of them could fit the bill and, without doubt, had pointed the finger at him after the bust.

Going against his instincts, he'd gotten involved in an FBI sting. Carter had asked and he'd reluctantly agreed. He'd figured he owed Carter a favor after all the assistance his team had given Jenna. Yeah, it had been dangerous, but acting as a go-between for a buyer of large quantities of US military weapons had come easy enough. During his career he'd handled just about every weapon available to a soldier and then some and could strip them all blind. Having knowledge of missiles, mines, mortars, and anti-tank missiles came with the job. Add his ability to speak many languages fluently, and an adequate disguise, made him appear legitimate and the deal went through without a problem. They'd exchanged the cash and weapons before the FBI took them down. The FBI arrested Kane as well, to cover his involvement. So who knew his identity? With the court case looming and Kane as the star witness, his testimony would ensure the main players in the cartel would serve jail-time. Assured the FBI had arrested everyone involved, he hadn't been overly worried about payback—until now. The four men standing in front of him proved there were more rats down the drainpipe.

"I can't believe a simple small-town deputy got involved in our business." Mateo stared at Kane. "Didn't you believe we'd find you? Now you plan to give evidence against us. That will never happen."

Keeping his expression neutral, Kane stared at him. "I have no idea what you're talking about. You've got the wrong man."

"Oh, I don't think so. It has taken us some time to hunt you down, but luckily for us, someone recognized your face. After discovering Agent Carter was involved, finding you was easy enough. He would have chosen someone he could trust outside the organization, someone unknown to us but in law enforcement, and where does he spend all his downtime? In Black Rock Falls." Mateo's highly accented English echoed in the small room. "I must give you credit for fooling me. For a local deputy, you speak our language like a native. I imagine you spent many years in my country, but I digress." He cracked his knuckles. "You have quite a reputation around these parts." He smiled and stared at him as if finding the situation amusing. "I'm going to tell you how this is going to go down."

Wondering where this conversation was leading, this time Kane remained silent. Mateo knew too much to deny his part in the bust. Likely he had a deal to offer. He leaned back against the wall and returned the man's gaze, listening.

"You are going to recant your testimony and refuse to give evidence for the prosecution in the case against my family." Mateo shrugged. "A simple request."

Amused by the idea he'd refuse to give evidence, Kane shook his head. "Request denied."

"Oh, that's too bad." Mateo shook his head slowly. "You could make life so much easier if you complied. Now I'll need to get my hands dirty but it's your choice. Walk into court and tell the judge it's all a lie and we all walk away, no harm, no foul."

Confused but not overly concerned, Kane straightened and looked along the line of men and back to Mateo. If they came at him, he could defend himself to some degree. They didn't plan on killing him, if they wanted him to recant his statement. If he died, his written evidence and the recording would be used as evidence. They'd go to jail with or without his testimony. "Do you believe if I arrive in court all messed up and then say I'm refusing to testify, the judge will just send me home?" He shook his head. "They'll know you're behind it and I'll be thrown in jail for contempt of court until I give evidence."

"Ah, well you see, I'm not going to torture you." Mateo shrugged. "That would get me nowhere, and like you say, seeing you battered and bruised would be counterproductive. Although, I'm sure you'd do anything to prevent your son being tortured, wouldn't you?" He chuckled. "You're chained to a wall and there's plenty of room in here to bring your son and beat him to the edge of death." His expression changed and his eyes turned to dark pieces of granite. "I can almost hear him pleading with you now." He pulled a sad face. "Make them stop, Daddy."

The need to tear out the bolts and wrap the chain around Mateo's scrawny neck rose up like a tsunami of rage, but reacting now would be suicide. Kane dropped deeper into the zone and just stared at him. He'd dealt with men like Mateo before, and thugs like him would have already paraded Tauri before him as leverage. He inhaled slowly. Jenna would keep their son safe, and he would deal with Mateo.

"I've seen men dig out their eyes to stop their sons from being tortured." Mateo shook his head. "Americans have no loyalty to family. You're all scum."

Rolling his shoulders, Kane met his gaze. He had nothing to lose, they'd already admitted they needed him alive. "The feeling is mutual."

"Tough guy. I'll see just how tough you are when we bring Tauri here. Yes, I know his name and where he is right now, but first thing in the morning when your lovely wife is tending the horses, he'll be all alone, asleep in his bed on your ranch." He shrugged. "I'll give you some time to think it over, huh?" He indicated to one of his men, who left the room and returned with a carton and stood looking at him.

Shaking his head, Kane moved his attention back to Mateo. "I don't make deals with criminals."

"Well, we have a week or so, and by then you'll come around to my way of thinking." Mateo chuckled. "Just how long can a five-year-old last? I guess that's up to you. When you decide to comply, I'll care for the boy until you do your part and then release him." He waved the man with the carton forward. "Don't move. I want you to appear fit and well when you arrive in court." Mateo pulled out a pistol and aimed it at Kane. "The chains will give you enough room to eat, drink, and use the bucket, but my aim is good and I will shoot you in the leg or arm if you cause me any problems. Everyone knows you wrecked your motorcycle by now, so a few scrapes and bruises will be acceptable. Don't make me pull the trigger, because when I start, I can't stop."

Mind reeling but refusing to ask questions or appear concerned, Kane remained emotionless as the man pushed the carton toward him and then backed away.

"I'll give you until noon tomorrow to think this over before I bring the boy here." Mateo nodded slowly. "Ah, I see you doubt me." He stared at Kane. "Don't for a second believe your fortress is secure. Like most places, there is always a way inside. Like you, the ranch has a weakness I can exploit." He waved a hand, encompassing the room. "This may look amateurish, but we have a network of people feeding us information via satellites. This is how I knew where you'd be this morning and how I know the movements of your family. Comply and you won't see us again."

If I comply and the judge holds me in jail for contempt, the cartel will attempt to murder me. Kane understood the implications of dealing with a cartel. No one lived to threaten their existence. It was a kill-or-be-killed situation. The moment the door closed and a key turned, Kane tugged at the chain. Freeing himself was a priority. He didn't appreciate threats to his family and they'd need to kill him to stop him escaping now. The faces of Jenna and Tauri tormented his mind, but right now they were safe. Mateo wouldn't get past the security system, and he and his men couldn't exploit anyone if they were dead.

SEVENTEEN

SUNDAY

Unable to sleep, Jenna headed to the barn before daybreak to tend the horses. Nothing had happened overnight. Not one whisper about Kane and she had no idea where to start looking for him. Surely after this long, he'd have managed to escape and call her, unless he was injured. Horrified at the thought, she tried to concentrate on her chores. The horses needed tending and she must keep placing one foot in front of the other. Allowing the panic to engulf her wouldn't find Kane. She tried to plan what to do next, but without any clues it was useless. Rowley and Rio would be heading to the office too. Right now, it was all hands on deck until they solved the cases and found Kane. Exhaustion tugged at her. She'd spent the evening with Tauri, reading him stories and sitting with him until he'd fallen asleep. They'd made his room special and filled it with things he liked. Posters of horses and a toy box overflowing with his favorite toys. Drawings he had done with Kane covered the walls, each one a special memory of their time together. Once Tauri had fallen asleep, she'd worked until late and had tracked down the biker gang to its new clubhouse in Blackwater. She'd contacted the local sheriff, and although he hadn't noticed any unusual behavior in his town, he did know a few buildings frequented by the gang and would check them out. Only one of the gang owned a truck. He doubted they'd abducted Kane. The five men who'd attacked Jenna had been released on parole a few weeks previously. All had reported to their parole officers and gained employment in town. The chances of them holding a vendetta, breaking their parole, and going back to jail was remote.

After repeated calls to Carter without any response, she'd called Blackhawk. He'd left a note on the door of Carter's cabin but hadn't noticed any recent signs of life. Perhaps Carter had gone to another town for a few days? With regret, she'd called Agent Styles. He'd be arriving at the ranch early to assist with finding Kane. Bringing in a stranger and not relying on her own skills weighed heavy on her but with Kane missing and two homicide cases, she had no choice. The sound of a chopper high overhead caught her attention. She hadn't expected Agent Styles to arrive so early. She hurried to finish her chores and pushed the loaded wheelbarrow out the back door of the barn to the manure pile. The sound of the chopper increased and she shook her head. No matter how early he'd arrived, she'd still need to get breakfast for Tauri. A rush of wind hit the barn door, sending a whirlwind of dust pinging against it. Adding feed to the mangers as fast as possible, she turned at the running of feet. Concern gripped her stomach. Had something happened to Kane? She ran to the barn door and hit the button to open it. It seemed to take forever for the door to slide open and she dashed outside in time to see two men on her porch. One carried a battering ram and smashed through the front door. The other ran inside. Beside her, Duke let out a howl of anguish. Horrified, Jenna ran toward the house when rapid gunfire burst into the air. A man dressed in black combat gear aimed an automatic assault rifle at her from the chopper. The sound of Tauri's screams tore at her heart as one man ran out the door with him wrapped in blankets. They'd dragged him sleeping from his bed. In panic, she ran toward him with Duke barking madly beside her. Shots cut up the ground at her feet, showering her with dirt. Duke veered away, barely missing the hail of bullets. Jenna stretched out her hands as if trying to reach her son as they handed Tauri screaming and fighting into the chopper. More bullets pounded the soil at her feet. She gaped in terror. "Leave him alone. What do you want?"

The men said nothing but, aiming the rifles at her, climbed into the chopper and it rose into the air. Screaming in terror, Jenna could only stare after them, trying to absorb as much information as possible. Shaking all over, she stumbled into the house and called Wolfe. Trying to control her sobs, she explained, giving as clear a description of the chopper and men as possible, plus the direction they were heading. "They have taken my son, Shane, and I was powerless to stop them. What am I going to do now?"

"I'm on it." Wolfe's footsteps echoed as he ran through the house to his private office. *"Explain everything to Styles and ask him to contact me. I'll get onto a satellite feed and see what I can find."* He disconnected.

Trembling, Jenna called Agent Styles and was surprised to find her call diverted to his partner, Beth Katz. Trying to keep calm, she explained the situation. "Is there any way of contacting him?"

"He left thirty minutes ago. He's in the air. That's why you were diverted to my phone." Beth let out a long sigh. *"I'll see if I can get patched through to him. He's not far from you. He might see the other chopper and be able to follow it. If you need me to run any info through the databases, call me. I'm in the office today."*

Glad of the support, Jenna sucked in a deep breath. "Thank you. I'd appreciate any assistance you could offer."

"That's what we're here for." Beth disconnected.

Unable to do anything but wait, Jenna notified Rio and told him to bring Rowley up to date. Forcing her mind to stop creating horrific images, she removed her dung-covered boots and took them to the mudroom. Needing to calm her racing heart, she straightened and took long deep breaths. Falling apart right now wouldn't help anyone. As she moved into the bathroom to take a shower and gather herself, the terrible realization of what had happened slammed into her. Wolfe had said Kane could endure torture but his Achilles' heel, the crack in his armor, would be her and Tauri. She slumped against the tile and shook with sobs. They'd taken Tauri to force Kane to do something. Her little boy's life was in danger and Kane would give his life to protect him. She could lose both of them.

Numb, Jenna sat at the kitchen table with Duke leaning against her leg. When the sound of a chopper came overhead, she went to her destroyed front door and stood waiting for it to land. The FBI chopper dropped into her front yard and she wished it were Carter climbing out, but it was Agent Dax Styles. She'd met him briefly in the hallway outside an examination room in the morgue some time ago. She had no idea what he was like, but she relied on Wolfe's recommendation. Remaining on the porch, she waited for Styles to climb down from the chopper, surprised to see him accompanied by a dog. When he walked onto the porch, Duke moved in front of her, barked, and showed his teeth. For Duke that was very brave as the FBI K-9 was twice his size but seemingly placid and under control. "Agent Styles. Thank you for coming. Did you see the chopper that kidnapped my son?"

"I'm afraid not or I'd have followed it." Styles removed his brown Stetson and frowned. "There was no sign of it on my radar, so they have either landed or headed in the opposite direction. May I come inside so you can bring me up to date?" He turned and gave a few commands to his dog. "This is Bear. He won't fight with your dog. He is ex-military."

Reluctant not to be going to find Tauri this second, Jenna nodded and led the way to the kitchen. She dropped into a seat and explained everything from the time Kane went missing.

"I believe I know what this is about." Styles fingered the rim of his hat. "It will take time to explain. Have you eaten today? I'll need you to be alert. Can I pour you a cup of coffee?"

Bursting into tears, Jenna shook her head. "You know? How can you possibly know? There's no possible local threat. I've been hunting down anyone who could possibly have a beef against Kane."

"First, take a breath." Styles stood and poured two cups of coffee. Without asking her, he added cream and sugar to both cups and pushed one in front of her. "Drink and I'll make you some toast." He pulled open the refrigerator. "No arguments. I can talk and cook at the same time. I know you're a tough sheriff, so don't fall to pieces on me."

Forcing her hands around the cup, Jenna nodded. "I don't fall to pieces. Spit it out. What do you know?"

"I know this isn't a local matter. This can only be about the weapons deal takedown your husband was involved in. He is due to give evidence soon and the cartel will do everything it can to stop him." Styles pushed bread into the toaster.

Unable to make sense of what he was saying, Jenna stared at him. She didn't appreciate his laid-back attitude when Kane and Tauri were missing. "That's impossible. Carter said they arrested the entire family and they're in remand."

"It's obvious we didn't arrest every member of the cartel. They have family members all over and they'll risk everything to prevent their hierarchy from being compromised. They probably believe they can make Kane recant his statement and refuse to take the witness stand. They'll use your son to force him into submission. This is crazy talk, but they can't murder Kane because his statement and the tapes will stand up in court. This is a last-ditch grasp at attempting to get a mistrial.

Whoever told them it could possibly work is giving them bad advice."

Angry at his nonchalance, Jenna glared at him. "Bad advice won't prevent my son and husband from being murdered by them. I know about cartels and how ruthless they are. They'll stop at nothing to get their own way."

"I know about cartels too. Time is of the essence and discovering where they're holding Kane and your son is my top priority. We have two choppers at our disposal. I'll find them but I'll need your assistance. I know you have urgent homicide cases to solve, but you'll need to organize your deputies to handle them in your absence. I'm sure this early in the investigation they'll be doing grunt work and won't need you to supervise them." He buttered the toast. "Eat the toast. We might need to leave in a hurry, and I'll need you alert and on your game if my plan is going to work." Styles slid the plate toward her and sat at the table opposite her. "My partner is a cybercrime expert and I gave her the approximate coordinates of the chopper. She is currently speaking with Wolfe and they're attempting to find a location. It might not be an exact match, but we'll have a few possibilities. It's hard to hide a chopper in this county. They can't land in the forest, so it has to be an open area. Wolfe and Beth have a good chance of finding it." His large hands closed around a coffee cup. "I'm not telling you to stop worrying, Sheriff, but rest assured everything possible is being done. Beth is one of the best and you've known Wolfe for years. They'll move heaven and earth to find them."

Taking a breath, Jenna looked at the handsome man opposite. His expression was sincere and not arrogant. He reminded her of Carter in his casual approach, but then this was a mountain man and they had a relaxed way about them. She could see the concern in his eyes. He hadn't tried to shield his feelings. "And when we locate them? What's your plan? If it's just you, me, and Wolfe, do you figure we can take down a cartel?"

"If you're as good as your reputation, yeah." Styles smiled. "They won't know we're coming, will they? And Kane is on the inside. Wolfe tells me he can take care of himself."

Swallowing the lump in her throat, Jenna nodded. "Yeah, and if we're going to risk our lives, Agent Styles, call me Jenna."

"Styles." Styles smiled at her. "While we're waiting, it's best to keep busy. Give me a rundown on the current homicides. I checked out what you uploaded to the server last night." He ran a hand through his collar-length light brown hair and turned his gaze on her. "If Carter is electrocuting women, I'll eat my hat." He leaned back in his chair and shook his head. "Although, considering the serial killers we've dealt with lately, anything is possible. I'm getting to the point where I don't trust anyone anymore. What you see is not what you get when it comes to psychopaths, is it?"

Calmed by his positive presence, Jenna nibbled at the toast. "No, we could be sitting opposite one right now and wouldn't know until it was too late."

"Ain't that the truth." Styles gave her a long look. "I hope not. My visit to Black Rock Falls is complicated enough right now."

EIGHTEEN

Dark skies and low cloud shrouded the snowcapped mountains, and the wind rattled the glass doors of the sheriff's department as Rio stared into the gloom. Winter was overdue and the late snowfall meant when it did arrive it would be brutal. The office, with its new furnace, was usually warm, but being Sunday, when he arrived with Rowley it was freezing. It hadn't taken long to set things right, but they both sat bundled up in their thick coats, gloves, and hats waiting for the temperature to rise. Jenna had made a frantic phone call earlier and he stood leaning on the front counter waiting for her to call again. She'd outlined what had happened to Tauri but had called in Special Agent Dax Styles from Rattlesnake Creek to assist. He scratched his cheek. They'd always worked as a close-knit team and her idea to change the system concerned him. He glanced up as Rowley handed him a steaming cup of coffee. "I feel useless just waiting here for something to happen."

"We're short of resources with Carter missing and Jo and Kalo on vacation. Jenna had no choice; she needs the backup of the FBI." Rowley blew across his coffee cup. "I figure calling in an agent with a chopper is a good thing. He can move from one place to another in less time than we can drive and he's a tough agent with an MP background."

Rio's phone vibrated in his pocket, and he took the call, putting the phone on speaker. "Any news yet, Jenna?"

"Wolfe is still hunting down the chopper's location with Agent Katz. I figure they're close. They're coordinating signals. Styles is doing a preflight check and then we'll be going to Wolfe's helipad to refuel. They have a plan, but I didn't call for that reason." Jenna took a long breath. *"We have two active murder cases with no credible evidence. I want you to hunt down the two possible suspects, Dallas Strauss and Chase Holden. Find out everything about them, where they live and work. Go and speak to the managers of the food market and the general store. Talk to the people working at the food bar. Show them pictures of the men and Carter. Ask them if they've seen any of the men in the stores over the last week or so. If you get a positive ID on Strauss or Holden, go and speak to them. See what you can find."*

"We've collected a ton of local footage from people via the hotline." Rowley sipped his coffee. "We'll need to go through that as well."

"That will take you forever." Jenna paused for a beat as if thinking. *"Call Agent Katz out at Rattlesnake Creek field office and ask her advice. With luck, she'll be able to run a facial recognition program incorporating our three suspects. Unfortunately, as Carter is missing, we need to include him into the mix. I don't believe he is involved for one minute, but we can't ignore the fact that he fits the description of the man seen with the murdered women."* She sucked in a deep breath. *"When you're done, start on the victims' laptops or tablets and hunt down their social media platforms. Check out their phones. Who did they call? Are they friends of one of the suspects? Does the killer work in an industry that involves the victims in any way? None of these*

things must be ignored. We can't risk missing a link between the victims."

Rio shot Rowley a glance and raised both eyebrows. "Okay, we're on it."

"I hope you find Kane and Tauri real soon." Rowley swallowed hard, making his Adam's apple bob up and down. "How are you finding Agent Styles?"

"Bossy but efficient." Jenna cleared her throat. *"I'll message you if we find any trace of them and then I'll maintain radio silence until we get them clear. Wolfe will be backing us up. Your priority is the homicide case. Get the job done."* She disconnected.

Heading behind the desk, Rio changed the 911 calls to his phone and looked at Rowley. "She's holding up well under the circumstances."

"She can maintain that tough exterior for a time." Rowley rubbed his chin thoughtfully. "I've never seen her fall to bits, but she's only human. We'll need to be here to take the weight as much as possible until this resolves itself one way or another. If the cartel is involved as she believes, it could be messy."

The phone on the desk rang and Rio picked it up. "Sheriff's office. You're speaking to Deputy Rio."

"This is Brian Rhoads, the manager of the pizzeria. I didn't want to call 911 as I might be worrying over nothing, but one of my long-time employees, Johanna Worth, didn't show for her shift last night. It's not like her not to call in if she's sick. She was due at six last night. I called at eight, mainly to see if she was okay, and got her machine. Same thing this morning. I know she goes out for a run every morning in the forest and I'm getting concerned. She lives alone out at Craggy Rock since her divorce." He let out a long sigh. *"I'd drive up there myself to check on her, but I don't have anyone to run the pizzeria. Weekends are always busy and I have dough to prepare."*

This is all we need. Rio ran a hand down his face and

blinked tired eyes. "Give me the details and we'll do a drive-by."
After taking down the details, he disconnected and looked at
Rowley. "We might have a problem. Another woman hasn't
shown for work and nobody can reach her." He pushed his hat
on his head. "Let's go."

The front door swung open and Rio's twin siblings, Cade
and Piper, walked inside in a blast of cold air. Their noses were
red tipped and their cheeks crimson. He came out from behind
the counter to greet them. "What's up?"

"Nothing." Piper smiled at him. "If you're working on a
Sunday and the sheriff isn't around, something is wrong. We
heard the news on the TV about the guy they're calling the
Casanova Killer. Does he really try and charm the servers in the
stores and then kill them?"

"So it would seem." Rio raised an eyebrow. "Why are you
here, Piper?"

"We heard about the request for camera footage of the guy
and figured you might need some help manning the phones, so
we dropped by." She shrugged. "We haven't anything to do
today. We're sick of studying. It's fall break next week. We have
plenty of time."

At twenty and college students, the twins were more than
capable of manning the phones. "Sure, we need all the help we
can get right now." Rio took two notepads from a drawer behind
the counter. "If anyone calls, make a note of the time, take their
details first, and then take down why they're calling." He took
two cards from a holder on Maggie's desk and handed one to
each of them. "Tell them to upload any footage to the link on
these cards. There's a page where they fill out details and a file
set up for the camera footage. They just have to click it and
upload."

"Anything else, say, if they're calling about the murders,"—
Rowley moved to Rio's side—"take their details and any information. Take your time and get them to repeat anything you

don't catch first time around. Again, times and dates are crucial evidence, but don't be surprised if the phones don't ring all day. It happens. Don't leave the office unattended. If you get hungry, order takeout and charge it to the sheriff's office. We're good at Aunt Betty's and the pizzeria. Coffee and cookies are in the kitchenette. Lock the door behind us." He zipped up his jacket and smiled at them. "We might be away for a time. We have a long list of things to do."

"Go." Cade shrugged out of his jacket and hung it on a peg by the door. "We'll be fine." He indicated to the TV in the corner of Maggie's office. "We'll watch TV and pig out on pizza. Same as at home." He grinned.

Rio nodded and headed out the door. He looked at Rowley. "Do you know Craggy Rock?"

"Yeah, it's close to Stanton Forest." He headed for his truck. "We'll take my ride. I know my way around better than you do and it will make life easier. Why don't you hunt down the details of our suspects, we can head there once we've done a welfare check?"

Icy wind cut into Rio's cheeks as he skirted the hood of Rowley's sheriff's department truck and climbed inside. "The wind is cruel. It cuts right through everything." He added information to the MDT. The mobile data terminal was a crucial piece of equipment in a patrol vehicle. The computer had many functions and locating people was one of them. Once located, he'd get a rundown of any outstanding warrants and criminal background.

"Yeah, it is but with luck it will blow away the clouds and hold off the snow for a few more days." Rowley backed out of his parking spot, spun the truck around, and headed out of town.

Raindrops splattered the windshield in a vague attempt to rain, the high wind more likely bringing with it small particles of snow or ice from the mountains. Rio climbed out of the truck and waited for Rowley. He scanned the immediate area, noticing the truck parked in the driveway matched the vehicle owned by Johanna Worth. "That's her vehicle. The plate matches." He headed toward the door. "If she doesn't respond, we'll head around back and check the doors."

"You mentioned she runs." Rowley indicated to a trail leading from her driveway. "That likely crosses Stanton and leads to the forest. If she went on a run this morning, maybe she was injured."

Rio shook his head. "If a bear took her, she'd be in trouble, but if she fell or hurt herself, she'd be carrying a phone. Do you know anyone who goes into the forest without a phone?"

"True." Rowley went to the front door and rang the bell. "Sheriff's department. Are you home, Ms. Worth?"

The sound of the doorbell filled the silence of the isolated building. No footsteps came down the stairs, no answering reply to Rowley's persistent and very loud calls. Rio pulled on examination gloves. "Go and check around back. I'll look through the windows. See those flashes? I figure that's a TV but I can't hear anything."

"Okay." Rowley hurried alongside the house, his boots crunching on the gravel.

Outside, Rowley's loud hammering on the back door echoed through the house, as did his callout. Rio moved to the windows, cupped his hands, and peered inside. A mudroom, foyer, and large windows of the family room loomed up on his right. He moved closer, noticing the flicker of a TV and peered inside. The chilling impact at finding a body is always the same. First a feeling of revulsion and the need to flee, followed by the tightening of stomach muscles and a wave of fear. He sucked in a breath and turned, almost jumping out of his skin when Rowley appeared out of the bushes. "This looks like another murder. There's a woman on a sofa before the TV. I can clearly make out burn marks to the back of her neck."

"I'll try the front door." Rowley moved forward. "The back door was locked. No signs of forced entry." His hand closed around the doorknob and it turned. "It's open." He looked inside. "The security system is turned off."

As the awful stench of death wafted out of the house, Rio turned back to Rowley's truck. "Masks and booties before we check the body."

They suited up, and taking a deep breath, Rio straightened his shoulders and walked inside. The victim was positioned on the sofa before the TV. A sandwich and a cup of coffee sat on a table beside her. He'd viewed Johanna Worth's image on her driver's license, not a great beauty but a pleasant face. His stomach roiled, threatening to eject his breakfast. Johanna Worth no longer existed. Wide black holes replaced her eyes, and blue lips drawn back into a hideous grimace gave the impression of a Halloween mask. "It's the same MO as the others. Don't touch her. It's pointless checking for vital signs."

The body made a sound like a moan and they both jumped back and looked at each other. The sound came again and Rowley's face drained of color, his brown eyes, wide and fixed on the victim. Recovering from the fright, Rio grabbed him by the shoulder. "She's dead. That's the sound of the body decomposing. A buildup of gas, is all. We'll need to call this in." He thought for a beat. "Not Jenna or Wolfe. I'll call Em and ask her who is available. We can't call in someone from Helena."

"Norrell will likely come with her and Webber. She is part of Wolfe's team and, as a forensic anthropologist, is qualified to do a sweep of the scene." Rowley shook his head. "Whoever is doing this is real sick."

Suppressing a shudder, Rio turned away. "We'll clear the house, but I doubt the killer waited around for us to arrive."

They rushed through the house, calling out "clear," and met back in the foyer. Nothing had been disturbed. Just like the other murder scenes, the killer hadn't left any sign of being there. "Let's get out of here before the stink permeates our clothes."

Outside, he stood in the wind with Rowley, glad of the fresh albeit damp wind rushing through his clothes, the sweet pine forest scents blowing the stink from his nose. He took out his phone and called Emily Wolfe. He spent most weekends with Emily. They had gotten closer of late, and he couldn't wait until she graduated from medical college. The internship would be with her father in the medical examiner's office or maybe a spell at Black Rock Falls General, but it would mean they could take their relationship a step further. He loved her dearly and wanted her as his wife but had promised her dad they would take things slow until she'd finished her studies. She'd turned twenty-two and knew her own mind. A determined woman, smart and great company, just hearing her voice turned him into a shy teenager. "Hi, Em, we've found a body. Another victim of the stun gun killer. I know your dad and Jenna are busy hunting down Kane. Can you round up a team to do a forensic sweep and collect the victim's body?"

"Sure, text me the address and I'll call Norrell and Webber." Emily sighed. *"Luckily, Julie is at home to watch Anna. I'd hoped you'd drop by today."*

Frowning, Rio glanced at Rowley, who'd climbed into his truck. "No, we're investigating the homicides. Jenna didn't want to lose any time. She must have figured he'd strike again soon. Once you're through here, we'll be hunting down suspects."

"I understand. Death waits for no man. I'm on my way." She disconnected.

NINETEEN

Somewhere in Black Rock Falls

It had been a long cold night but Kane hadn't wasted any of it. He worked at loosening one bolt and then the other. Pulling them completely from the wall was counterproductive. If his captors discovered him lose, they'd likely either shoot him or hammer the darn things back into place. If he pulled himself free, he'd never make it out of the metal door or barred window. No, he needed to outthink this band of men, who threatened his wife and son. So far, they'd fed him, changed the slop bucket, and given him adequate amounts of water. He found this highly unusual for the cartel. The usual mode of torture or persuasion didn't involve food or water. It came with blows to the body that could be covered by clothes, sleep deprivation, or water torture. One thing, moving and using his muscles to pull at the chains had eased the stiffness from his injuries. Keeping moving even when chained was a priority. Killing each and every one of them his motivation.

A chopper passed overhead and he hoped Jenna had Wolfe or Carter out searching for him. His phone or belt locator should have pinpointed his location hours ago, which made him wonder why nobody had found him. He'd expected a rescue by now... unless they had Jenna. He shook his head in denial. She had Duke and the Beast for protection. Duke was a great early warning signal, and she had the panic room and Wolfe. When the sound of footsteps came from outside the door, he kicked away the brick dust from the wall behind him and leaned against it. If he turned to one side, he could use one hand, but the chains restricted him from using both at the same time.

The lock in the door clicked and the metal door swung open. Two men, one with a carton, the other with an automatic weapon, moved into the room. They didn't speak to him but, using a broomstick, pushed the carton within reach. Kane could smell coffee and wondered briefly if they planned to lure him into a false sense of security with the food. He waited for them to leave and pulled the carton toward him with his foot. He turned to one side and reached for the one of two to-go cups of coffee. One bag held bagels and cream cheese—Jenna's favorite —and the other six fresh donuts sprinkled with powdered sugar. He sniffed each item and sipped the coffee and waited. Nothing happened. They hadn't drugged the food.

He ate everything, drank the coffee, and then stood the four bottles of water in a line within reach and waited. It had been at least forty minutes before the footsteps came again and Mateo stepped into the room. Acting nonchalant, Kane eyed him and the three men with him. He made a mental note of each man's features. These were the same men all the time. He figured the extent of Mateo's team was four. They had a chopper, which added another problem. They had the ability to move fast and over vast distances. If they had taken Jenna or Tauri they could take them anywhere and he'd never find them. He waited for Mateo to speak.

"How is your eyesight?" Mateo held out his phone.

A shiver of concern slithered down Kane's back. It was easy

to recognize Tauri's tear-streaked face. He pushed down a rush of anger so intense it sent a shudder through him, but he said nothing and listened.

"Daddy, this baddy man broke the front door and took me in a chopper. Can you come get me?"

"Your ranch isn't so safe, is it?" Mateo grinned at him. "I have your son and you have three hours to make a decision. Until then, I won't touch a hair on his head. I've already fed him but that all stops at noon." He waved his men from the room. "If you don't agree to my demands, the consequences to your son are out of my hands. I have a man who is highly skilled in keeping a person alive during torture. He can't wait to start on Tauri."

The sound of Tauri's name on this animal's tongue sent bile rushing up Kane's throat, but he remained emotionless. Allowing the enemy to get the upper hand was a mistake he'd never make. Anger smoldered into a volcano of destruction and he welcomed it. He'd use it to protect his son and strike so fast their weapons would be useless. Oh, how he'd make them pay for touching his family. Breathing in through his nose and out slowly through his mouth, not one muscle twitched. This man was a fool to reveal his intentions to him and he could use that knowledge to his advantage. They had underestimated him and now it was time to make his own plans. The moment they produced Tauri it would be game on.

TWENTY

The noise of the chopper surrounded Jenna and for once the vast beauty of Black Rock Falls had become a massive haystack hiding Kane and Tauri. She used field glasses to search all around the coordinates Agent Katz was feeding through to Styles and Wolfe. To her surprise, Nanny Raya had arrived to assist in the search. As a retired operative, she could use her in-the-field knowledge to their advantage. She had nodded to Jenna and climbed into Wolfe's chopper. Trying hard to control the waves of rising panic as the hours ticked by, Jenna listened to the transmissions between Styles and Wolfe or Agent Katz. Flying with Styles was very different from Carter or Wolfe. She'd always believed Carter to be a little crazy and take too many risks, but Styles was a whole new ballgame. He tossed his chopper around swooping up and down, and moving so close to the roofs of houses she clung to the seat in terror. After half an hour Jenna had experienced every ride at the fair and had her stomach in her mouth more than once.

During lulls in the radio conversation, he didn't speak to her. Keeping her attention on any buildings they flew over, she flicked him a glance. "Have you been flying long?"

"Yeah." He flicked her a glance. "Beth asked me the same thing first time we flew together." He swung the chopper to the right. "Do I make you nervous?"

Dropping the field glasses as they banked, she looked at him. "My nerves are shot, so it's difficult to say, but you do seem to take risks."

"I know the capabilities of my bird." Styles dropped down low and then without warning rose very high. He used the radio to contact Wolfe. "Possible target in sight." He gave the coordinates. "Two black SUVs, a chopper, and a small brick building set beside the burned-out ruins of a ranch house. Maintaining altitude to avoid detection. Suggest stealth. Over." He looked at Jenna. "Look down on the left. I'm sure I saw someone moving outside. I'll do another sweep, but I'll need to maintain altitude or they'll get suspicious. Check it out."

As the chopper made another sweeping turn, Jenna aimed the field glasses down to the brick building. A jolt went through her stomach. In front of the building, a man dressed in black combat gear with a submachine gun slung over his shoulder leaned against the wall. "Yeah, one man, armed. He's wearing the same gear as the men who took Tauri." She moved the glasses over the chopper and her heart raced. "The chopper has a blue emblem on the tail. It's the same chopper. We've found them."

"Positive ID on the chopper. Armed guard on patrol. Over." Styles contacted Wolfe and then looked at her. "The problem is we can't just land and storm them." Styles frowned at her. "They wouldn't hesitate to kill Kane and your son. They're witnesses. I'll search for a place to land where we won't be seen, but we'll be going in on foot." He peered out of the window. "Looking at the terrain, it will be a mile or so. I'll take a look around, but we don't want to alert them we're here."

The radio came to life. It was Agent Katz.

"I'm detecting something strange at those coordinates. There

was a signal interference when you first called in. I figure they are using a signal disruptor. Over."

Jenna swallowed hard. That would account for not detecting the tracker in Kane's belt. His phone could have been smashed but no one knew about his belt. These men were covering every angle and not taking chances of being detected. Concern for Kane's and Tauri's safety growing by the second, she ran a hand down her face. "That means we won't be able to use our comms on the ground."

"That won't be a problem." Styles lifted one shoulder in a half shrug. "We've all used hand signals during missions. Wolfe will be able to communicate with me as long as we have eye contact."

Blowing out a breath, Jenna nodded. "That's good to know."

"Over there, a wooded area with grasslands behind." Styles used the radio to speak to Agent Katz. He gave her the coordinates. "Check for any mineshafts in the immediate area. I'll need room for Wolfe to land as well. Over."

It seemed a lifetime before the response came back and Jenna listened with interest as the all-clear came over the radio. They sped off in the direction of the trees and from another direction she made out the white ME's chopper, speeding toward them. When Styles landed. Jenna ripped off her headset and climbed into the back to retrieve their backpacks. Bear licked her hand and Duke barked a warning. She rubbed his ears. "It's okay, Duke. We'll find them. Now make friends with Bear. He is here to help too."

"Bear hasn't got a bad bone in his body." Styles jumped down from the chopper and took the backpacks from her and set them on the ground. "He nurtures and protects. He was trained to do a wide variety of maneuvers on the combat field, since then I've trained him to track. With the pair of them, we should be able to locate Tauri." He gave her a long look. "Carter has told me how much he admires your husband's abilities, so

I'm sure he'll be fighting back from the inside once he knows we're there. He was a Marine like Wolfe, I believe?"

Jenna nodded. "Yeah, there's no 'was' in the Marines. It's lifelong, in or out of the service."

"I understand. I was an MP in the Army. We had a close-knit team but we weren't popular on base. I don't miss being in the service at all. I like the slower pace of Rattlesnake Creek, although of late, since Beth arrived, we've been working all the darn time. It's her expertise in cybercrime. Someone is always needing her for something, so we travel all over." He held out a hand to assist her from the chopper and winced. "It's a long way down and I don't want you to turn your ankle."

Reluctantly, Jenna took his hand. Because of her size, many people believed her to be incapable of jumping down from heights, but the ground was littered with rocks and she didn't plan on limping behind the others when they hunted down the cartel. "Thanks." She hit the ground and turned to lift Duke down, her knees buckling from the weight of him.

The moment Wolfe landed he made his way to her side. He carried a backpack and a medical kit over one shoulder. On his hip, his M18 pistol was evident, and his jacket was weighed down with spare ammo clips. She turned to see Styles spin the cylinder of a Magnum revolver and pat his pockets for extra ammo. She blinked at him. "You're bringing a six-shooter to a gunfight against automatic weapons?"

"I have a Glock as a backup weapon, just in case things get nasty, but I figure four bullets will be enough." He pushed on his Stetson and turned to Wolfe. "Are you leaving the nanny behind?"

"Yeah. Raya is going to man the radio." Wolfe pulled on a pair of gloves. "If Beth believes they're using a signal blocker, it's better someone remains here to see what happens. She can call Beth for assistance if we need it. Beth can alert the Black-water sheriff. They have a chopper at their disposal."

"That sounds like a plan." Styles looked over his shoulder at Jenna. "Are you ready to move out, ma'am?"

Jenna opened her mouth to tell him not to call her ma'am, but military men were all the same and she just nodded. "Absolutely. That's my family being held hostage by mercenaries."

TWENTY-ONE

Craggy Rock

It had taken longer than expected for the forensic team to process the crime scene, and hunched against the cold, Rowley made another sweep of the house perimeter, searching for anything of interest. One footprint could make so much difference in a murder investigation. Rio had walked the entire driveway, up one side and down the other, searching for tire tracks. They'd found no trace of the stun gun killer. It was like hunting down a ghost. How could a guy move around without leaving a trace behind? Heck, he'd made footprints alongside the gravel pathway to the back of the house and yet they'd found no trace of anyone. As he walked, his mind flicked back to Jenna. They'd heard nothing from her since she'd left with Agent Styles, and no news wasn't good. The choppers could cover a wide area in a short time and it had been three hours since she'd left.

Pushing the concern to one side, he concentrated on the murder cases. Jenna had taught him well and Rio had handled his fair share of homicides. There was no reason they couldn't find this killer alone. It would be nice to be able to remove some of the burden from Jenna's shoulders right now. She was holding up well, but he suspected the brave exterior was hanging on by a thread. They must move on with the murder case and have something for her when she returned. He walked back around the front of the house and met Rio. "I've found nothing at all. You?"

"Nope and I've just spoken to Norrell." Rio blew out a long sigh. "She gave me the laptop and phone, but she didn't find any fingerprints not belonging to the victim. No signs the place was wiped clean either. The only thing she believes might me a possibility is that the killer moved the hair to one side to get access to the neck." He shrugged. "He might have left something on her skin, a trace of sweat, something. So she'll be concentrating on that. She also believes that as there is one sandwich and one cup of coffee, the victim wasn't expecting company."

Rubbing the back of his neck, Rowley looked at him. "The place has high security and yet the alarm was switched off and the front door unlocked. How did he get in if she didn't open the door to him?"

"This is something we need to concentrate on." Rio stared into space. "Why did she just sit there and allow him to touch her hair? Why didn't she run? Victims are usually found in hallways or places where they've tried to escape. All these victims just sit in front of the TV and there's no indication they were moved postmortem."

Putting himself in the victim's shoes for a while, Rowley frowned. "Maybe he knew the code for the door, and most guys carry a weapon out here. He maybe walked in and held a gun on her." He looked at Rio. "She's alone, no neighbors, and a guy sticks a gun in her face. She's not going anywhere, is she?"

"That makes sense." Rio stared at the door as Webber pushed a gurney with the body out to the ME's van. "What doesn't is his motive. This is a serial killer and they usually have something that makes them kill. They enjoy the kill and it's usually messy. This is almost nice in comparison to what we usually see. I can't see the thrill in killing someone with a stun gun."

Sickened by the sight he'd witnessed of the wide-open black holes for eyes in each victim, Rowley shook his head. "Maybe he gets his thrill after the kill. He likes the look of what he's done. He enjoys ruining their faces. Maybe eyes are a trigger and he wants to destroy them. Don't ask me to figure them out or I'll be as crazy as them."

TWENTY-TWO

Somewhere in Black Rock Falls

Watery sunlight peeked through the boards over the barred window, marking the floor with bands of gold dancing with sparkling dust motes. Jenna always referred to the shimmering particles as fairies. They swirled around, tossed by the wind for a few seconds before a cloud hid them from sight. Where was she? Free and searching for him and Tauri or tied up somewhere to use as leverage. As there'd been no mention of her by any of the men, and Kane had understood every word they'd uttered, even though they'd changed from their initial Spanish tongue to Portuguese in an attempt to outwit him. If they had Jenna, one of them would have mentioned her as they had often mentioned Tauri. At only five, his son, although strong and very smart, would be terrified. He wished he could reach out to him and tell him all would be well. He drank water and got slowly to his feet, stretching a little and then relaxing at the sound of footsteps and grunts in what he imagined was a small passageway outside the metal door.

The door swung open and the rusty hinges complained

with a high-pitched whine. Kane's attention moved to them. A well-placed kick might break the bottom hinge and make it easier for him to escape. The door opened to reveal two men carrying a heavy metal table. Red-faced with effort, they fought to guide it through the door and once inside they pushed it into a corner. Amused, Kane bit back a smile as they bent over breathing heavily, with their rifles swung over their backs. They were prime for the taking and, muscles bunched in anticipation of lethal action, his hands closed around the chains. He froze at the sound of Tauri's protests from the passageway. The next second, Mateo walked in dragging his son.

"Daddy." Tauri wild-eyed and frantic turned and bit down hard on Mateo's hand. The man released him in a string of curses and Tauri ran to Kane and wrapped around his legs. "Daddy, Daddy." His face crumpled and tears flowed down his cheeks.

Kane had seconds to react, he assumed all the players were in the room with him. Taking in the position of the men and the actions required to take them down, he scanned the room. His main objective was to protect his son. Using the chains was his only option. His gaze rested for a split second on the heavy metal table against the wall and his plan slid into place. Holding up a hand to Mateo, Kane gripped Tauri close to him. "If you want my cooperation, give me some time with my son."

"Ah, at last you are taking me seriously." Mateo shook his injured hand. "Think long and hard about what might happen to the kid because he won't be leaving my side until you've testified in our favor."

Any moment, Kane could attack but he needed precious seconds to get Tauri to safety. He allowed his combat face to fall into place and raised his chin. "You think long and hard about touching my son, because if you do, you'd better kill me now because one thing is for darn sure, I'll hunt you down and tear you apart. Nothing or no one will be able to stop me. I'll never give up and you will die slowly and in agony."

"This is trash-talking. You're my prisoner and I'm no fool. I know you're a law-abiding deputy and must play by the rules of the law or you'll go to jail." Mateo stared at him. "You do know what happens to cops in jail, right?"

After seeing the sudden shift from bravado to uncertainty, Kane needed to even out the odds. The cartel knew little about him and these people lived in a world of uncertainty and violence where threats had substance if used in the right way. Not wanting to alarm Tauri he slipped into Spanish and smiled at Mateo. "You see what I want you to see. You have no idea who I am or what I'm capable of doing. I ripped the head off the last man who touched my family and fed him to the pigs. I'd be a hero in jail, but they'll never catch me. I'll be too busy hunting down your family and killing each one of them."

Bending, Kane pulled Tauri close and spoke to him in his native tongue. "I've got you. Everything will be okay, but I need to get free. When I say 'go,' hide under the table, against the wall. Curl up like a little mouse. Close your eyes and cover your ears until I come and get you. Be brave, my little eagle."

"Okay." Tauri nodded like an automaton and wiped his eyes on a shirt two sizes too big for him. His feet were bare and dirty.

Anger shivered through Kane. It was something that rarely happened to him. With one hand on Tauri's shoulder, he straightened and relaxed, combat ready. He'd get Tauri out of this situation or die trying.

TWENTY-THREE

Kane stared at Mateo, waiting for his next move, but a man walked into the room interrupting any further conversation. With a nod from Mateo, the man lined up instruments on the metal table. He gave Kane a satanic smile and held up a scalpel before adding it to the line.

Kane glared at Mateo. "There's no place you or your goons can hide from me. Each time you threaten my son, your time left on earth is growing shorter."

"Wait outside." Mateo turned to the man. "I'm sure Deputy Kane understands why you are here." He rubbed his knuckle where bite marks stood out sore and swollen. "If he denies my request, I will get much pleasure in watching you use your skills on the boy."

Rolling his shoulders, Kane moved his attention back to Mateo. "I don't lie and the bit about feeding you to the pigs is a promise."

Time was running out and he needed all the players in the room. He couldn't risk leaving anyone behind who might hurt Jenna before he could get home. Eyes fixed on Mateo, Kane took a step back and wrapped the chains around his hands. Beside him Tauri trembled but his grip had lessened and he'd turned ready to run to safety. He sucked in a breath. "Go."

Without a second's delay, Tauri ran past Mateo dodged out of the grasps of the other men and slid under the table. He pushed himself so tight against the wall that in the shadows he'd become almost invisible. In the distraction the armed men turned their backs on Kane. It was a fatal mistake and one he'd counted on. He had a split second to react before the men reached for their rifles. Timing now was everything. The move must work or Tauri would become a target of Mateo's twisted mind. He could never allow that to happen. Bunching his muscles, he pulled down hard on the manacles, testing the resistance. He gathered his strength and roared.

In a controlled burst of rage, Kane ripped out the bolts in a shower of broken bricks. Armed with two lengths of chain, he spun one of them around his head like a lasso. Time spent on Rowley's ranch lassoing cattle quickly became an asset as he wrapped it around the neck of the closest man. Dancing forward, he wrenched down hard, dragging the gasping man toward him. The rifle clattered to the floor as the man, eyes bulging, raked at his throat, gasping for air. Kane tightened his grip, squeezing the life from him until he fell limp in his arms. *One down.*

Free to move, Kane held the man before him as Mateo reacted first, drawing his weapon and firing. His shots slammed into his guard's vest, protecting Kane as Mateo emptied the clip. Before Mateo could reload, Kane tossed the body at him, knocking the gun from his hand. He spun around using the chain to take out the second man before he had the chance to pull his rifle from his shoulder. As the life drained from the man, he ripped the chains from his inert body. *Two down.*

He turned. He wanted his prize, the man who dared to

kidnap his son. He would make him pay. He stalked calmly toward the unarmed man, fingers flexing. "Now it's your turn."

"I don't think it's my day to die." Mateo pulled a hand grenade from his pocket, backed away, and pulled open the door. He stepped into the doorway, grinning.

Fear for Tauri's safety gripped Kane and he froze on the spot. If he attacked Mateo now, it was instant death for both of them.

"You've made a big mistake, Deputy. This could have been easy, a small retraction of a statement and everyone would have been happy. I never lose and now there won't be enough of you left to testify. I would have killed you before, but we needed to be sure my family would be set free. Now I know you'll never cooperate we'll take our chances in court." As he backed out, he laughed. "I would have taken much pleasure in killing the boy and will enjoy watching my men with your wife. Think about that in your last seconds on this earth. I'm going to get her now and I promise her death will be slow." Mateo ran along the passageway.

As Mateo disappeared, Kane heard the familiar bounce and roll of a tossed grenade on cement. The brown ball of destruction rolled toward the entrance to the room. With seconds to live, survival instinct took over. He ran at the doorway, kicked the metal door shut and chains trailing behind him, dived beneath the table. Gathering Tauri in his arms he wrapped his body around him. "It's going to be okay, cover your ears. There's going to be a loud bang."

In his arms, Tauri sobbed and trembled. Pain of deep loss rammed through him. He'd let his family down. His mind counted down the seconds before the explosion would change the world forever. He tightened his grip around Tauri, using his body to protect him the best he could. Maybe one of them would survive, but alone, Jenna would be in a fight for her life because of him. He'd been such a fool to risk everything and to trust the FBI had planned everything down to the last second. The takedown should have worked out fine, the cartel arrested, and his name suppressed for the trial. No one outside a small circle should have known his identity. The time counted down, one second left to live or die. He tensed for impact. *I'm so sorry, Jenna.*

TWENTY-FOUR

Craggy Rock

Rio fiddled with Johanna Worth's phone as they followed Wolfe's van back to Black Rock Falls. He'd never found it too difficult to access someone's phone—most who used fingerprints or facial recognition left the numeral password intact and those people usually used a very simple four-digit code. The most popular was the year of the person's birth. The three phones he'd examined belonging to the victims he'd opened in the same way. He scrolled through the calls. Recently she'd called the pizzeria, made a call that had the ID tag of *Mom*, one was to the beauty parlor, and that was just about it. He accessed her social media via the phone and the passwords popped up on their own. After scrolling through her twenty or so social media friends, he found one of the suspects, Chase Holden. Johanna had followed a page for his business, Living Things, a woodcarving store in town. Rio followed this with a background check but no red flags went up. Chase Holden had arrived in Black Rock Falls in summer to open a store to sell his artwork. He carved animals from wood using a chainsaw. Rio found reels on his page demonstrating his ability.

He'd noticed a carving of a bear cub in Johanna's family room and closed his eyes, filtering through information in his cluttered mind. His retentive memory was a curse as well as a blessing. Some things he'd rather forget, but in times like these it did come in handy. He did recall seeing a sculpture of an eagle in the home of Dakota Slade. This was one of the links Jenna had mentioned. Sometimes the simplest of things linked people to killers. He thought for a time but couldn't recall any wood sculptures in the home of Jennifer Kriss, but perhaps they were expensive and she doubted any of them had spare cash for artwork. He turned to Rowley. "I've found a small link between Chase Holden, Dakota Slade, and the last victim."

"If that's the case, then you'll need to take a look at the social media of Jennifer Kriss." Rowley pulled into his spot outside the sheriff's office. "If they're all social media friends, we'll need to grab the keys to Jennifer Kriss' home and look for a wooden sculpture. I must admit, I'm usually looking for evidence and not appraising artwork."

Nodding, Rio used the phone to hunt down Chase Holden's social media followers. He entered the names of the victims one by one and found all three followed his page. "He has three thousand followers, but I found them."

"Now what?" Rowley headed up the steps to the office. "If we find his sculpture in Jennifer's home, do we go and confront him or hunt down the other suspect first?"

Considering the facts, Rio nodded. "We go and speak to him. He has a store in town. He works and lives in the back. His page says his store is open seven days most times, so even though it's Sunday, we'll find him there or at home." He followed Rowley into the office. "I'll get an update from Cade and Piper."

"We've had three calls." Piper handed him three sheets of

paper. "I've entered the details into the daybook as instructed. These are copies." She smiled. "Two people with dashcam footage have sent it in and the other was from the bank manager. The ATM has a camera and he went by to check it when he heard the news report. It picked up a cowboy fitting the description: blond untidy hair, brown Stetson, snakeskin boots, walking to a white truck, with an airport rental sticker on the back."

Impressed, Rio smiled at them. "You have the pictures of the suspects. Can you make out who it is?"

"It could be any one of them and I'm not so sure this guy has blond hair. He's kind of hunched up against the rain." Cade raised both eyebrows. "It looks like Carter, right down to the snakeskin band around his hat."

"Everyone has those around here, along with the boots and the Stetson." Piper shook her head. "All the guys wear cowboy hats, ball caps, or hunting hats in this weather, so hair color is hard to distinguish." She looked at Cade. "They need more evidence than that before they send a guy to jail for murder and I don't believe it's Carter. He wouldn't kill women for fun. He loves women."

"Maybe he loves them so much he doesn't want to share them with anyone so he kills them." Cade grinned at her. "They do that, psychopaths. I'm reading Jo Wells' books on criminal behavior. That is one of the signs."

"You're impossible." Piper turned her back on him and headed down to the kitchenette. "I'm taking a break."

Rio watched her go. At twenty they were forging ahead with their own lives but he didn't see them leaving home anytime soon. Neither had wanted to go off to college, both happy to attend the local one, although they'd gone through the usual application process and he'd been surprised at the number of colleges offering them scholarships. Both had decided on a career in law enforcement to various degrees.

Piper wanted to be in the justice system, working in the courts, she'd wanted to work alongside a judge and listen to court cases. Cade, after a very bumpy adolescence, had made up his mind to become a law enforcement officer and was working toward the necessary qualifications. He'd even mentioned the FBI. He turned as Rowley came back from the evidence locker. "When we've searched the Kriss home, we'll go to Aunt Betty's and plan our next move. I want to see if there are any more links between the victims before we go and speak to Holden and have a list of questions in my mind rather than go in unprepared."

"That works for me." Rowley slid behind the wheel. "Do you figure we should call Jenna and bring her up to speed?"

Rio shook his head. "Nah, if she's in the chopper, she won't hear the phone. She'll call us when she finds Kane. We can tell her then, if she's in any fit state." He gave him a long look. "If the cartel has him, his chances are one in a million to get out alive and now they have Tauri. I want a good outcome, but I've seen what they do to people. The best thing we can do to help right now is to take some of the burden from her shoulders by solving this case."

"Kane is as tough as they come." Rowley backed out of the parking space and headed along Main. "He was buried alive, struck by lightning, and survived. I don't know many men who could take him down alone. My money is on him. He'll make it out, he always does."

Surprised by Rowley's obvious hero worship, he cleared his throat. "He's flesh and blood like all of us, Jake. If he hadn't been unconscious, there would have been signs of a fight and Jenna found nothing. Blackhawk examined the scene as well and both concluded Kane must have been out cold when they took him. He must weigh at least two-fifty and they would have needed at least four strong men to lift him into a truck." He frowned. "Put Kane out of your mind for a time until we know what's happening. Keep your head in the game. We must be the professional team that Jenna needs right now."

"Okay." Rowley turned into Jennifer Kriss' driveway and pulled up beside her old truck. "Let's do this." He pulled examination gloves from the console and tossed a pair to Rio. "This is still a crime scene and I'm betting it still stinks in there." He grabbed two masks and handed him one.

Using the keys, they went inside, ducking under the crime scene tape. It did stink of death and they split up to look through the lower floor. They didn't need to go far, the moment Rio walked into the family room, he spotted the small carved bear on a table in front of the window. "I found a carving, but this is way too small to have been carved using a chain saw." He picked it up and turned it over. "It has the initials CH carved into the bottom. It's one of Holden's. I'll bag it and take it with us. We'll enter it into evidence. I figure we go and get all three of the sculptures. They're crucial evidence and prove that Holden came in contact with all of the victims."

"I had a strange feeling you'd want to visit the other crime scenes today." Rowley patted his pocket. "I have the other victim's house keys with me."

Rio smiled at him. "That's what I call thinking outside the box." He headed for the door.

TWENTY-FIVE

Running on adrenaline, Jenna bounded over the uneven ground toward the red-brick building. "Seek Dave, Duke. Seek Tauri." The dog moved out in front of her, Bear running alongside him sniffing the air.

In the distance she'd spotted one man walking from the truck parked outside to what was left of an old barn. One section was intact, the other half damaged. Bars covered a boarded-up window, and a passageway inside was evident. Was this where they were holding Kane? Where was Tauri? The field ahead was covered in waist-high wheatgrass. Once inside, it would be difficult to see the building, but the grass offered them cover. Panting after the sprint led by Styles, Jenna pushed on, moving through the space in the wheatgrass cut by Styles. The wet blades soaked her jeans and the seed-covered tips stuck to her clothes or whipped against her face. Underfoot, the uneven ground made the way difficult. Behind her, Wolfe pounded along, his heavy medical bag swishing through the grass as he ran. Rain spots hit her hot cheeks and ran down her neck but as they broke out of the wheatgrass. The view ahead was clear and Styles slowed, held up a hand, and scanned the area. She went to his side. "Can you see anything?"

"There's a chopper parked some ways from the building and two trucks close by. We don't have any cover. If they come out and see us, hit the ground." Styles moved forward. "Keep behind me, Jenna."

One man appeared, lit a cigarette, and walked around to one side of the building. They all moved forward in a line, trying to cover the ground as fast as possible before the smoking man came back. The next moment, someone burst from the passageway, stopped and tossed something, and then ran yelling toward a chopper, sitting about thirty yards away from Jenna but a hundred yards from the men trying to reach it. Ahead of her, Styles stopped moving and drew his revolver. She ran to his side. "Don't stop."

"Grenade." Styles pushed her down into the wheatgrass and Wolfe dropped beside them. "Bear, down."

Jenna snagged an arm around Duke and grabbed his harness. "Down." She tugged hard and the dog flopped, panting beside her.

Slapping hands over her ears as an almighty explosion shook the ground, Jenna rolled into a ball. Moments later she opened her eyes as dust climbed into the sky in a cloud of blood red. Bricks and debris flew into the air. Before she could react, a wall of heat rushed over them, sucking up the air around them. Gasping for breath, Jenna coughed. The smell of gunpowder and burning wood and flesh filled her nostrils and coated her tongue. Fragments of bricks and mortar fell from the sky, thumping into the ground all around them. She covered her head as flaming splinters of wood cartwheeled in all directions in a fireworks display of flaming embers that sizzled out in the soaked wheatgrass. Horrified and shaken to her core, Jenna crawled to her feet, oblivious of the falling debris. Where the

EYES TIGHT SHUT   125

old barn once stood was a blackened hole surrounded by broken walls and twisted metal. "Nooooo."

Wolfe's arms came around her waist and she struggled against him. He was saying something but the ringing in her ears obliterated his voice. She needed to get to Kane and Tauri. Styles took one arm and Wolfe the other and they hightailed it back into the long grass. The next second, automatic-weapons fire cut up the grass around them. She hit the ground hard and all the air rushed out of her lungs. Bullets pinged above them, slicing the tops from the long grass and sending up clouds of chaff. When silence fell, she tried to move but Wolfe was pinning her down. Beside her, Styles crawled forward, went to his knees, and poked his head up.

"FBI. Put down your weapons." More gunshots peppered the ground around them, and Styles lifted his heavy revolver in both hands and took aim. "Stay down, this ain't going to be pretty."

The sound of the revolver boomed and the men's chopper exploded into a fireball. More gunshots hit the ground around Jenna, but pinned beneath Wolfe, she couldn't move. Sobbing, she tugged at his arm. "Fire back, for heaven's sake. They'll get away."

Two more booms came from Styles' 351 Magnum and his face poked through the long grass in front of her. "Both men are down."

As the ringing in her ears lessened, an eerie silence descended on the quiet landscape. Beside her, Duke trembled and she rubbed his ears. "It's okay, Duke."

Desperate to look for Kane and Tauri, Jenna wriggled to get free. "Let me up, Shane. Duke, seek. Find Kane, find Tauri." Duke took off toward the pile of rubble.

"Let me go in first." Wolfe's hand closed around her arm. "Please, Jenna."

She stared into Wolfe's concerned face and dragged her arm free. "No. Look at Duke. He hears something."

Before he had the chance to argue with her, Jenna pushed to her feet and ran, tripping over pieces of broken bricks and dodging smoldering pieces of wood. She stopped on the edge of the blacktop and stared in horror at the pile of smoking rubble. Refusing to believe the inevitable, she ran across the road. "Dave, Dave. Where are you?"

Behind her, Wolfe grabbed her around the waist and she hammered at his arms. "Let me go. I must go to them."

One corner of the building remained standing, the jagged broken bricks and blackened walls the only sign a building had once stood there. The rest was little more than a pile of rubble. Two bodies with parts missing had been tossed around like rag dolls. She moved closer with shaking legs and stared at them. She choked back a sob. Neither was Kane. Shocked to her core, Jenna pointed a trembling finger toward the remaining wall and pile of broken bricks. "Something moved. I saw it. Look there." She raised her voice. "Dave, we're here. Call out."

Duke took off with Bear at his heels. Both dogs stopped and barked at the pile of rubble. Duke made a mournful whining sound and started to dig furiously at the smoldering pile of debris.

Running, Jenna stared at Styles. "They're under the rubble. Help me."

The bricks slid, tumbling away from the pile, and a metal plate sparkled in the watery sunlight. Wolfe and Styles ran across the road and plunged into the smoldering ruins, tossing bricks in all directions with their bare hands. Duke was going crazy, barking and trying to move mountains. The metal plate moved again and then slowly rose spilling bricks in all directions. Jenna ran toward the shaking pile as the top of a metal table speared up through the bricks. Styles and Wolfe ran forward, pushed away bricks, grabbed it, and tossed it aside.

Jenna gaped in disbelief as Kane, dust-covered and hardly recognizable, uncurled and straightened, lifting Tauri into his arms. The little boy was liberally coated in red dust, but waved at her. Stumbling through the rubble, she fell against Kane and wrapped her arms around them. "Oh, thank you, Lord."

"We're okay." Kane kissed Jenna and then shifted Tauri onto one hip to hold her against him, but the long chains attached to his manacles were pinned under the rubble, preventing him from moving far. "A few bruises maybe and my ears are ringing some, but the metal table protected us and they'd locked us in a room with a metal door. That wall took most of the impact. The door flew straight past us and then the roof caved in." He looked at Styles. "Thanks for coming. Can you get me out of these things?" He passed Tauri to Jenna.

"Yeah, sure." Styles pulled out a small leather kit from his pocket and went to work on the locks.

Unable to stop the tears from flowing, Jenna checked Tauri all over. "Are you okay, sweetheart?"

"Daddy saved us from the baddy man." Tauri snuggled against Jenna. "I bit that man hard."

Jenna brushed the dust from his head and shoulders. "You were very brave. I'm so proud of you." She looked at Kane. "And Daddy too."

TWENTY-SIX

Shaking the dust from his hair, Kane looked at Jenna's tear-streaked face and his stomach twisted. Thankful she had eluded Mateo's clutches, now all he wanted was to hold her close and convince her all was well, but Wolfe was busy wiping the dirt from his eyes. He blinked away the dust. "I figured you'd find us." He smiled at Duke. "I heard Duke barking and whistled. The table was so darn heavy, but I pushed up on it and hoped you'd see the bricks moving."

"I'd never give up." Jenna took bottles of water from her backpack and gave Tauri a drink and handed one to Kane. "It was fortunate that Styles arrived to help out, as Carter is still MIA."

"Did you recognize any of them?" Wolfe was in doctor mode and checking Tauri for injuries and then flicked a light over Kane's eyes.

Trying to put Wolfe at ease about his abductors, Kane gave him a meaningful stare and a slight shake of his head. "It was the cartel, and Mateo got away. He's the one who threw the grenade. I'll need time to hunt him down. He should be in jail.

Carter assured me he'd put him on the bus to County personally."

"No need, they're all deactivated." Styles flicked a glance at Tauri and smiled as he dropped the manacles to the ground. "No more baddy men. They've all run away." He raised both eyebrows and much to his surprise spoke to Kane in Arabic. "I know you understand me. Wolfe mentioned you speak many languages. There are bodies in pieces all over. You'll need to leave before the little one sees anything. Maybe cover him with your jacket? There are two trucks outside. Give me five to see if I can get them started. It would be easier to drive back to the choppers. They used some type of signal-blocking device and I'm hoping it's in one of the trucks. If not, I'll call in a cleanup crew when I get back to the chopper. I put my bird down out of range."

Kane nodded and indicated to Jenna and Tauri with his chin. "Thanks, can you fly us back to the ranch? I need to get my family home."

"That's the plan." Styles glanced at Wolfe, who was listening with interest. "Are you staying to supervise the cleanup?"

"Yeah, for the time being, but the bodies will need to be taken to California for identification." Wolfe scratched his cheek. "These men were part of a federal investigation, and a California medical examiner will need to be handling the case. Plus, right now we have two ongoing homicide cases. I'll call in the Helena team and they can hand over to the team in LA."

Concerned about sensitive information getting into the wrong hands, Kane swung his attention back to Wolfe. "I hope they left my weapon and phone in one of the trucks." He turned to Styles. "The second explosion I heard. Please tell me you took out Mateo's chopper?"

"Yeah. I hit the gas tank." Styles' mouth twitched into a smile as he reverted to English. He pushed his hat firmly on his head and climbed over the mounds of debris. He looked over one shoulder. "Stay there, I'll bring a truck closer. Best you cover Tauri's head against the dust on your way out." He climbed over the rubble and headed along the sidewalk.

Nodding, Kane sipped the water. His throat was parched. He looked at Jenna's sheet-white face. "A signal blocker, huh? No wonder you couldn't find me." He held out his hand to her.

"We did it old-style." Jenna slid under one of his arms and a tremble went through her. "Shane and Styles worked a grid across the lowlands. We figured they'd need space to land a chopper, so we discounted the forest or wooded areas."

Kane frowned. "How did you know they had a chopper?"

"Y'all have a fault in your security we've never considered." Wolfe met his gaze. "While Jenna was tending the horses early this morning, they dropped a chopper into your front yard, broke down your door, and took Tauri."

"I told you, Daddy." Tauri rubbed at his eyes and then dropped his head on Jenna's shoulder and closed his eyes.

"I was expecting Styles and was hurrying to finish up and didn't head out to meet him right away. I heard a smashing sound and ran out of the barn. As I came out of the barn I came under fire and couldn't stop them taking Tauri." She shook her head. "I'm never doing anything without carrying a weapon from now on. Dammit. In my own home, I should be safe."

Hating to see Jenna so distressed, Kane rubbed her back. "All this is my fault. I've become so comfortable here. I honestly never expected the cartel would find me." He shook his head. "No one spoke my name. I was in disguise and spoke Spanish the entire time. Not one person was suspicious of me. The sting went down perfectly. Everything was caught on film, with the audio from my nosepiece. I drove away with the cash. The FBI apprehended the dealers after I'd left. They couldn't know I was involved. Carter and three other agents made the plans, and I went over them with Shane before I decided to take the mission. It was a few hours out of my day, is all. I couldn't tell you the plan beforehand, Jenna. It was classified."

"Do they know who you are? I mean your job before you came here?" She indicated to Tauri and raised both eyebrows in warning not to say anything that could be repeated.

"Not one hope in hell." Wolfe shook his head. "Dave was there because he could pass as an arms dealer. He was set up with a cover story, creds, and he fooled them. Nope, for something to go wrong, one of the men in the team is a mole. When we eventually find Carter, we'll get an investigation underway."

Kane indicated with his chin to where Styles had gone. "Could Styles be the mole?"

"Nope." Wolfe narrowed his gaze. "He's solid. Former MP, high-ranking Army. You can trust him."

"He speaks Spanish and would have a knowledge of arms. Why didn't they use him?" Jenna narrowed her gaze. "Why when everyone wants someone to do something life-threatening do they call Dave? Why can't they just leave us be? We've paid our dues. They owe it to us."

Holding Jenna closer and more concerned about her trembling, Kane nodded. "They didn't use an FBI agent because they'd have their ID in a second. They took pictures of me the moment I stepped out of the truck. No doubt, they ran my image through their database to make sure I wasn't a fed before they allowed me to meet anyone. I had a choice this time and made the wrong choice, is all. It happens, but I'll be more careful next time."

"Next time?" Jenna twisted to look at him. "You're batshit crazy, you know that?"

Blowing out a breath, Kane shook his head slowly. "I'm still active, Jenna. When and if a call comes, I have no choice but to go. One in five years isn't so bad, is it?" He touched her cheek. "I'll keep clear of the FBI missions from now on, but I figured I owed Carter for everything he's done for us."

"It's his job." Jenna's eyes flashed with anger. "And right now, when we needed him most, he didn't pick up his darn phone."

Beside him, Wolfe's phone chimed, and he frowned. "My satellite phone is working." He took the call. "We have Kane and Tauri. Yeah, just found them. They'll be fine. I'll give you the details when I get back to the office." He listened for a time and frowned. "Upload all the information to the server and I'll inform Jenna. Our phones have been out. Yeah, Tauri is right here. I'll give him your love when he wakes. He's asleep right now." He disconnected.

Kane looked at him. "Bad news?"

"First up, Emily sends her love and she's very happy you're okay." Wolfe pushed a lock of hair from Tauri's face and smiled at the sleeping child. "The stun gun matter we discussed yesterday? There's been another incident. Rio and Rowley are handling it just fine. Emily and Norrell have done a forensic sweep and are on their way back to the office. She mentioned that Rio has everything under control and they're heading out to interview a suspect known to the three women. All the current files are on the server."

"I need to be in the office." Jenna stepped away, swallowing hard. "He's escalating." She looked at Kane. "We must stop this killer before he takes another life."

"There's no way I'm passing either of you fit for work." Wolfe looked from one to the other. "You're in shock, Jenna, and y'all need to be at home with your son to reassure him. Dave is bruised all over and could have delayed concussion. Y'all have two very capable deputies investigating the case. Take the rest of the day and come back fresh in the morning. By then Rio and Rowley might have hunted down a few suspects or arrested the killer."

"Uh-huh." Jenna shook her head and looked at him. "I asked for a miracle. I guess I can't expect two in one day."

TWENTY-SEVEN

Rain fell in icy sheets as Rowley turned into Main and headed to Chase Holden's store. As he drove, Rio dictated some of the rave reviews Holden had received for his artwork. He lived above the store and had built a workshop out back. The store was open seven days a week, nine until three, and the front door held a sign: *I'M CREATING MAGIC. RING THE BELL AND I'LL BE RIGHT ALONG.*

Bending against the rain, he looked at Rio. "Now that's a guy who is super confident at what he does. Let's go around back. It's better to speak to him away from prying eyes. We'll be noticed inside the store, and if he's innocent, seeing us will ruin his business."

"I doubt it." Rio pulled down his hat, allowing the rain to pour off the rim. "From what I see, his customer service is as good as his product." He frowned. "What a unique way to meet women, and think about it, it's also a great excuse to get inside their homes if he delivers his artwork."

Rowley nodded. "True."

The sound of a chainsaw came from a shed out back, and Rowley followed Rio to the open door. The smell of freshly cut

wood came from inside. Holden was busy creating a magnifi-
cent eagle in full flight and hadn't heard them approach. His
workbench was covered in tools, and a counter along on one
side of the room held a variety of sculptures, all different but
incredible. Some depicted animals and birds, others leaves,
fruit, and vines. Not just statues but intricately crafted mantel
pieces and bed ends, all polished to a high shine. This guy was
talented, and Rowley could imagine some of the pieces in his
home. *I hope this guy isn't a psychopath.*

He waited for Holden to pause and look at his work before
he raised his voice. "Mr. Holden. Can we have a word with
you?" As the man turned, he noticed he did indeed resemble
Carter. He had the same untidy blond hair and his build was
identical. They could have been brothers.

"Come in out of the rain." Holden turned off the chainsaw
and removed his safety goggles, earmuffs, and face mask. After
brushing wood shavings from his clothes and hair, he sat on a
stool beside the bench. "What can I do for you?"

"We're investigating the deaths of Dakota Slade, Jennifer
Kriss, and Johanna Worth." Rio crunched over the wood curls
on the floor and took out a notebook and pen. "We're working
down a list of anyone who came into contact with them so we
can get a timeline of their movements prior to their deaths."

"Okay." Holden shook his head. "Those women are all
dead? That's terrible news. How did that happen? Were they in
a wreck?"

The sound of a dust extractor hummed above his head as
Rowley took in the blank expression on Holden's face and
exchanged a knowing look with Rio. "We don't know the cause
of death at this time. Can you give us some details of when you
last saw them?"

"Johanna came by on Friday last to collect a small bear."
Holden smiled. "It was actually part of a set, but she loved it so
much I made one especially for her. The other women, I recall

their names, so I figure they bought things from me. I'll go check in my files. Each piece I create is numbered and listed with the name of the owner." He looked from one to the other. "You'll need to follow me to my office." He waved a hand toward the door.

Not wanting to turn his back on a possible suspect, Rowley stepped to one side. "Lead the way. Do you live on the premises?"

"Yeah, my apartment is above the store." Holden glanced at him. "If you'd rung the bell out front, I'd have come around, rather than you getting wet walking back here."

"How do you hear the bell with the noise from the chain-saw?" Rio hunched against the rain.

"Flashing lights inside the workshop." Holden smiled. "They're hard to miss." He walked to a door in the back of the main building and opened it with a key. "The office is through here." He led the way.

Rowley remained in the doorway and Rio followed Holden inside, keeping a distance between them. Not knowing if this man had a weapon stashed in a drawer or was a threat, they watched Holden closely, but he sat down at his desk and booted up a computer.

"What were their names again?" Holden looked at Rio over the flat screen.

"Dakota Slade and Jennifer Kriss." Rio moved closer. "You have pictures of your customers?"

"Yeah, along with their sculptures." Holden smiled. "It makes it easier for me to recognize them if they call me to ask about new pieces, and I have many customers who come back time and time again." He frowned at the screen. "Ah, yes, I recognize Dakota. She works at the general store. I've often seen her there. With so many people living in town, it's difficult to recall who is a customer and who is someone I see behind a counter in town." He thought for a beat. "I went by the general store Thursday last. I believe she was there. I can't swear on it, but I was there on that day."

"What about Jennifer Kriss?" Rio leaned on the desk staring at the screen.

"Yeah, she purchased one of my sculptures three months ago." Holden looked at the image and frowned. "She hasn't been by since and I don't recall seeing her in town, so I can't help you." He pushed a hand through his hair dislodging small pieces of wood and looked at them. "Is this anything to do with the Casanova Killer who's all over the media? Some blond-haired guy has been seen chatting with these women and then they're found dead? You figure that's me?"

Shaking his head, Rowley stared at him. "We're running down a list of any blond-haired men who came in contact with the victims over the past two weeks. It's normal procedure to ask questions to eliminate people. There's no reason to believe the man or men seen talking to these women are involved, but it's a place to start. We can't leave any stone left unturned."

"If these men spoke to the victims, they might have information we can use." Rio straightened. "They might have mentioned going somewhere or doing something in general conversation. It's that type of information we require to find and stop whoever is murdering them."

"Wow!" Holden blew out a long breath. "I don't want to be caught up in the system again."

"How so?" Rio's hand rested on the butt of his pistol.

"I was arrested and did time for the rape of a woman in Colorado." Holden leaned back in his chair shaking his head. "I'd never met the woman, but she picked me out in a lineup and I was sent to jail."

"How come you're walking free?" Rio raised both eyebrows and flicked a glance at Rowley. "Your name didn't come up with any priors."

"I didn't touch the woman." Holden blew out a long sigh. "I

changed my name, but my prints still come up as my old name. It's a long story, I had a court-appointed lawyer. He didn't request DNA samples and the woman pointed me out in court. I was inside for two years. My wife divorced me. My parents turned their backs on me. I couldn't get an appeal without new evidence, so I made a deal with a lawyer. If he could get me an appeal, I'd give him a percentage of the damages. He agreed and they had the woman's clothes DNA-tested and it wasn't a match. It was some other guy, who is still out there somewhere. I walked and received damages. I came here and purchased the building, set up my workshop." He opened his hands and gestured to the works along the benches. "The only good thing that came from being in jail was that I learned how to make sculptures. I've made them in clay, but a chainsaw is a different matter. After two years I was pretty good and the pieces were sold, the money going back to the prison."

Surprised by the confession, Rowley nodded slowly. "Thanks for letting us know. Do you mind if we run your prints for elimination processes?" He pulled a scanner from his pocket.

"Not a problem." Holden held out his hand. "I've nothing to hide."

"I'll run them." Rio took the scanner and headed for the truck.

Keeping his mind on the investigation, Rowley turned his attention back to Holden. "So did you become friendly with any of the women?"

"I'm a friendly guy." Holden shrugged. "Did I find them attractive and ask them on a date? No, they were clients, is all, who appreciated my art." He frowned. "I'm sorry they died. No one deserves to be cut down like that in their prime."

Rowley nodded. "No, they don't."

"The prints confirm his story." Rio glanced at Rowley.

Convinced they'd covered all angles, Rowley nodded. He

looked at Rio. "Do you have any other questions for Mr. Holden?"

"No, I figure we have everything we need." Rio folded his notebook and pushed it inside his jacket. He handed Holden a card. "If you think of anything or see anyone who resembles you around town, give me a call."

"Thanks." He pushed the card into a jar filled with a variety of junk and loose change. "I hope you catch the Casanova Killer soon. I hope he's not targeting my customers."

"Oh, we'll catch him." Rio touched his hat. "Thank you for your time." He headed for the door.

TWENTY-EIGHT

Rio looked at Rowley as they climbed into the truck. "Wow! I sure didn't expect a confession like that from a suspect."

"I guess he figured we'd find out sooner or later and fessed up." Rowley let out a long sigh. "Two years in jail and innocent. That must have been soul destroying."

Taking the interview into consideration, Rio snorted. "Don't allow a sad story to sway you about his true character. Most psychopaths are nice guys until they're cornered."

Rio's phone buzzed as they headed back to town. It was Emily. His heart warmed at the thought of her. They were officially dating now, but he respected the fact her career and studies came first and any talk of marriage would need to wait. Once she graduated and began her residency, things would be different. "Hey. What's happening?"

"My dad called. They just found Dave and Tauri. They're okay but a building exploded and they're staying at the ranch today to rest, all of them. They'll be back at the office in the morning." Emily cleared her throat. "He said maybe you shouldn't call Jenna about the new murder. She's in shock and it might make things worse. Styles is heading home but he said Agent

Katz will be available to assist if you need her to run any checks."

Nodding, Rio climbed out of the truck and followed Rowley to Aunt Betty's Café. The delicious aromas of fresh coffee and barbecue ribs filled his nostrils, making his stomach growl. "Thanks, Em. I'll call you tonight at nine as usual. Bye." He disconnected and gave Rowley a rundown of what she'd said.

"Okay, we have a ton of work to get through before Jenna gets to the office in the morning." Rowley walked to the counter, ordered ribs, peach pie, and coffee and then headed for the reserved table at the back of the diner.

Shrugging, Rio ordered the same and followed him. "Now we find Dallas Strauss." He removed his damp coat and hat and dropped into a chair with a sigh, smiling at Wendy as she filled cups with steaming hot coffee. "You don't by any chance know a guy by the name of Dallas Strauss, do you?"

"Dallas?" Wendy placed the pot of coffee onto the table and nodded. "Yeah, he drops by for a meal from time to time. Blond hair and he has unusual black eyes. Like lumps of coal in a snowman." She giggled.

"Do you know what he does for a living or where we can find him?" Rowley sipped his coffee.

"He lives and works out at the Diamond Bar Ranch." Wendy smiled. "He drops by when he's in town buying supplies. I saw him in the pizzeria on Friday. Don't tell Susie but I dropped by for a pie to take home. A change is as good as a vacation they say."

Recalling that Johanna Worth worked at the pizzeria, Rio put down his cup. "Did you see him chatting with Johanna Worth, one of the servers, by any chance?"

"Well just about everyone speaks to the servers, don't they?" Wendy balled one hand on her hip. "Look at us chatting away. Anyone watching us would figure we're up to no good." She raised her eyebrows. "I don't know Johanna. There are so many new people in town these days." She shrugged. "Dallas always chats to me when he drops by. He leaves a big tip as well."

"What about Carter? Have you seen him lately?" Rowley looked up as Susie came with their meal and raised both eyebrows at Wendy.

"Carter, yeah, he has been by a few times over the last week." Wendy looked at Susie. "When did you last see Dallas or Carter?"

"Hard to tell them apart when I'm in the kitchen. Carter I've seen more last week than for a time. He mentioned he was staying out at his cabin on vacation. Dallas came by on Thursday. Come to think about it, so did Carter. He ordered a pile of takeout. He was dressed nice, clean shirt and jeans, and he smelled good, like he was going on a date." Susie blushed. "He has such a nice smile."

Blinking, Rio covered a smile. "Thanks, you've both been really helpful." As they walked away, he pulled his plate toward him and stared at Rowley, who was chuckling. "Well, Carter is never going to live that down."

"You can say that again." Rowley tucked a napkin down his shirtfront and tackled the ribs and moaned. "The best ribs in town."

Rio swallowed and nodded. "You said it. Have you heard of the Diamond Bar Ranch?"

"Yeah. They run beef cattle and horses. It's between here and Blackwater. Before the mines, down along the riverbank where it's green. The bigger ranches usually hire hands after the melt and through to the first snow. If Dallas Strauss works there now, he works year-round. To get a position like that, he must have been there for a time. He might be a family member. If I recall, the folks out there go by the name of Hill. Ethan is the owner as far as I know. He has a contract to supply beef to some of the finest restaurants in Montana. He has a manager who runs the place, and he handles the business side of things."

Enjoying having Rowley's local knowledge, Rio nodded. "Good, once we're done here, we'll head out and see if we can locate Strauss." He glanced at his watch. "As Jenna will be back first up, once we've spoken to Strauss, I'll grab Cade and Piper and head on home. I figure we'll be pulling double shifts until we find this killer."

"That works for me." Rowley nodded. "Although, we haven't looked through the victims' laptops and phones or located next of kin. If you can open them, I'll go through them tonight."

Shaking his head, Rio smiled at him. "I'll do it. You go and spend some time with your family. If I find anything interesting, I'll call you."

They ate in silence for a time and then Rio looked at Rowley. "Did you figure Chase Holden was just a little too cooperative? Too nice?"

"I was just thinking the same thing." Rowley looked at him over his cup. "I sure as heck didn't want to turn my back on him."

The hairs on the back of Rio's neck prickled. "Neither did I."

TWENTY-NINE

Rain pounded against the windows as Jenna tossed more logs on the fire. They'd arrived home to a damp freezing house. Rain had blown through the gaping front door, bringing a scatter of fall leaves across the highly polished floors. Jenna had closed as many doors as possible before she'd left with Styles, but she'd stared in dismay at the damage to the front door. Needing the security and the warmth, Kane had gone to the best source he knew, and within the hour, Wolfe had arrived with a new door. It seemed that Wolfe had the ability to obtain just about anything, no matter what the day of the week or the time of day. They'd had time to tend the horses, shower, and eat and then she'd tucked Tauri into bed and they'd sat with him until he'd fallen asleep. The little boy was so exhausted he'd struggled to stay awake at the kitchen table.

Unable to do anything to help with the repairs, Jenna made a fresh pot of coffee and then wrapped herself in a blanket on the sofa. Pumpkin, her black cat, curled up beside her, her silken black paws kneaded the blanket, purring in contentment. Jenna tried to relax but couldn't push the day's events from her mind. The fear of losing Kane and Tauri had been too much to bear. Flashes of the explosion and the dropping of her stomach came in waves. Right now, she didn't need to be alone. Her mind would settle soon, but the reason Kane had allowed this to happen baffled her. He and Wolfe were usually so security conscious, so it was obvious Wolfe hadn't been involved from the get-go. No doubt, because if he'd notified his chain of command, they'd have gone ballistic. They didn't take chances with an asset like Kane.

The voices from the front door stopped, but it wasn't Kane's footsteps in the hallway. The distinctive sound of Duke's claws clicking on the polished floor announced his arrival. The dog walked onto the rug before the fire, turned in three circles, and dropped with a sigh. He eyed Jenna with his huge brown eyes for a few seconds before he fell asleep.

A few minutes later, Jenna turned as Kane came into the room, exhaustion etched in his face. She'd seen the scrapes on his knees from the tumble from the motorcycle. Wolfe had checked him out before they'd left the crime scene and hadn't seemed worried, but she'd noticed him moving stiffly when he'd headed for the bathroom in the spare room for a shower. He'd not wanted her to see his injuries, not yet anyway. He didn't appreciate sympathy and somehow just seemed to keep going no matter how he felt. He hadn't had time to sit for longer than it took to eat the scrambled eggs and toast Jenna had hastily made on their return before Wolfe had arrived in the chopper with a new front door. He'd insisted she go and sit down and then spent a long time fitting it. Without stopping to say good-bye, Wolfe left, and Kane washed up.

Appalled, she stared at his wrists as he pulled down the arms of his sweater and grimaced. "You're bruised to the bone from those manacles. Do you want me to bandage them?"

"Nah, nothing's strained. It's bruised, is all. I'll be fine." He dropped onto the sofa and held out his arms for her. "Come here. Right now all I need is you."

Moving into his arms, she didn't snuggle against him but touched his chest gently. "Why are you hiding your injuries from me? I could see the grazes on your knees and the tear in your jeans. It wasn't difficult to see the gravel rash on your hip. They must be so sore. Can't I do anything to help?"

"I've taken care of them." Kane shrugged as if his injuries meant nothing. "Our first aid kit holds everything we need, from grazes to gunshot wounds. That's why I went into the spare room. I didn't want Tauri walking in on me tending my wounds. He's been through enough." He cupped her chin, rubbing his thumb tenderly over her cheek. "You have too. I'm sorry I put you through all this stress. It's unforgiveable. I shouldn't have believed the FBI intel and should have used my own brain. They intimated that they had eyes on the entire cartel and the lesser members were being arrested at the same time as we made the bust." He pushed one hand through his hair and his eyes flashed with anger. "Mateo was the main player in the arms deal, not the boss. They already had him under surveillance and once the deal was made moved in to arrest him. Yet somehow Mateo and some of his men escaped arrest. I wasn't there. Carter handcuffed me and bundled me into an FBI SUV and drove me straight to the airport." He frowned. "Then they identified me, which would be near impossible unless someone told them. They have a mole in the FBI, someone who works for the cartel." He sucked in a long breath. "Now Carter is MIA. Where the heck is he?"

Shrugging, Jenna traced the frown lines on Kane's forehead and sighed. "I wish I knew. What's happened to you is bad enough, but we have two homicides, identical MOs and the description that the witnesses gave us of the man seen hanging around both victims fits Carter." Reluctantly, she stood, shedding the blanket. "Unless he's suddenly turned his coat, I'm at a loss what to believe." She indicated to the kitchen. "I made a pot of coffee. Wait here, I'll grab us a cup."

"I don't want to be away from you for a second." Kane pushed to his feet. "We'll look in on Tauri again too. Wolfe mentioned he might have nightmares and we'll need to be there for him."

They checked on Tauri, but the little boy was curled up around the purple spotted dinosaur they'd given him for his birthday sleeping peacefully. Jenna poured the coffee and they took their cups back to the family room. The house was warming up. With the heating turned up and the wood fire, it was starting to appear normal again. Even the broken door and wood had been removed and carried out back of the barn. Seeing it only brought back memories Tauri didn't need. It had been fortunate the trip back in Styles' chopper hadn't caused him any problems either. Tauri loved to fly.

Jenna sat on the sofa and sipped her coffee. "So this sting operation was compromised by persons unknown and I gather you can't ask for intervention by Wolfe's usual sources because you'd rather keep the fact someone abducted you a secret?"

"Not a secret." Kane frowned. "Wolfe won't mention it unless asked specifically. He doesn't have anything to do with the FBI. It's not in his chain of command, so he doesn't need to report it specifically. As far as Carter is concerned, Wolfe was out of the loop. It was a need-to-know operation. He has no idea that Wolfe is my handler or the need to know that either." He shrugged. "In my capacity as a deputy, I answered a request by our local FBI field office for assistance. That's all anyone needs to know. It went sideways after the fact and that's something Carter and Styles will focus on going forward." He reached for his cup. "It's not our problem. The mole didn't know about me, as in who I am. He didn't know all the members of the cartel involved would be killed either. They expected me to fold under pressure." He gave her a long look. "The mole is still out there, Jenna, and I'm still going to testify. I need to do this to ensure those remaining members of the cartel will never be set free." He shook his head slowly. "This time, when I'm away, I'll arrange the security for you and Tauri."

Jenna looked at him. "How so?"

"You'll both be with me." Kane smiled at her. "I had plenty of time to think when they chained me to the wall. Wolfe will arrange federal marshals to escort us. We'll travel on a commercial flight. Federal marshals, Wolfe, and Carter, or Styles if he's still missing, will be with you when I testify. Once it's done, we all come home together."

Jenna turned to look at him. "In the meantime, we have targets on our backs and a murderer who resembles Carter electrocuting women. When I took the job as sheriff, I never realized life in a backwoods town would turn out so complicated."

THIRTY

Concerned, Kane wanted to remove the worry from Jenna's shoulders, but in truth the next couple of weeks wouldn't be easy for any of them. The one thing he could do would be to help her solve the current homicides. He finished the cookie he'd been eating and sipped his second cup of coffee. "How far have you gotten in the cases?"

"Zip." Jenna blew out a long breath. "I haven't spoken to Rio or Rowley since I left this morning, but I gave them a ton of grunt work to do. They're hunting down CCTV footage of this Carter-like guy and sending it to Agent Katz as Kalo is on vacation. They have a couple of people of interest, mainly because they resemble Carter. We're grabbing at straws." She shrugged. "I'm sure if they'd had a breakthrough, they'd have called me by now."

Nodding, Kane leaned back on the sofa, pulled her close, and moaned with delight at just holding her. "I guess, we'll find out in the morning. There's just one thing I need to know."

"Shoot." Jenna rested her head against his shoulder.

Kane stared into the fire. "No one has mentioned my Harley. Did you find it and just how bad was it damaged?"

"It's in the garage." Jenna chuckled. "Wolfe and Atohi collected every fragment and bagged them." She rested her head on his shoulder. "It's okay to look at. The mirrors came off when it got wedged between the trees. It has a couple of scratches but it doesn't look as bad as you do."

Relieved, Kane smiled. "That's good to know. The cosmetics I can fix. Parts might be difficult but parts can be repaired. Does it run?"

"Heavens above, Dave." Jenna sat up and turned to look at him, eyes wide. "You were missing. There was blood on the blacktop. The last thing on my mind was if your motorcycle ran or how bad it was damaged." She shook her head slowly. "I did look at it when Atohi pushed it out of the trees, since then I've been a little busy, with my son being kidnapped and all." She rolled her eyes. "Why don't you go and look for yourself... Oh and I drove the Beast. Maybe you need to make sure it's okay too."

Surprised, Kane examined her face and the slight tremble in her hands. The shock was setting in just like Wolfe had warned him. He pulled her close and held her against him. "It was just a question. Material things can be replaced. You and Tauri are my first concern and always will be. Okay?"

"Okay." Jenna nodded against his chest. "I know that. I'm still a little stressed. I didn't mean to snap at you, I'm sorry. It was a perfectly logical question. You worked for months building the Harley. It's only natural you wanted to know what had happened to it." She waved a hand. "All this, the cartel, you and then Tauri, a case we can't solve. It's like trying to climb the side of an iceberg. I keep slipping down and having to start again."

Kane stroked her hair. "You're just tuckered out, is all." He wrapped his arms around her and stood, lifting her into the air. She weighed nothing and snuggled into his arms. He kissed her forehead and smiled. "I know it's only eight but we're going to bed. Everything can wait until the morning." He carried her into the bedroom and kicked the door shut behind him.

* * *

Rain streaked down the windows when Kane woke at five the following morning. He dragged on his clothes and checked on Tauri. Once asleep, Tauri and Jenna slept like the dead. He slept like a cat with one eye open. Until the trial date came and went and for some time after, he'd be watching his family very closely. He went to the mudroom to push his feet into ice-cold work boots. He filled the coffee pot and then headed out in the dark to tend the horses. It would be a long day and he set up the stables so they could swap the horses into clean stalls when they arrived home. The scent and warmth of the stables were soothing to his aching muscles as he mucked out the stalls and groomed each horse until they shone. Being exhausted after a long day, any shortcuts were welcome. If it hadn't been raining, he'd have turned out the horses into the corral for the day, but they'd be comfortable enough in their large stalls with the radio on to keep them happy.

His usual workout could wait. He'd had all the exercise his body could take this morning. The deep grazes to his hip and knees restricted his movement, the areas both stiff and sore, with skin so tight the healing flesh tore open with each movement. He'd tend to them once he'd had a shower and in a day or so he'd be fine. The antibiotic shot Wolfe had insisted administering before he left last night would prevent infection. Sitting in a rat-infested barn with open cuts had been one of his concerns. The idea vermin might try and feast on him the moment he fell asleep had kept him awake all night.

He closed the barn door and stared at the garage for long seconds. He'd pushed the accident and the potential loss of his Harley to the back of his mind, but just looking at the garage pulled everything into focus. Wolfe had mentioned finding wire at the crash site and he recalled the blow to his chest before he hit the road. He walked to the garage door, used his handprint to unlock it, and waited for it to slide open. Inside, the Beast was parked where he usually left it and set beside his partially rebuilt Indian motorcycle was his Harley. On the bench against the wall, someone, he assumed Wolfe, had laid out all the parts they'd collected. Alongside them sat his helmet. He turned it around in his hands and stared at the dent. He'd have died in the wreck without it, but that was easy to replace, not so the damaged parts of his motorcycle. He looked over the Harley and winced. He'd restored it to its former glory and now the tank had a long line of scratches on both sides. The mirrors were missing, torn off, and the saddlebags caked with mud all along one side. Taking a deep breath, he pulled out his phone and took images of the damage and then sent them to one of the restorers he'd met during his journey with his motorcycle. He could fix just about anything but trusted the paintwork to a specialist. When he had time, he'd drain the tank and send it to his guy. The broken parts might be more difficult to find. He ran his fingers over them, deciding if any could be saved or repaired. Sadly, they were just mangled pieces of metal. The saddlebags would clean up. Leather was very forgiving and a once-over with saddle soap would have them clean again.

He climbed into the Beast and drove it to the front of the house. There was no need for Jenna and Tauri to get wet this morning. His mind went to his little boy. The kindergarten was a safe place, but so was his ranch and the cartel had gotten to them. He had no idea how many more of them were out there planning on taking him out. He'd speak to Nanny Raya. Maybe she needed to stay with Tauri at the kindergarten, just to be safe. He climbed out of the Beast and headed to the front porch. He used the retinal scanner to gain entrance and removed his boots before padding softly back to the bedroom. As he undressed and headed for the bathroom, Jenna's voice came from behind him.

"Why didn't you wake me?" Jenna stared at his bruised and battered body, and her eyes widened. "Look at you. You should be resting up today. Is your head, okay? The helmet has a huge dent in it."

Nodding, Kane stood motionless as she examined the bruises and scrapes. "I'll be fine. These are more of a nuisance than anything else. A straight cut can be stitched and then forgotten. Large areas of grazes from the blacktop have two problems: they're part scrape and part burn, plus they have dirt in them. I'd rather leave them open to dry, but Wolfe insisted I cover them with a dressing after my shower and use ointment to prevent infection." He rubbed his hip. "He gave me a shot before he left last night and that hurts more than the grazes." He bent to kiss her. "I stink of horse. Give me five minutes. The coffee is ready." He headed for the shower. "Then we can discuss the case before Tauri wakes up."

"That sounds like a plan." Jenna yawned explosively. "I hope the guys made progress in my absence."

Kane smiled at her. "So do I."

THIRTY-ONE

Being an early riser, with chores to do on his ranch, Rowley called Rio early and they decided to get to the office at seven. They wanted to go and speak to Dallas Strauss at the Diamond Bar Ranch before he disappeared again. The previous afternoon they'd driven to the ranch only to find he'd left earlier to move cattle down from the high country to the winter feed pastures before the snow came. He'd been due back later that evening, but waiting hours in the cold was a waste of valuable time. They'd returned to the office to finish up loose ends and then headed on home.

When the call came from Jenna at five after seven, Rowley put the phone on speaker and they both looked at each other as she spoke.

"Dave and Tauri are okay, a few scrapes and bruises but nothing serious." Jenna breathed a sigh of relief. *"We'll be in once we've taken Tauri to the kindergarten. Any breakthroughs in the case?"*

Swallowing hard, Rowley glanced at Rio and he just shrugged. He was no help at all. "Yeah, first up, we've had another murder, same MO. I've uploaded all the files to the server. The young woman's name was Johanna Worth out of Craggy Rock. She worked at the pizzeria and her boss, Brian Rhoads, called it in when she didn't show for work. We did a welfare check and found her."

"Why didn't you call me?" Jenna's annoyance came through the speaker. *"I need to be in the loop at all times, Jake."*

Groaning, Rowley glared at Rio. "We handled the situation. You had enough on your plate with Kane and Tauri missing. We followed procedure, and Norrell and Emily did the forensics, but we did notice a similarity between the victims." He told her about the carved wood figurines and the interview the previous afternoon with Chase Holden.

"Okay, I'll read your reports." Jenna paused a beat. *"What was your take on Chase Holden?"*

Nodding, Rowley stared at his phone. "Relaxed, very informative. He wasn't worried about speaking to us at all. He admitted knowing all the murder victims and about his time in jail." He rubbed the back of his neck. "He was asking questions about the cause of death. He made like he was upset about them dying, but I figure it was just a show for us." He took a deep breath. "We're heading out now to speak to Dallas Strauss. He's a ranch hand out at the Diamond Bar Ranch."

"Where is that?" Jenna tapped on a keyboard. *"I have it. It's halfway between Blackwater and Black Rock Falls. Okay, talk to him but be careful. If this is our man, we know what he is capable of doing and a stun gun is very easy to conceal in a pocket. Don't trust anyone we consider a possible suspect in this case."*

Raising his eyebrows at Rio, Rowley breathed a sigh of relief. "We'll take all necessary precautions as usual. I'll call you when we leave the Diamond Bar Ranch."

"Before you go, did you find anything of interest on the phones or laptops? Have you checked out their call logs?"

"This is Rio." Rio leaned toward the phone. "I checked

them all out and found nothing of interest. Calls to their employment, takeout, calls to family. No one outside the usual framework we'd see for most people. We know Jennifer Kriss contacted Brian Lock a few times. He's the carpenter who called in when she wouldn't answer the door when he arrived to do some work. That's all. Nothing of interest on social media."

"We still need positive ID on the victims." Jenna covered the mouthpiece and spoke to someone. *"I'm guessing Wolfe is on that, but he's been with me, so no progress there, I guess."*

Rowley shrugged. "Emily didn't mention anything and we uploaded all the information we discovered onto the server. I doubt much progress has been made with the murders coming along so fast."

"Okay. I'll hunt down the next of kin and get the identifications rolling." Jenna sucked in a breath. *"Get at it and we'll see you at the office later. Thanks for working yesterday and starting early this morning. Don't forget to put in for overtime."* She disconnected.

"She sounds a little overprotective toward us today." Rio left a message for Maggie, the receptionist on the front desk, to let her know where they were heading. "Is this the mothering instinct?"

Pushing on his hat and collecting a fresh statement pad and a couple of pens from behind the front counter, Rowley looked up and nodded. "Yeah, Sandy has been the same since the twins arrived." He straightened and smiled. "I kinda like the attention. When the twins were newborns, I felt like a third thumb. Sandy had her mom and dad staying at the ranch to help out. It was a bad winter, if you recall, but the crime rate didn't slow any. I was glad of the help around the ranch, but I didn't get much time to get to know my kids."

"That must have been difficult." Rio frowned and buttoned his coat and then pulled on gloves. "You and Sandy must have needed the help. I recall when my brother and sister were born my mom was up all hours with them. My dad worked and I helped when I could, but you know how cranky moms get when they don't get enough sleep."

Laughing, Rowley headed for the door. "Tell me about it. By the time the melt came and her folks moved back home, I'd become more confident with the twins. You know, they were so little I was frightened of hurting them every time I picked them up. Now I'm worried they'll hurt me." He chuckled. "They hurled themselves at me when I got home the other night and almost knocked me flying."

"Wait until they're teenagers, then the fun begins." Rio shook his head. "I became a surrogate father to teenagers at twenty-one. This is why I ended up here. Cade and Piper were out of control. Anyway, it's all good now." Rio followed him to the truck. "Let's hope we can find and speak to Dallas Strauss."

Rowley headed along Main and then onto the highway that led to Blackwater. It was a cold, crisp morning and mist still swirled across the blacktop, moving in great waves as traffic pushed it this way and that. The rain had cleared overnight but the lowlands glistened in the lingering wet sheen. He spotted a herd of bison wandering through the thick wheatgrass, their backs darkened with patches of soaked fur. The beasts moved slowly, spreading out in an arrow formation, yellow teeth snatching at anything edible as they went. Under the protective eye of a proud bull, whose massive head swung back and forth, its nose sniffing the air for any male intruder, the cows moved easily, unafraid of predators. It wasn't mating season, but he'd seen the bulls fight, charging each other at high speed and butting heads. He'd often wondered if that's where the expression *butting heads* came from.

Rowley had lived in Black Rock Falls all his life and had no hankering to leave. He owned his ranch, ran a few beef cattle, had chickens, and a kept a cow to supply more milk than they needed. His wife, Sandy, was born and raised on a ranch, had been making cheese and butter with her mom and aunts since she was five. Nothing went to waste.

"You're miles away." Rio turned up the radio and listened to the dispatches from Blackwater. "Nothing is happening in Blackwater. They have it easy over there. I can never figure out why all the serial killers come to our town."

When Rio's voice burst into his thoughts, Rowley glanced at him and then fixed his attention back to the highway. "If you think about it, it's the size of our county and the varied terrain. There are so many places a person can vanish off the grid and so many places to commit murder. For a killer, the isolated homes are like a brochure of possible victims."

"You'd figure as most people have weapons, they'd be cautious and stay away." Rio shook his head. "It's not logical."

Rowley chuckled. "Okay, you're the one with the super brain. I know for a fact that many women don't make it a habit to carry a weapon. They might have one in a gun safe at home, but from all the murders our team have investigated, few have them at all and those that do often have them used against them."

"We know about sixty percent of Montanans have weapons in their houses, but the national average is about twenty-two percent for women." Rio blew out a long breath. "Serial killers here seem to have the uncanny ability to know which ones to pick."

THIRTY-TWO

Slowing to take the exit, Rowley left the highway and then turned right at the crossroads. "Our town has another problem. We're visited by tourists, rodeo riders, and fairs, all types of shows, from cattle to cakes, then add the seasonal workers, the miners, and ranch hands. It's a perfect environment for people to move around unseen. This is why we're finding it so difficult to pin down suspects across the board. The locals recognize locals, but we have so many strangers moving through town at any one time they hardly get a second glance."

He drove through a set of gates under a sign with DIAMOND BAR RANCH depicted in cast iron and along a gravel driveway. They'd made the same journey the previous afternoon and parked outside the main ranch house. To one side was another building with a sign saying OFFICE on the door. They climbed out of the truck and crunched in the damp gravel toward the office. Rowley knocked on the door and then pushed it open. The same ranch manager they'd spoken to the previous day was sitting behind a desk staring at a computer screen. "Morning."

"Ah, morning, Deputies." The man leaned back in his seat and peered at them from under the brim of his hat. "You'll be looking for Dallas. It must be important to drag you all the way out here so early."

"Maybe." Rio smiled at him. "Don't bother to get up, just point us in the direction and we'll be out of your way before you know it."

"He's in the barn tending the horses." The manager indicated toward the door with his chin. "Turn right and follow your nose. It's the red building, smells like horses." He chuckled and turned his attention back to the screen.

As they walked outside the manager's voice followed them.

"He knows you're coming."

Rowley hunched his shoulders against a blast of cold wind whistling between the buildings. It was a usual setup for a cattle ranch: corrals and pens, cattle trucks, and the flies and smell of once-dried cow pies that had moistened since the rain. Having the cattle so close to the house wasn't something Rowley would allow. The flies and smell crept in everywhere and made life miserable. They followed the driveway, marked with deep ruts from the trucks, and made their way to the barn. The warm smell of the stables greeted them and as they walked inside, Rowley blinked to allow his eyes to adjust to the dark interior. He looked around as a tall blond-haired man chewing on a strand of hay walked toward them. "Dallas Strauss?"

"In the flesh." Strauss walked toward them, his stride easy and relaxed. He met them with a casual almost condescending smile. "Who has complained about me this time?"

"Do you have many complaints made against you?" Rio straightened and stood one hand resting on the handle of his weapon. "I haven't found any priors. Or are you speaking about misdemeanors in other states?"

"Nope, no one has ever made a complaint to the cops about me, well, not yet anyway." Strauss leaned casually against an empty stall and shrugged. "So what has you driving out here to speak to me? Someone die?"

How perceptive. Rowley took the statement pad from beneath his arm and rested it on a feed bin close by. "Have you heard the news reports about requests for CCTV footage?"

"Nope." Strauss shrugged. "I don't have time to watch too much news. It's depressing. I don't have a dashcam in my truck, so I can't help you. Is there anything else?"

"Do you know a woman by the name of Dakota Slade? She works in the general store in Black Rock Falls." Rio was watching Strauss closely.

"Yeah, I've spoken to Dakota a few times in the general store. I asked her to the Halloween Ball." Strauss shrugged. "She was busy that night." He rubbed his chin slowly. "I figured we were getting along just fine. She was as nice as pie when I went to the store."

Noticing the confused look on the man's face, Rowley nodded. "That's all part of their customer service. They're nice to everyone. It's not a come-on."

"I didn't bug her." Strauss shrugged. "I was just being friendly. Did she complain about me?"

"Nope. She hasn't said a word to us." Rio raised one eyebrow and shifted his gaze to Rowley. "It's just you were seen in the store talking to her before she went missing."

"She's missing?" Strauss pulled the straw from his mouth. "When?"

"Last Thursday." Rio stared at him. "Which brings me to Jennifer Kriss. A man fitting your description was seen talking to her at the hot food bar in the food market three times up to Friday last."

"I don't know anyone by the name of Jennifer, so it wasn't me. I go to Aunt Betty's Café if I want a meal. I don't need to go into the market. All my meals are provided. If I want a few luxuries, I grab them from the convenience store." Strauss straightened. "Is Jennifer missing too? Maybe they went out somewhere together."

Rowley stared at him. "We'll ask the questions. Do you know Johanna Worth? She works at the pizzeria."

"Who doesn't know the girls working at the pizzeria?" Strauss barked a laugh. "Yeah, I've spoken to Johanna. I didn't know her last name, but they all have their first names on their uniforms. She's a plain Jane. Why would I be interested in her?"

"Well, you looked interested in the CCTV footage we viewed recently." Rio leaned in a little closer, but Strauss didn't seem intimidated. "Care to explain that?"

"Just being social." Strauss shook his head slowly. "Seems to me, being cordial is acting interested. This seems a little one-sided to me, Deputy. She was being nice to me and it's fine, but me being nice to her when I'm ordering a pizza is a problem. I figure you have the problem not me." He blew out a long sigh. "If there's anything else you need to ask, get on with it. I have chores to do."

"Do you recall when you last spoke to these women?" Rio inclined his head. "Have you asked Johanna out on a date?"

"No and no." Strauss looked from one to the other. "You have CCTV footage, so you have the dates I was in the stores. I take my downtime when the workload is low. It's a ranch. Surely you know the days all run into each other." He shook his head slowly. "I shouldn't have asked Dakota to the Halloween Ball. You know, I regretted it the moment it came out of my mouth. I felt kinda sorry for her."

"How so?" Rio rolled his shoulders.

"She wasn't my type." Strauss removed his hat and ran his hand through his hair. "She was friendly enough and it just slipped out, is all. I figured she'd be grateful." He smiled. "I don't have a problem getting dates, so when she refused it surprised me some." He lifted his chin and replaced his hat. "The next girl I asked came to the ball with me."

Rowley nodded. "Are you an item now?"

"Nope." Strauss smiled flashing uneven teeth. "I'm not planning on being restricted for some time yet. Maybe never."

Glancing at Rio and seeing he didn't have anything further to ask, he turned back to Strauss. "You live here on the ranch?"

"Yeah, in the bunkhouse. There's four of us who work here year-round." Strauss looked from one to the other. "We done here? I have work to do."

"Yeah." Rio nodded. "Thanks for your time."

Outside Rowley turned to Rio. "What's your take on him?"

"I'm not sure." Rio tipped his hand back and forth. "I'm of two minds about him. One thing's for sure, I'm going to look into him a little closer when we get back to the office."

THIRTY-THREE

Relieved to see Nanny Raya waiting inside the kindergarten when they arrived with Tauri, Jenna took her to one side. "Are you carrying?"

"All the time." Nanny Raya squeezed her arm. "What happened was out of your control. Don't blame yourself, Jenna. All the intel Kane had going into this situation indicated the arrests had been made."

Frowning, Jenna kept her voice to just above a whisper. "Styles called Dave this morning. He told him, as far as he was aware, Mateo was arrested in the raid. So someone took his place and his prints were switched. There's a rotten apple in the sequence of events, and Dave's not convinced we're safe until he's been identified."

"Maybe not." Nanny Raya raised an eyebrow. "The problem has been neutralized. The chances of any intruders are negligible. From what I understand, the FBI is running an investigation to find the mole. There is no reason to believe the cartel will cause you any more problems."

Shaking her head, Jenna stared at her in disbelief. "The families of the cartel are spread out all over and they're loyal. It would be impossible to find them all. If they have a vendetta against Dave, then we'll never be safe."

"As far as I know, only the men who took Kane were involved." Nanny Raya gave her a long, concerned look. "Speak to Wolfe. He's been working closely with Styles to get the information you need. Styles was a highly trained military investigator and he's working on the problem. The FBI isn't too happy about the leak either. If the information was passed using the dark web, he has the best cybercrime expert as a partner. Sometimes you must trust in the system."

Not happy in the least, Jenna nodded. "Fine, but you watch Tauri like a hawk."

"I'll keep him safe, Jenna. You have my word." Nanny Raya smiled at her. "Don't worry."

Turning and looking for Tauri in the mass of kids, she spotted him close to Kane. They walked along the display of paintings of Thanksgiving the kids had pinned to a board along one wall. That morning, although a little more clingy than normal, Tauri had spent the entire time over breakfast telling Jenna how Kane ripped the chains from the wall and roared like a great warrior. He had hidden, covering his head, and the gunshots had frightened him, but his daddy had curled up around him and saved him. He was so proud of Kane and kept on looking up at him and squeezing his hand. She went to them and smiled. "We need to go to work now. Nanny Raya would like to stay and help out today. Is that okay?"

"Yes, maybe she can tell us a story?" Tauri hugged Kane's legs and then lifted his face to kiss Jenna's cheek.

Jenna hugged him close. "I'm sure she will if you ask her in story time. We'll be close by and come and get you and Nanny Raya this afternoon."

"I'll look after her." Tauri smiled.

"See you later." Kane ruffled his son's hair and gave Jenna a meaningful stare. "Ready?"

Lingering would be unusual and Jenna wanted everything to be as normal as possible for Tauri. She gave him a wave and they hurried reluctantly from the room. She turned to Kane. "I hate leaving him. Are you sure this is our best option?"

"No one can get through the front gate." Kane blew out a breath. "Nanny Raya is armed. Everything is as safe as we can make it right now. The FBI is on the job. I figure Styles is solid, and his military record is exemplary."

Jenna climbed into the Beast. "So why did he leave? No one that overqualified ends up in Rattlesnake Creek."

"Wolfe checked him out." Kane started the engine and headed for the office. "Apparently, his wife tried to kill him. He needed to get away and went back to his roots. His great-grandfather was a miner there way back, and it seemed like a nice quiet place to settle."

As they stopped outside the office, she looked at him. "You mean a nice quiet place like Black Rock Falls?" She snorted. "They sure made a mistake sending us here, didn't they? I was supposed to blend into the local population and now we're in books. So much for a quiet life."

Beside them, Rowley slipped into a parking spot and nodded to Jenna. She turned to Kane. "I sure hope they've found something on the homicides. What with the cartel and everything that's been happening, I don't know which way is up right now."

"Following the investigation will clear your head." Kane gathered his things and climbed out, opened the back door, and helped Duke from the seat. "Has Wolfe mentioned anything about autopsies? We have three victims and need more information."

Sighing, Jenna headed for the door. "I guess we're going to find out once Wolfe gets organized, but I do know he has positive IDs on the victims. While we were busy, Emily found the next of kin and organized everything. They've all viewed the bodies and given DNA samples. I feel sorry for them. Seeing their loved ones like that would have been harrowing." She caught Rowley's and Rio's attention and waved them toward her. "In my office ASAP."

"Yes, ma'am." Rowley tipped his hat and followed them inside.

In her office, Jenna surveyed the whiteboard. In her absence, Rio had added all the current information about each case. Complete with crime scene images and information they'd gathered about each victim. The suspects list included Carter, but he'd added nothing to his list. The other men, Dallas Strauss and Chase Holden, had information on each man and when they were spotted on CCTV cameras around town. She perused the information and then went to her computer to view all the recent uploaded files on the server. She found a file added by Agent Beth Katz out of Rattlesnake Creek and a message. She looked at Kane across her desk. "Agent Katz has requested the password for the surveillance array we have on Main. She's going to collect footage from any CCTV cameras around town and run them through a face recognition program."

"That would be just a formality." Kane rubbed the back of his neck. "She's like Kalo. She could hack into the Pentagon without leaving a sign. Give her what she needs. Until Kalo returns from vacation, she's our go-to for assistance." He leaned back in his chair, making it creak, and looked at her. "By now Kalo would have dredged up every dirty little secret he could find on our suspects and found the victim's next of kin. I sure miss having him around."

"Did you miss me too?" Carter walked into the office smiling around a toothpick, his Doberman, Zorro, at his heels. "I found a note stuck on my front door asking me to come by. What's been happening?" He dropped into a chair in front of her desk. "Rio gave me the evil eye when I walked in before and Maggie ignored me."

Jenna waited as Rio and Rowley came into the office and pulled up chairs to sit down. She moved her attention to Carter. "Three homicides and you just happen to match the description of the killer. You go MIA, leaving us to wonder if you've turned rogue." She sucked in a breath, taking in his astonished expression. "So where the heck have you been?"

THIRTY-FOUR

Shocked that his friend would consider him to be capable of murder, Carter listened with incredulity as Jenna went on to bring him up to date about Kane's and Tauri's abductions. He tossed his toothpick in the trash and blew out a long breath. After staring at his hands for some moments to allow his time-line to fall into place, he lifted his head and met Jenna's eyes. "First up, my intel on the members of the cartel was solid. I had copies of the arrest warrants and we had everyone in the immediate circle." He flicked a gaze at Kane. "We all know the families are large and widespread. We can't arrest every member of the family. Some have never committed a crime. Mateo we arrested. I was there when they put him on the bus to County. Check the records. They'll show he is still there. He must be because I've received no reports of an escape from the prison. If I had, you'd be the first person I'd notify, and Styles would know as well. I can assure you no one outside of the team knew your name, Dave."

"Somehow, he got out or was never there. Someone gave them my name. There's a mole in your team." Kane glared at him. "Mateo planned to torture my son, Ty." He ran a hand down his face. "I'm hoping the threat has been neutralized for now. Styles took out Mateo and one of his men. I took out two in the barn before Mateo tossed a grenade into the room. We barely escaped with our lives. In fact, it was pure dumb luck that before all hell broke loose, they dragged a heavy metal table into the room and laid out the tools to dissect my son. I used it as a shield."

"I don't know how that could possibly happen." Carter looked from one to the other. "I imagine Styles is investigating a mole in the FBI?"

"Yeah, he called this morning." Jenna nodded. "With all this happening and you MIA, it's been a difficult time."

Carter removed his hat and tossed it onto the desk. "And now I'm implicated in three murders. Anyone I know?"

He listened with interest as Jenna went over the cases and the times he apparently met the victims. In his mind's eye, he made out the faces of the women. He stood to stare at the whiteboard and swallowed hard at the crime scene images. He recognized all of the victims and had a vague recollection of when he'd last seen them. "Yeah, I've spoken to these women."

"Do you want a lawyer?" Jenna leaned forward and read him his rights. "Before you incriminate yourself any further, I suggest you get legal advice."

Shaking his head, Carter stared at her. "No, I don't want a lawyer because I haven't killed anyone." He shot Kane a look. "You know me, Dave. I figure we're friends. How could you possibly believe I'd do such a thing?" He moved his gaze to Jenna. "You honestly figure I'd be stupid enough to commit murder in your town?" He waved a hand around the room. "With this team and Wolfe? I'd need to be crazy to attempt something like that, and I'm not."

"The evidence is there. You're one of three current

suspects." Kane flipped around his laptop to show the CCTV footage from the general store and the hot food bar. "Don't tell me this isn't you. All of these women are dead. Explain that if you can."

On vacation, the last thing Carter worried about was time or the day of the week. He had six months leave due and had taken two weeks. He'd planned to call Jo and ask her if everything was okay in a day or so. They'd had all their calls diverted to other field offices. He did recall going into the stores and speaking to the women working there. In fact, he always talked to women in stores. Being a sociable guy, it was part of his personality, but that shouldn't make him a suspect in three grisly murders. Nodding, he looked at Kane. "Days kinda roll together when I'm on vacation but I'll do my best. One is easy to check because I recall asking Jennifer to recommend a beauty parlor for me. I went and got my hair cut the same day. The stylist that cut my hair went by the name of Donna. We got along real well and she didn't care that I was FBI, in fact, she gave me her card." He pulled out his wallet and extracted a card and handed it to Kane. "Trudy Newman. She'll verify the day. I think it was Friday last. In fact, it was because I dropped by the pizzeria and took home a pie. That's where I met Johanna." He stared at the ceiling. "Give me a few minutes and I'll try and recall what days I was in the stores, because most of the time I was fishing or hiking in the forest."

"Why were you in the general store three times in a week?" Jenna leaned on the table. Her expression was unreadable.

Carter shook his head. "I wasn't." He frowned. "I purchased a new lock for my cabin, is all. We chatted like you do, being social." He pointed to the whiteboard. "That would be Dakota. She found the lock I needed. I paid and left. I had no need to go back three times."

"What about visiting the market and the hot food bar?" Kane leaned forward and indicated to his screen. "The manager said you were seen there numerous times. Both of the victims worked there. You've admitted speaking to them. We have CCTV footage of you in the stores." He opened his hands. "What would you do in our position?"

Mind rushing a thousand miles per hour, Carter tried to think rationally. He hadn't murdered anyone, so someone was trying to frame him. It was the only explanation. "You're making assumptions on two short pieces of footage. I'd want all the footage analyzed using facial recognition before I jumped to conclusions." He sighed. "If this takes a court order, I'll lawyer up to get justice because while you're blaming me, a killer is still out there hunting down women."

"You deny going to the market and hot food bar?" Kane's expression hadn't changed. "When we have you on CCTV?"

Annoyed but determined to keep calm, Carter nodded. "I've already admitted going there. I purchased food a few times, coffee and milk most times. I purchased a to-go cup of coffee one day and donuts." He moved his gaze back to Jenna. "The problem is I didn't murder anyone. Just how were they killed? Shot in both eyes?" He swung his gaze back to Kane. "That would take your degree of skill, not mine."

"They weren't shot." Kane raised both eyebrows. "See if you were the killer, I'd expect a comment like that. You're digging a hole for yourself, Ty."

"Do you honestly believe I'd plot to kill you, Dave, or commit murder? Give me a break."

"Personally, no, I don't believe you killed anyone." Kane met his gaze. "You took charge of the team in the sting, so the blame of who leaked information on me rests on your shoulders." A nerve in his cheek twitched. "Mistakes on missions cost lives and not checking the backgrounds on all operatives is unforgiveable."

Unnerved, Carter straightened. "I checked them out. Kalo checked them out. They were all solid. If there was a leak, it came from somewhere else. Or one of Mateo's men recognized you. It's the only explanation."

"If my family is going to continue living here, I need answers." Kane shook his head. "There must be a communications trail. Find it."

Meeting his gaze head-on, Carter glared at him. "Don't you figure that's all I've had on my mind since I walked in here?" Trying to remain calm, he turned back to Jenna. "You gonna hold me on suspicion of murdering those women or do you want me to help you solve these crimes and get to the bottom of the darn leak?"

"That depends." Jenna leaned back in her chair, staring at him. "I don't believe you'd murder anyone, so I'll wait until Agent Katz is done with the CCTV footage. She has everything we've collected plus she's hunting down cameras all over town. It is part of her special skills." Her lips flattened into a thin line. "Here's the deal. I want you to be in communication with us at all times. Keep your phone and satellite phone at hand. As soon as we have the footage analyzed, I'll call you." She met his gaze. "This is in your best interest. Think about it, Ty, if you spoke to Jo about profiling this guy, the fact you want to insert yourself into the investigation would be a major red flag. You know that, right?"

Nodding, Carter pinched his bottom lip considering her suggestions. Jenna had acted in his favor by trusting him not to take off. She believed him and it warmed his heart. He shrugged. It was obvious Kane blamed him for the leak in the FBI. He understood his anger and the team's suspicions. "Yeah, and I'm a nice guy. I was in the vicinity of the victims. I'd hold me for questioning." He nodded and offered Kane his hand. "I did my best to protect you and I know what happened is unforgivable, but I'll find out who did leak your name." He waved a hand toward the whiteboard. "I haven't touched one hair of those women's heads and I'll be proved innocent. I'll be in my cabin or close by waiting for your call. You have my word."

"We're trusting your word, Ty, so see that you pick up." Kane stood and narrowed his gaze. He took his hand in a vice-like grip and his expression hardened to ice. "After what happened to my son, if I discover you're involved, you really don't want me hunting you down."

THIRTY-FIVE

After believing that Kane and Jenna had become part of his surrogate family, a heavy weight landed on Carter's shoulders. He couldn't stand around and wait for his friends to make a case against him and he had to admit right now the evidence was compelling. He clicked his fingers and Zorro, always loyal and his constant companion, walked beside him. Zorro wore his FBI coat, because in truth, an FBI agent was never really off duty. He needed to walk and think. Soon he found himself at Aunt Betty's Café. He needed a familiar sanctuary to think and walked inside. He smiled at Susie, the manager, and ordered a slice of apple pie and coffee. "How's your day been?"

"Busy as usual." Susie smiled at him. "The FBI has been all around town of late. I was informed my CCTV footage would be confiscated. Do you know what's going on?"

An uneasy feeling crept across Carter and he shrugged. "I'm on vacation, so out of the loop right now." He leaned closer. "What do *you* figure is going on?"

"I know for a fact two of the women working at the market went missing. The manager came by earlier and told me. He said a man who looks just like you came by his store and talked to both women."

Scratching his cheek, Carter stared at her. "It could have been me. I did go into the market and buy a new lock. I spoke to the server but I'm guessing she spoke to many people over the same day. Why do you believe they're targeting someone who looks like me?"

"I'm not sure but I did see a guy who looks like you." Susie leaned closer. "The chef needed a couple of extra pans and I dropped by the general store to see what they had available. I almost stopped the guy to chat, then when he turned around it wasn't you. He had black eyes, not green like yours, and wasn't as tall."

Interested, Carter nodded. "Was he talking to anyone?"

"Yeah, he was real chatty with Dakota, like they knew each other." Susie rolled her eyes. "I'm waiting in line to pay for the pans and he's talking up a storm like he has all the time in the world."

Nodding, Carter blew out a breath. Susie had been up and personal with a potential killer. She could identify the man everyone believed was him. "What day was this?"

"That would be Thursday last." Susie looked at him. "Do you figure he could be involved with Dakota going missing?"

Not wanting to alarm Susie, Carter shrugged nonchalantly. "Like I said, I'm out of the loop right now. Keep the information to yourself but tell Jenna if she asks you. If he's involved and knows you can identify him, you might put yourself in danger."

"My lips are sealed." Susie smiled. "I'll have Leona bring out your meal. It won't be long."

Carter returned her smile. "Leona? I don't believe we've met."

"She started a couple of weeks back." Susie leaned in again conspiratorially. "Married six months and her husband had an affair. They moved here for his job and he's hightailed it back to

Texas, left her the house, so she's working two jobs to pay for it." She pointed at him. "You be nice to her. She's fragile."

Holding up both hands and backing away, Carter chuckled. "I'm always nice." He headed for a seat near the window and sat down to watch the people walking along Main.

A young woman arrived a short time later with a tray carrying a pot of coffee, the fixings, and a very large slice of pie with ice cream on the side. Susie always spoiled him and he appreciated her. He looked up at the young woman, her face flushed from running around. He put her age at around twenty, and her heart-shaped face held exquisite eyes of the darkest violet-blue he'd ever seen. "You must be Leona." He smiled at her. "Agent Ty Carter, nice to meet you. How are you settling into life in Black Rock Falls?"

"Not so good." Leona pushed a strand of hair behind one ear and poured his coffee. "I'll be happier when I can sell my house and move closer to town. I don't need a big old house. The apartments in town, the ones they're building in the old industrial buildings on Maple, are more my style."

Carter smiled at her. "I'm sure it will sell. The real estate is in demand in this town."

"Oh, do you live in town?" Leona smiled at him. "I haven't seen you come by."

Shaking his head. "Right now I have a cabin in the woods, but I live out at Snakeskin Gully. I'm on vacation right now." He leaned back in his chair. "I'm in town often, so I'll be around. Maybe we can have a drink sometime?"

"I'd like that." Leona blushed prettily. "It will need to be when I sell my house. Right now, I'm working all hours. So I'll take a raincheck if that's okay?"

Nodding, Carter smiled at her. "Sure. I'll be dropping by again real soon."

He watched her go, wondering if Agent Katz was monitoring his every move via the CCTV cameras around town.

Being a social animal, changing his usual character and friendliness toward women just to please a murder investigation was never going to happen. He hadn't done anything wrong and refused to play their game. The problem was, restricted to his cabin he couldn't investigate anything. He needed help. Going to Jenna or Kane and giving them the information Susie had divulged only made him look guilty, as if he needed to point the blame elsewhere. Reluctantly, he pulled out his phone and called Kalo's burner. The FBI computer whiz kid was his chance to get out of this mess—if he could reach him. To his surprise, Bobby picked up after a few rings. "Bobby, it's Carter. Are you back from vacation?"

"Yeah, we came back last night." The squeak Kalo's office chair made when he moved from one computer to another came through the earpiece.

Grinning at his good fortune, Carter added the fixings to his coffee. "You're in the office?"

"I live here, man. Remember?" Kalo's chair creaked again. "I'm playing four online games at once. If you're looking for Jo, she's not planning on coming into the office for another week."

Carter took the time to explain the situation and the involvement of Beth Katz. "I need you to get involved. I figure someone is trying to frame me. First, they make me look like an ass with Kane by letting his name out to the cartel and now someone is making like I'm murdering women."

"If you imagine that it's impossible for an outsider to gain information from the FBI files, then you're wrong." Kalo's chair squeaked as he moved from screen to screen. "That's how I ended up here. The hackers are getting better not by the month or day but by the second. Look what's happening around the world. Seemingly impenetrable companies are being hacked. Our minds are moving so fast. Kids are phenomenal at their knowledge of technology. It's as if another part of their brain has just been switched on. Trust me, a ten-year-old could hack the Pentagon now. Sure, my mind is growing too, but trust me, nowhere is safe. When these hackers start getting into satellites and weapons systems, we're all dead. Trust me, it's not far away."

Thinking over the information, Carter nodded slowly. "So someone planning to commit the perfect crime could be setting me up? First by destroying my support and then by murdering women. Who would be doing this to me and why?"

"You've upset many people in your time, Ty." Kalo chuckled. "Put names in a hat and pull out one. You have a better chance of finding him that way." He sobered. "First up, you know he is impersonating you or looks like you. I'm sure Jenna and Kane already have men of similar appearance on their list. You were in Jenna's office. What did you see on the whiteboard?"

Carter stared into space visualizing the whiteboard and only seeing the murdered women. He moved his mental image to the right and made out three names. "Three suspects and I was on the top of the list." He pulled his pie toward him. The ice cream had melted all over the plate and dripped off onto the table. He dropped paper napkins on the mess and picked up a spoon. "You can get into the casefiles. Get me the names of the suspects and then see what you can discover about them."

"Sure." Kalo took a deep breath. "When I'm done, I'll go through a back door and find out what Agent Katz is doing. Chances are she won't be guarding her files as she'll be running a routine facial recognition program on the CCTV footage. I'll try and download copies of the interesting files and look at them. One thing, next time you call my burner, use a burner. Agent Katz could get through my firewalls. She's darn good."

Breathing out a sigh of relief, Carter smiled. "Okay, but you didn't ask me if I was guilty."

"I didn't need to." Kalo tapped away at his keyboard. "I'll contact Jo the moment she gets home. She told me she'd call me this evening. I'll let her know what's happening. She'll have your back too." He paused a beat. "Maybe stay away from town for a

*day or so. Just in case someone else gets murdered. Stay at the
cabin and give us time to find some answers and leave your
phone on, so they can track you."*

Carter chuckled. "That won't help. If I was killing women,
I'd have the sense to leave it at the cabin. No, I'll call when I'm
at the cabin and make sure the people I speak to in town know
me and not a doppelganger, if that's what's happening here."

"I've already started to access files." Kalo chuckled. *"Wow!
Agent Katz has accessed nanny cams and local security footage.
It's going to take some time to run a facial recognition over all of
them. Man, she's good. Message me your new number and I'll
call as soon as I have something."*

Carter smiled to himself. He'd conduct his own investigation, and just like Jenna, he had a darn good team behind him.
Knowing Kalo was back and Jo on her way, it was as if a great
weight had been lifted from his shoulders. "Thanks. Talk later."
He disconnected and dug into his pie. Not even runny ice
cream could spoil an Aunt Betty's pie. He'd hang around for a
time and might just have a piece of the cherry one next.

THIRTY-SIX

I could not believe it. It was as if the planets aligned or something. There, in full view, I made out Agent Carter chatting with Leona. I've been watching Leona since she started working at Aunt Betty's Café. I try and avoid that eatery as often as possible. You see, the servers there are very friendly with the sheriff's department. I see them making special deliveries. All the cartons specially sealed to avoid tampering. It makes me laugh. I could easily inject poison through a carton if I really wanted to—but the sheriff and her deputies aren't my targets. Killing is an artform, but my special skill is making it appear to be someone else.

It was only by chance that I happened to be in the Cattleman's Hotel bar and noticed Carter. He's known around town, and with his FBI jacket and Doberman at his side, he's a hard one to miss. I watched him play pool along with a few of the locals. He was openly chatting about his vacation and his cabin in the woods. He'd planned to go off the grid and joked about dropping into town only for pizza and supplies. He was perfect and making myself resemble him was too easy. We have many characteristics the same. I needed to add some highlights to my hair, which was easy enough—women do it all the time—and then it took a change of clothes, a pair of snakeskin boots, and shades. In my new persona, many people assume I'm him. I tried the disguise a few times, even dining at his favorite restaurant. He'd been there three times since he'd arrived in town and servers in Antlers even called me Agent Carter at one time. I made sure to pay in cash. A credit card would have given the game away.

Now, you may ask me why I picked Leona this time. She's divorced and I just happened to have run into her—literally outside Aunt Betty's Café. She was coming out carrying a to-go cup and walked right into me, spilling the coffee. I apologized, mainly because she had tears in her eyes, and I love a vulnerable woman. I asked her to wait and I'd replace the coffee. I purchased one myself and, seeing her distressed, offered to walk to the park opposite with her, saying that sitting in the quiet park was a good way to gather herself. We sat talking for a time. She sure talked up a storm, telling me about her divorce and how her husband cheated on her, and how she needed to work two jobs to keep the house—blah, blah, blah.

Dressed in my work clothes, I probably didn't smell so good and all she needed was a sympathetic ear. It was a long hour of wasted time because the moment I offered to meet her for coffee again sometime, she looked at me as if I were last night's leftovers and shook her head. I mean, really? One long hour of listening to her moaning and she couldn't give me the same in return. When I watched her toss her coffee into the trash, blow her nose, and walk away without so much as a "thank you," the need to remove another heartless woman from existence became an obsession. From then on, Leona became my priority. I needed to know everything about her. Where she worked, where she lived, her schedule, and when I could get to her. It sure is easy when people stick to a schedule. I can spend all the time in the world, making sure when the time comes I can just walk into their house and... well, you'll find out soon enough.

I just need a little more time to make sure Agent Carter is a suspect without an alibi. The CCTV footage the media has been requested was collected and uploaded to a server. That was their first mistake but a big break for me. Ah, I see I have your attention now. Don't worry, give me time and everything will become clear. I've waited and watched Agent Carter because they say everything comes to people who wait, and the stars aligned when I walked past Aunt Betty's Café and there, right before my eyes, was Leona in her new job. Agent Carter was chatting with her and she was smiling. Her fate is sealed. Remember that I'm not responsible for what happens next. It's her fault she's going to die.

THIRTY-SEVEN

After being brought up to speed on the interviews conducted by Rowley and Rio, Jenna looked from one to the other. "Do you believe that either could be suspects?"

"They both have the same characteristics and, like Carter, made contact with the victims before their deaths, although Strauss says he doesn't know anyone by the name of Jennifer." Rio leaned back in his chair. "If he were our only suspect, we'd haul him in for further questioning and even consider having him charged on suspicion of murder. The problem is, we have three men, all moving around town at the same time and the victims all worked in places where they were in contact with any number of members of the public in one day."

Nodding, Jenna twirled a pen around in her fingers. She looked at Rowley. "What do you think, Jake?"

"I don't believe Carter would murder women, for a start." Rowley turned his hat around in his hands, fingering the brim. "The other two, maybe, and the woodcarver, Chase Holden, has been to their homes. He knows the victims. He didn't appear to be nervous at all when we spoke to him. I've been talking to people for a time now as a deputy and anyone you stop to speak to is always wary." He shrugged. "Both Holden and Strauss didn't have a care in the world, as if deputies dropped by every day to ask them about missing women." He indicated to the door with his chin. "Carter, on the other hand, was visibly shocked and I could see by his expression that doubting him was cutting deep. Whoever murdered those women doesn't have feelings and that's all I have to say."

"Allowing a killer to lure you into a false sense of security is a big mistake." Kane moved his gaze from one deputy to another. "I'm not saying that Carter is guilty of murder, but he is capable of taking lives and not letting it worry him." He lifted one shoulder. "SEALs are trained to kill. Never forget that part of his makeup. He could take out a battalion and not break a sweat. Some can't take the killing and have mental breakdowns and the suicide rate in troops returning from tour of duty is skyrocketing." He drew a deep breath. "We know Carter suffered from PTSD due to an incident he won't discuss. What if something triggered him?" He raised both eyebrows. "Let's look at the facts: Is he capable of making the changes to the stun gun? Yes, he is." He looked back at Jenna. "That is one thing you need to be checking. Do our other suspects have the knowledge. Is it available on the internet?"

Making notes, Jenna lifted her eyes back to Kane. "Do you honestly believe Ty is our killer?"

"Nope, but we can't go easy on him just because he's our friend." Kane shrugged. "Trust me, if the boot were on the other foot, he'd be doing the same. It's better we make sure he's innocent rather than leave any room for doubt. Just don't ever underestimate a SEAL. He has far more knowledge and capabilities than any of you are giving him credit for. Plus the fact he knows how to react. That's part of his training too, and working with Jo, he could fool anyone."

Troubled, Jenna looked at her deputies. "Okay, Rio, go and see what you can find about changing the amps on a stun gun, and Rowley, take another look at the suspects Strauss and Holden. Don't go poking around Carter's files or you'll stir up a wasp's nest."

She stood and refilled her coffee cup and one for Kane and then sat down at her desk and stared at him. "That was harsh. Carter looked stunned when you shook his hand and threatened him. What's gotten into you, Dave?"

"That wasn't a threat. It was a promise and he knows it. You don't want him flying back to Snakeskin Gully and out of our jurisdiction, do you? As a suspect, that would show incompetence on our part." Kane pulled his coffee cup toward him, took a sip, and swallowed. "He screwed up on the sting operation and put lives in danger. He didn't follow up with the prison to make sure they ran Mateo's fingerprints when they took him into custody because it's as obvious as the nose on my face that Mateo escaped in the bedlam that followed the raid. Someone took his place and likely the switch was planned ahead of time, just in case something went wrong. I wouldn't be surprised if the same switch was made by Eduardo Souza. The cartel is well organized and makes contingency plans."

Jenna rubbed her temples, wondering where this conversation was going. "There's nothing he can do about it now. Mateo's dead."

"Yeah, but the man who took his place is still alive and I'll call Agent Styles and make sure Eduardo Souza is actually on remand." Kane's lips curled up in one corner. "I know Ty, and he'll break a world speed record to discover how it played out and if there are any players left in the field for us to worry about."

Jenna poked one finger on the desk and stared at him. "Is that your only concern? We have homicide victims in the morgue and a killer on the loose. Can you focus on the cases for a time?"

"Your and Tauri's safety is my priority. I don't like

surprises. Being ambushed so easily, and not knowing if they were hurting you and Tauri, isn't something I'm going to forget." Kane stood, walked around the desk, and pulled her into his arms. He held her tight against him, with his face buried in her hair. He stood there just holding her, as if gathering himself, and then stared into her eyes. "I know you're strong and independent, but so am I and they still got to me, Jenna. They abducted Tauri before your eyes." He held up his hand and closed his finger and thumb a quarter inch apart. "We came this close to dying because someone conveniently forgot to run Mateo's prints. This means the cartel has someone inside the prison and I mean to find out who it is." He pressed a kiss to her cheek and then met her gaze. "The current caseload is well in hand. We're investigating the murders. In fact, Rio and Rowley have made progress in a very short time. Has Wolfe added any files to the server? The autopsy was scheduled for eleven on Saturday." He went back to his chair and peered at his laptop screen.

Unable to believe that Kane actually believed life went on as normal when he went missing, she gaped at him. "He completed the autopsies and gave me a verbal rundown but as the living take priority, I gave Rio and Rowley orders to proceed with the investigation. Wolfe and I dropped everything and started searching for you. After we'd searched all around the ranch, we waited for you to show or for a ransom demand. When nothing happened, we alerted the FBI and then Agent Styles arrived and we began a grid search."

"Yeah, but that wasn't until Sunday, right?" Kane tapped away at his laptop. "I see Wolfe completed the autopsies on Saturday. Let me see, electrocution using a stun gun with high amps, as we thought. No sign of trace evidence, nothing found on the skin of both victims." He looked up at Jenna. "His note says if there'd been a stun gun at the scene, he'd have considered suicide as means of death." He raised his gaze from the screen.

"So, we have nothing apart from the suspects seen speaking to the victims?"

Opening up the files, Jenna swallowed hard at a partial report from Agent Katz. "I have something." She looked at Kane's inquisitive expression. "Not all of the CCTV footage gave a clear indication of the man seen with the victims. She mentions they all appear the same build and wear the same type of dress and boots, but so did another twenty or so men who appeared on the footage. The ones she clearly identified all gave a positive for Carter."

"Does she give a time and date?" Kane raised both eyebrows. "He did admit to speaking to the victims."

Jenna nodded. "Yeah, and strange as it may seem, none of the times Carter said he was speaking to them are on the footage. The times were in the days before the murders but not on the days of the murders as Carter seemed to remember." She looked at Kane's startled expression. "So is this proof he's lying to us?"

"It's a problem I didn't envisage." Kane blew out a long sigh. "Send her a message and ask her to upload all the incriminating data to the server so we can view it."

Nodding, Jenna picked up her phone and sent the message. "Now what?"

Before he could answer, Jenna's computer signaled an incoming video call. She looked at Kane. "Jo's back and she's asking for a video call." She turned her screen around and joined the conversation. "Hi, Jo, did you enjoy Disneyland?"

"I figure I've come back to it." Jo's eyes flashed. *"You have Carter as a suspect in three homicide cases? Have you lost your minds?"*

"He was the last person to see them alive." Kane gave her an intent stare. "Have you read the files?"

"Yeah, I have, and they mean nothing. The CCTV footage that we obtained from the Rattlesnake Creek field office shows

many men spoke to the women over the same time. This accusa-tion is ludicrous." She blew out a long breath. *"He'd no more commit murder than you would, Dave."*

Jenna raised both eyebrows. "We don't believe he did it either."

"The other matter, the so-called mole in our team..." Jo stared into the camera. *"I can imagine how upset you are, Dave. What happened to you and Tauri is unforgivable, but you can't lay all the blame on Carter."*

"Why not?" Kane leaned forward on the desk. "He informed me he'd seen Mateo onto the bus to County. There's been no escapes and yet Mateo was free to organize my abduction and Tauri's. He planned to torture my son to make me recant my evidence against Eduardo Souza. What happened?"

"I spoke to Agent Styles just before and told him I'd call. He smelled a rat after he spoke to you and flew straight to LA to discover the truth. He's still there on the job. The prints of all the prisoners were taken on arrival and all are still in jail. Styles ran the prints of the prisoner by the name of Mateo and they didn't match the ones on record. The man who claims he's Mateo is in fact his cousin. They look alike. After Styles interrogated him and informed him he'd have the kidnapping and assault of a law enforcement officer, plus the abduction of a child, added to his sheet unless he cooperated, he buckled. He planned to switch places with Mateo as soon as the deal was agreed on, he would easily get out of most of the charges on a technicality later." She paused a beat. *"Before the deal was completed Mateo had already slipped away. It will interest you to know the kingpin, Eduardo Souza, had a double as well, but he didn't escape capture. The cartel members on scene were arrested and processed. Carter was there with others to make sure they all made it to jail. The doppelganger would have fooled anyone, Dave. As soon as they discovered the prosecution had an eyewit-*

ness, they needed to protect Eduardo Souza. He's the reason they hunted you down."

"There is one person you need to pursue and that's the guard responsible for checking the prisoners' prints." Kane stared at Jo on the screen. "He's working for the cartel and either switched the prints or didn't conduct a search for a match. You need to find that man and charge him. He will be acting as a go-between from the kingpin to the remaining cartel members on the outside. While he's moving around freely, nobody is safe."

"We were going to ask for an internal investigation on how that oversight happened, but I'll contact Agent Styles and inform him of your concerns." Jo made notes and then glanced up at the screen. *"I see why we need to get involved. An internal investigation can be manipulated if there's a cartel member working at the prison."* She smiled at Kane. *"Don't worry, we'll find the worm in the apple."*

Glancing at Kane, Jenna turned her attention back to Jo. "So how did Mateo find Dave?"

"One of Mateo's men took a photograph of him during the deal. They used their extensive family members in jail to move it across the country, asking other prisoners until someone recognized him. It took less than twenty-four hours to get a result."

"Who was it?" Kane leaned forward in his chair.

"I don't have the details, but Styles got a name. It is a member of the biker gang you shot for kidnapping Jenna at the Triple Z Roadhouse. He was doing time in County in Black Rock Falls and released last week. He contacted Mateo to give him Kane's name. That's how they found you."

"So prisoners all over now know my face?" The nerve in Kane's cheek twitched. "Nice."

"I'll send you a copy." Jo suddenly smiled. *"It looks more like your evil brother, maybe. The expression is wrong and you darkened your skin. I'd say you maybe looked that way when you*

took down the biker gang. I personally wouldn't worry. As this came through the cartel, and the men who saw it are in jail, I'd figure they wouldn't want to get involved. I'd say the biker had a score to settle."

Jenna ran a hand down her face. "Send me his name. If he's been in contact with a felon, he's broken his parole. The money he received from a felon will have him back in jail. I'll send the information to the Blackwater sheriff. It's his problem to deal with parole violations."

"Not a problem. I'll contact Styles when we're done here." Jo looked from one to the other. "You guys are like family to me. I don't want Carter's apparent involvement in a crime to come between us. You have my word we'll share all the investigations we're conducting to prove his innocence. He is innocent and I'll stake my professional reputation on it. You need to be looking elsewhere."

"We are, and we have two other suspects." Kane twirled his coffee cup around in his fingertips and stared at the screen. "Right now we need information on the tampering of the murder weapon. When we discover which of the two suspects is capable of changing the amperage on the stun gun, we'll have a case. There are many factors involved to do that and I'd expect the weapon isn't one purchased and altered, that's near impossible. I figure it was built by the killer, because any readily available are restricted in their capability to produce high amperage. Rio and Rowley are searching the suspects' backgrounds and the internet as we speak for more information."

"That's way over my head." Jo rubbed her temples. "Where exactly is Carter?"

Jenna blew out a sigh. "I have no idea. I gave him the benefit of the doubt and let him go. I assume he's at his cabin. He said he'd leave his phone switched on." She frowned. "Can't you reach him?"

"Right this moment, no. My call went to voicemail." Jo held

up a hand. *"He might be out of range. I'll try the satellite phone. Oh, and Kalo is back on the job. He's hunting down a few things for Carter. They spoke after he left your office. I'll be in touch."* She disconnected.

"She's not very happy with us." Kane rolled his eyes skyward. "Yet she'd do the same. Look what happened when Rio was found with a victim. We followed procedure then too. Nobody is above the law."

Losing Jo and Carter's friendship would be a disaster, but Jenna had no choice. She looked at Kane and shook her head slowly. "There goes Thanksgiving."

THIRTY-EIGHT

The library was deserted when Carter walked upstairs and set his laptop on a table next to a window overlooking Main. Hours later and mentally depleted from reading all afternoon, he finished a can of soda, and leaned back in his chair, staring at the computer screen looking for answers. His FBI access codes had gotten him into Jenna's files. He'd always had access but had expected Jenna to restrict him during the investigation. He read through the autopsy reports. The forensic conclusions Wolfe had supplied had been extremely interesting. Only a stun gun with high amperage could have caused the damage to the victims. From the information Kalo had sent him, the background checks of the suspects didn't show the electrical engineering attributes required to make electroshock weapons. Not intending to put anything in writing, because he couldn't trust anyone right now, he called Kalo's burner. "Is it possible to buy a high amperage stun gun on the dark web?"

"I haven't found anything you can't buy on the dark web." Kalo unscrewed the top of the jar of candy he always had on his desk. It made a familiar spinning sound, and a clatter as the top fell on to the desk. *"Do you want one?"*

Smiling to himself Carter smothered a yawn. "Nah, I'm just hunting down all possible ways a person could obtain a stun gun capable of killing someone. I'm finding it difficult to believe that either of the suspects in the current case has the intelligence or training to be able to change the amperage on a stun gun. So, I'll need you to check out if either of them has any skill when it comes to IT. If they're capable of negotiating the dark web, it opens up a whole can of worms."

"I don't have to check that out, I already know. They have intelligence in spades." Kalo tapped on his keyboard. *"The answer to that question is both of them. Holden obtained a scholarship to one of the most prestigious colleges in the state. He was writing software for some of the major companies and making millions until his security program was hacked offshore. He walked away and ended up in Black Rock Falls, carving wood. Strauss had a similar background in IT but his specialty was gaming. From what I could dig up about him, he left the company due to burnout. He was raised on a cattle farm and decided it was time to go back to his roots to get his karma back— I found that info on his social media page."* He paused for a beat. *"Where is this line of investigation leading?"*

Carter digested the information and ran a hand through his shaggy blond hair. "I'm not sure but I'll need to go and look at the crime scenes. My movements haven't been restricted by the local sheriff's department, so I'll be calling in where I'm going, just in case anyone asks questions. I don't want them to believe that it's the killer returning to the scene of the crime."

"I'll add it to my daybook." Kalo's voice dropped to just below a whisper. It was obvious that Jo was close by. *"I strongly suggest you don't let anyone see you. The information I'm seeing from the Rattlesnake Creek field office, comes close to implicating you in both murders."*

Stunned, Carter swallowed hard. "How so?"

"To date, Agent Katz's recognition software has you identi-

fied as the blond-haired man who spoke to the victims prior to their death. The times and dates don't tally with what you told Jenna. There are days of difference between the times. In Jenna's files, it says you admitted to being one of the last people to see the women alive, and yet the CCTV footage put you in contact with them days prior."

Rubbing a hand down his face, Carter stared out of the window and along Main. "Then we have a problem. I wasn't in town prior to when I spoke to them. I was in Snakeskin Gully."

"There's another problem." Kalo's squeaky footsteps sounded on tile and a door opened and closed. *"The flight plan that you filed to travel to Black Rock Falls was not the time that you said you arrived in town."*

Astounded, Carter shook his head. "What? That's impossible." He thought for a beat. "Wolfe will remember the time I arrived. My chopper has been parked on his helipad on top of the medical examiner's office since I arrived."

"Maybe, but can you prove you didn't drop the chopper somewhere else beforehand? You need to make sure you have everything in place, because if you didn't murder those women, someone out there is setting you up. If they have the ability to hack into aviation logs, anything is possible."

As Carter stared out of the window, he noticed Leona from Aunt Betty's Café walking toward her pickup truck. Not far behind her, a man who looked remarkably like him went up behind her and struck up a conversation. "Just a minute." He accessed his phone camera and took a string of rapid shots, capturing the man climbing into Leona's pickup truck. She drove away and he kept clicking until they mingled into the line of traffic. "I need to send you images of something I've just witnessed. How can I do this without anyone hacking the file?"

"Hang on for five." More footsteps as Kalo returned to the office. The sound of drawers opening in a filing cabinet and plastic ripping. *"Okay, send them to this burner, I'll download*

them onto a stick and then nuke the phone. I suggest you do the same. Send me your new number. My burner is bouncing off towers around the world. Conversations will be safe but documents might be vulnerable."

Carter pulled a thumb drive from his pocket and stuck it into his phone and downloaded the files. He sent a copy to Kalo and then pressed the phone to his ear. "Done. I gotta go and buy a new burner. I'll send the number to the office as an invoice, call me when you get it." He disconnected and removed the SIM from the phone and scored it with his knife before leaving the library. As he walked along Main, he dropped the SIM and phone down a drain.

Rain had started to fall again and large spots hit his cheeks like tears. Beside him, Zorro shook his head and moved closer to the stores lining the sidewalk. After buying another burner from a convenience store, he headed back to his rental. He opened the door for Zorro and sat in the front seat for a time, thinking through Kalo's information. Evidence was stacking up against him and every last piece of it was false. Determined to find the real killer, he started the engine and headed out to the first crime scene.

THIRTY-NINE

Kane made the call to Agent Styles and explained his concerns about Eduardo Souza. He found Styles likable and efficient. His military police background showed through. "I understand that you checked Mateo's prints against the prisoner with his name in jail."

"I checked them but I didn't collect them. I asked a local FBI agent in LA I trust to go to the prison and take his prints. I ran them against the copies of Mateo from the previous arrests we had on file. When they didn't match, I jumped on a plane and went to LA to interview the doppelganger. I forwarded all the information to Jo Wells out at Snakeskin Gully as she is your go-to person."

Drumming his fingers on the desk, Kane stared to space. "Yeah, she called. Did you by any chance check Eduardo Souza's prints while you were there?"

"Oh, yeah." Styles chuckled. *"I figured if they tried it with Mateo, they would definitely try it with Souza. I scanned the mug shots of the arrests made that evening and noticed two of the men looked very similar. So I personally took Souza's prints and*

ran them through our software when I got home. I can personally guarantee that Souza is in jail awaiting trial."

Relieved, the tension in Kane's jaw relaxed. "That's good to know."

"I hear that you have Carter as a suspect in your current homicide cases." Styles cleared his throat. *"From what my partner is telling me, the evidence is stacking up against him. I've known him for a time, and he sure doesn't act like any serial killer I've met. I hate to play devil's advocate but I figure we need to get to the bottom of what the heck is happening here."* He blew out a sigh. *"Anything you need me to do, I'm there."*

Running a hand down his face, Kane thought for a beat. "It's pointless searching Carter's cabin or his apartment at Snakeskin Gully. If he was involved, he'd hide the murder weapon." He thought for a beat. "I know for a fact that Carter is more than capable of building a high-amperage stun gun. No doubt you could as well. We're in the process of determining whether or not the two other suspects have the knowledge to do this as well. If one of them does have this ability, then we know to concentrate on him instead of Carter."

"Beth... ah, Agent Katz, believes there is more to this that meets the eye. Hang on a sec, the coffee's ready and I've been out all day." Styles' spoon clinked in his cup as he stirred his coffee. *"Beth believes it's possible the stun gun was purchased on the dark web. She was able to access Carter's devices and he hasn't been near the dark web or anywhere else online where he could purchase such an item. The only way we'll be able to discover if the other two suspects use the dark web for whatever reason, is if Beth gets the hard drives from their media devices. It doesn't matter how hard they try to delete information from their history. She'll find it."*

Leaning back in his chair and staring at the ceiling, Kane sighed. "Without probable cause, that ain't gonna happen. We've got two men who admit speaking to the victims, and that's it. Sure, they fit the description of the people who saw them speaking to the women. Both men have been interviewed and although they could fit the profile of a serial killer, we have absolutely no motive. There are no links to the women in any way whatsoever. Holden sold them carvings. Strauss spoke to them at work casual-like. Both admitted to speaking to them."

"No, not enough probable cause for a search warrant, that's for darn sure." Styles' chair creaked. *"Leave it with me. I'll see what I can do about it. Having someone like Beth Katz in the office, sometimes miracles happen. Her expertise in cybercrime has given her access to more places than you would imagine."*

Glad of the support, Kane pushed a hand through his hair. "Thanks, I'd appreciate any assistance you could offer."

"Anytime." Styles disconnected.

"Get any information?" Jenna peered at him from across her desk.

Nodding, Kane stood and went to the kitchenette to pour a cup of coffee. He hunted through the cabinet below, looking for a jar of cookies. "Yeah. The man they have on remand is Eduardo Souza. Styles took his prints while he was there to interview Mateo's doppelganger." He grabbed the jar of cookies and straightened. "The general consensus of the FBI is that something unusual is going on. We have Beth Katz working on it. She's an expert in cybercrime but really needs access to the suspects' computers to get anywhere."

"I'm sure Kalo will get involved as well." Jenna indicated to her screen. "I've been scanning our suspects' files right back to grade school. They're both smart. They have strong IT backgrounds, which are at odds to their current employment. This wouldn't assist them with the stun guns, but it could easily give them the skills to gain access to the victims' homes. We know how easy it is to hack a security system or any local cameras. Either of them has the skills to have been watching the victims undetected."

Nodding, Kane poured two cups of coffee and sat at Jenna's desk. He went back for the cookies, and a doggy treat for Duke. "Yeah, since I discovered that just about all Wi-Fi cameras can be hacked, even nanny cams and robot vacuum cleaner cams, it opens up a whole new world for Peeping Toms."

"Or the best time to lie in wait for a victim to arrive home from work." Jenna sipped her coffee and munched on a cookie. "How can we eliminate either suspect or Carter without gaining access to their computers or other devices?"

Kane shrugged. "We're between a rock and a hard place. I guess we could haul them both in for questioning and see what happens when we shake the tree. Other than that, I guess we wait for him to make a mistake."

"You mean when he kills again?" Jenna grimaced. "That can't be our only option. I'm writing down what we have and we'll take it to the judge. Circumstantial evidence might be enough." She gave him a long look over the rim of the cup. "We'll pull the suspects in first. If they're not involved, they might just surrender their devices voluntarily. Stranger things have happened."

Kane snorted and tossed a doggy treat to Duke. "One day pigs might fly too, but I'm not holding my breath."

FORTY

Carter had driven deep enough along Dakota Slade's driveway so that his truck would be hidden from view by the trees. He sat in his vehicle with Kalo on speaker, trying to think like a tech-savvy killer. "You have the coordinates. Can you check to see if there are any CCTV cameras anywhere around the outside of the property?"

"Nope, you're good to go." Kalo tapped on his keyboard. *"The victims have security systems. Nothing was activated when the deputies arrived."*

Rain splashed against the windshield as Carter drove along the driveway to the house. Apart from the pine trees, all the other vegetation had dropped their leaves, and the blackened trunks gave an eerie feeling to the surrounding area. Fall leaves of every color appeared glossy as the rain soaked the gravel driveway. He pulled the truck to a halt outside the front porch and, moving a toothpick across his mouth, stared at the house, trying to think like a killer. What would he do if he wanted to murder someone? "Do you figure he was inside the house before Dakota got home from work?"

"Well, from the crime scene photographs she wasn't

expecting a visitor, as in a date. Seems to me she'd gotten ready for bed and was having a snack in front of the TV." Kalo moved his chair, the wheels running across the tile in a familiar sound. *"They all seem to be like that, just sitting staring at the TV but dead. It's real creepy, man."*

Carter turned up the collar on his jacket and pushed his Stetson firmly down on his head. "I'm going to take a look at the lock on the front door and try and establish if the security system was compromised."

"If it had been damaged in any way it would have been in Wolfe's report." Kalo tapped away at his keyboard. *"Even if the killer used some of his IT skills, it would be too difficult for him to manipulate the security system. Unless he was spying on the girls some other way. You need to look for any type of cameras. You would be surprised how many people leave their laptop cameras switched on, and there are others in the house. For instance, many motion detectors have security cameras. Nanny cams, robotics all have cameras and all are easy to tap into. If he was watching the victims, he could easily discover the code to the security system, which would give him immediate access. He would know their movements to the minute and, as you suggested, have been inside when they arrived home. They wouldn't know because the moment he was inside he'd have reactivated it."*

Carter walked up to the house and peered through the window. The security system was blinking green, which meant he was good to go. It only took him a few seconds to get through the lock on the front door. The stink of death still lingered inside the musty house. It was getting late in the afternoon and the rooms were in shadows. Using his flashlight, he examined each room, searching for any evidence of cameras. "See if you can access the motion sensors and the robotic vacuum cleaner. The motion sensors are only in the foyer of the house over-looking the front door, so I would imagine she used them for her own peace of mind. Someone would have to be inside the house before they gave her any warning."

"Yeah, I can get into them. Wait up." Kalo chuckled.

At a whirring sound close by, Carter pulled his weapon and turned toward the noise as a vacuum cleaner lit up and came out of its docking station and began to move around the house heading straight for him. "Did you do that?"

"Yeah, that basic model is easy to manipulate by anyone with a few programing brain cells. They could make it follow the victim around, constantly sending a stream of video back to the person who's watching. People don't realize how easy it is to be under surveillance when you're surrounded by tech. Think about it, your phone is listening to you... your TV, tablet. Well, some people even have Wi-Fi in their air conditioners. Any type of Wi-Fi can be manipulated if you have the right skill set." Kalo snorted. "Stop aiming that weapon at me, it's disturbing."

Slowly sliding his pistol into his shoulder holster, he made his way into the family room and stood at the entrance, looking at the setup. It would be very easy to approach the victim from behind as she was watching TV and kill her, but what was the motive? Hitting a victim with a stun gun from behind didn't really tick any of the thrill boxes of the psychopaths he dealt with in the past. From the many cases he'd worked on, it seemed that psychopaths got thrilled from killing. So where was the thrill here? "Has Jo worked out a profile on this guy yet?"

"Yeah, she believes he exerts some type of power over the women." Kalo opened a candy wrapper, the sound of the plastic absurdly loud in Carter's ear. "I mentioned I believed he must be watching them using various cameras around the houses and she believes this is part of the domination. Getting inside their houses without them knowing is another power play. She doesn't have any doubt that he makes himself visible to them prior to their deaths, so she assumes he is carrying a weapon to keep them subdued before he murders them."

Carter nodded and headed back to the front door. "He gets his thrill out of seeing them terrified of him, maybe? Motive?"

"I asked her the same question and she replied that psychopaths don't need a reason to kill people." Kalo blew out a long breath. *"She suggested maybe look at something that connects the women together—their age, looks, marital status, that type of thing. Something that makes them targets to him."*

Heading out the door, Carter ducked his head against the sheets of rain and ran to his rental. He rubbed Zorro's head and then removed his dripping hat and dropped it into the seat well. "Three women isn't really enough to make a victims' profile. I can see these women lived alone in remote areas. They followed a schedule, didn't date, and more or less kept to themselves. I can't see how their lack of actions made them targets."

"They all worked the same type of job and came into contact with a variety of people over their day." Kalo munched on his candy. *"Maybe their customer service wasn't good and they upset the wrong person?"*

Starting the engine, Carter backed out of the driveway, not wanting to leave any tire tracks in the softer gravel around the front of the house. "I've met them and they were fine with me. Helpful and friendly but way too reserved for me. Had I found them attractive, I wouldn't have asked them out to dinner or even a coffee. They had that line well and truly drawn the moment I started to make conversation. That is something common to all of them, and the fact they were single at the time of their deaths, with no men in the picture at all, according to the report Rowley filed on their backgrounds."

"Well, the other murder scenes are the same as the one you just left." Kalo stood and walked across the tile, his shoes making squeaky sounds. *"Everything as if he was just repeating the crime, like it was his fantasy or something."*

Carter swung his truck around and headed back to his cabin in the forest. "Maybe that's the clue. The sneaking into a house and killing a woman is his fantasy. I'm heading to my cabin. It's wet and cold and I need to get a fire going or I'll be a popsicle by morning. Catch you later."

"I'll call if anything else comes up." Kalo disconnected.

As Carter turned into the fire road that led to his secluded cabin. He glanced at Zorro in the rearview mirror. "Let's just hope while I've been MIA again no one else has been murdered."

FORTY-ONE

Despondent, Jenna walked back to the office, avoiding the puddles deepening by the second. The gray skies didn't lighten her mood. She'd given the judge a list of reasons why she required a search warrant and had been refused in a few seconds. The proof they needed to stop a killer could be right under their noses and they couldn't reach it. Hauling the suspects in for questioning wouldn't get them anywhere. They'd already been cooperative and explained their where-abouts at the time of the murders. If she kept pushing as Kane suggested, without more evidence against them, they'd be making complaints about harassment. As if he knew she needed support, Duke walked beside her. Rain splattered his coat, but he held his head high and his thick tail swung back and forth. She looked down at him and smiled. "At least you're happy. Did the judge's receptionist give you a cookie?"

She couldn't resist Duke's wide doggy smile and innocent brown eyes and bent to rub his ears. "Dave will dry you when we get back to the office, although I'm not sure why you insisted on coming with me today. Not that I'm complaining." She headed up the office steps and waved to Maggie at the counter.

She moved through the office and along to Rio's and Rowley's desks. "Come on upstairs. I had no luck obtaining a search warrant and we need to discuss what we've found today and the next steps." She looked at Rio. "Thank Cade and Piper for dropping by to help yesterday. I really appreciate it, but shouldn't they be studying for the December examinations?"

"Yeah, but they can't study all the time and they're good." Rio smiled. "They already know the work. I've quizzed them on everything I can think of and they're doing fine. They want to come by tomorrow as well. It will give Maggie a break. I'm sure she'd like a couple of hours to organize the food for Thanksgiving."

Nodding, Jenna smiled at him. "She would indeed and with the hotline open, although we aren't getting a ton of calls, it does take up Maggie's time. I could make them interns, so they can use the work experience on their resumes."

"I'll ask them." Rio smiled. "That sounds like a great idea. Piper is completing a social work degree. She has always been interested in the work done by the Her Broken Wings Foundation. She believes working to help people in bad situations is her calling."

Thrilled, Jenna's heart lifted. She had watched Piper grow from a troubled teen to a strong and reliable woman. Her twin brother, Cade, was also making great strides toward a law degree. Rio had raised them after his parents were killed. It was his only choice after the kids ran away from their grandma's house and were constantly in trouble. "I know how difficult it's been for you raising them, but you've turned their lives around."

"Yeah, and now maybe it's time for me to have a life." Rio chuckled. "Those early teenage years were something I wouldn't wish on my worst enemy."

Happy, Jenna turned to the stairs and reality hit her the moment she walked inside. Kane had already dried Duke and had made a pot of coffee. When he gave her an expectant look, she shook her head. "The judge denied the search warrant. He said it was a blatant invasion of privacy, fueled by speculation and hearsay." She removed her coat, shook off the rain, and hung it behind the door. With a sigh, she dropped into her office chair. "I felt like a kid in the principal's office. I'm surprised he didn't give me detention."

As Rio and Rowley filed into the office, Kane stood to make coffee. Jenna smiled at him as he walked past. "I did my best."

"It was an outside chance we'd get the search warrant." Kane bent and, to Jenna's surprise, ignored the deputies and cupped her cheek and pressed a kiss to the top of her head. "Don't worry, we'll find other ways to catch this killer."

A warm glow rose from the tips of her toes right through her, and her cheeks heated. For Kane, public showing of affection wasn't in his wheelhouse. She moved her attention back to Rowley and Rio, who grinned at her like demented baboons, and cleared her throat. "Did you discover anything interesting in the backgrounds of our two suspects?"

"Not mechanical engineering, no, but both have considerable talent in various fields of IT." Rio leaned back in his seat. "I've uploaded everything we found into the current files. Although, I'm not sure how this is going to help the investigation."

Jenna lifted the cup Kane set beside her, blew over the contents, and sipped the rich aromatic brew. "We figured bringing in the two men for questioning might shake a few incriminating answers from one of them, but after speaking to the judge, we need to tread carefully. We don't have a solid reason to pull them in."

"As there's no forced entry, we know they entered the houses without any difficulty, but if they'd met and spoken to the victims beforehand, it's possible they were invited inside— or they had a weapon." Kane handed the cups around and then sat down. "I ran checks via the companies who made the security systems on the victims' homes. Both were different and installed by different companies. The systems would send out an alert if someone tampered with them, so unless the killer has the codes, the victims opened the doors."

Jenna's phone rang. She listened to Maggie and her heart sank to her boots. She swallowed hard. "Okay, thanks, tell them we're on our way. Get all the information you can and ask them to remain on scene. I'll need you to call Wolfe and give him the details." She placed the phone back onto the receiver and lifted her gaze to her team. "There's a body in the Triple Z Roadhouse parking lot. The caller said the victim has no eyes. The body has been there for only around two hours. The truck driver was at a stopover. He went to his truck around three and didn't see the pickup parked beside him."

"We'll need to know the whereabouts of the suspects over the last two hours." Kane glanced at Jenna. "I'll call Carter. He has a tracker on his phone now by his insistence." He stood and went outside to make the call.

Standing, Jenna looked at her deputies. "You already know the suspects. Hunt them down and find out where they've been these last two hours. Check out their stories. We'll go and secure the crime scene." She moved to the door to retrieve her damp coat and looked at Duke. "Maybe you should stay here." She took down a container of dog food and filled his bowl. "You have plenty of water and we won't be long."

"Good idea." Kane walked back inside. "Stay, Duke." He looked at her and raised both eyebrows. "Carter is at his cabin, and his locator confirms it. He was in town earlier at Aunt Betty's for lunch and grabbed takeout. I didn't tell him about the body at the Triple Z Roadhouse."

Relieved Carter was away from town, she handed Kane his coat. "I hope this isn't the Casanova Killer. If he's changing his MO, it's going to make a difficult case impossible."

FORTY-TWO

The wind rushing down from the mountains drove the rain at an angle, lifting the hood of Jenna's slicker and wetting her face as she walked toward the eighteen-wheeler parked beside a pickup at the Triple Z Roadhouse. Kane had parked some ways away, to allow Wolfe access to the victim. She glanced at Kane beside her. "If this is the same killer as before, this won't be nice."

Taking a deep breath, she walked slowly toward the pickup and peered inside. Although she'd been prepared for the horrific sight, the blackened eye sockets shocked her to her core. She laid one hand on Kane's arm and looked at him. "Wolfe is two minutes away. I don't think we should touch anything. It's obvious the victim is deceased."

"That must be the guy who found her." Kane indicated with his chin toward the man observing them through the window of his truck. "We'll get his statement before Wolfe arrives."

Nodding, Jenna waved the man down from the truck. The man nodded and pulled up the hood of his slicker. As he climbed down, Jenna accessed the record function on her phone. "Do you mind if we record your statement? Paperwork is impossible in this weather."

"I'm good." The man turned his back into the wind.

Jenna moved closer and used her sleeve to protect the phone from the downpour. "If you could state your name for the record and details, we'll type this up when we get back to the office, and if you could drop by to sign it, we'd appreciate it."

"Not a problem." Rain dripped from the man's hood. "I'll be back first thing in the morning, I'll drop by then." He gave his details and stared at Jenna expectantly.

"If you could give us a timeline of events, it would help." Kane moved closer to Jenna. "What time did you arrive?"

"I've been here about two hours, maybe a little longer. So I arrived around two. I went to have a meal. Met a couple of buddies and we talked about the weather. We waited for the next weather update as the road to Blackwater is prone to flooding. That came at three-thirty. I called my boss about the pickup in Blackwater. I needed to know when they'd be ready to load my truck. Then I came out here at four and found the body. I didn't touch anything just jumped into my cab and called 911." He shuddered. "That pickup wasn't there when I arrived, so it's been there about two hours, maybe more now."

Nodding, Jenna had just about everything she needed. "Did you notice anyone leaving around the time you found the body?"

"Nope." The man shrugged. "Vehicles come and go all the time. I don't usually take much notice, but you can see how close the pickup is to my truck. It would be difficult to miss it."

Wolfe's medical examiner van drove into the parking lot and stopped behind the pickup. Jenna looked back at the man. "Thank you for your assistance. I'll have the statement typed up and ready for you to sign before I leave this afternoon, so whenever you can drop by, we'd appreciate it."

"Okay." The man turned away and climbed into his truck

and then started the engine. In a cloud of diesel fumes and crunching of gravel, the eighteen-wheeler headed for the highway.

"What have we got here?" Wolfe circled the pickup as he pulled on examination gloves. "Has anyone touched anything?"

"Not that we're aware." Kane pulled on examination gloves, went to Wolfe's side and brought him up to speed. "It can't be a copycat because we haven't released anything to the press about the other murders."

"It appears to be the same MO, but why the sudden change of location?" Wolfe leaned inside the pickup to examine the body. "No smell of decomposition yet, which would make me believe that the timeline offered by the witness is correct." He went to his bag to collect instruments to take the temperature of the body. He turned to Colt Webber, who was waiting for instructions. "Record the air temperature, the temperature inside of the truck, the weather, and the time."

Jenna stood back to give him room to move. "Is there anything you want us to do?"

"Yeah. Take a video of the scene." Wolfe bagged the victim's hands. "I recognize her. Doesn't she work at Aunt Betty's Café?"

"I'll run the plates." Kane walked back to the Beast to use the mobile data terminal.

Stomach rolling, Jenna peered closer at the victim. The face was distorted and the mouth hung open. "Yeah, it could be the new girl. Ah... what was her name? Leona?"

"I think that's her." Wolfe straightened and gave the body temperature reading to Webber to add to his notes. "It's too wet to do a forensic sweep here. I'll need to tow the vehicle back to the morgue garage. We'll remove the body out of the rain." He reached for his phone. "I'll call Miller's Garage and they'll send someone out. You might as well head back to the office. I won't have anything for you today. I'll call you in the morning." He straightened and shut the door. "I'll wait in my van for the tow truck."

"Thanks." Kane slapped him on the back, sending splashes of water in all directions.

Jenna peered around the parking lot. Being a back lot, usually used for parking trucks overnight, it wasn't overlooked by the roadhouse. She looked at Kane. "I would go and ask people at the roadhouse if they'd seen the victim's pickup arrive, but unless they followed them into the parking lot, the pickup would have been hidden between the eighteen-wheelers."

"I guess we should cover all possibilities." Kane turned toward the Beast.

Inside the roadhouse, they went to the four people eating and asked them about the pickup. Not one of them had seen it arrive. One man did mention a hitchhiker dropping by and taking a ride into town with one of the drivers. "What did he look like?"

"Six-feet, brown jacket, cowboy boots and hat. He was wet through." The customer shook his head. "I didn't see his face."

"What time was this, do you recall?" Kane stared at him.

"Around three, I believe." The man rubbed his chin. "I can't swear on it."

"Okay, thanks." Kane looked at Jenna as they walked to the door. "Sounds like the same guy."

Once inside the Beast, Jenna called Rowley and brought him up to date. "Did you find the two suspects?"

"The woodcarver, Holden, wasn't home. There was a sign on his door saying he'd be back in one hour and we're just leaving the ranch now." Through the speaker came the sound of footsteps on gravel and then the slamming of a door as Rowley climbed into the truck. *"Strauss isn't there either. His boss said he's been back and forth all day. Couldn't say what time."*

Sighing, Jenna pushed wet hair from her face. "So we have nothing."

"I'm sorry, Jenna." Rowley gave a slight shake of his head. *"We spoke to the store holders either side of Holden's store and neither noticed when he left."*

Wiping her face on a tissue, Jenna shrugged. "Okay. You might as well call it a day. We believe the victim is Leona, the new server at Aunt Betty's Café. We'll drop by and speak to Susie. I'll need next of kin and she'll have that on her records."

"I wouldn't like to be identifying the body, if it's the same as the others." Rowley grimaced. *"I hope Susie can help."*

Jenna disconnected and they drove through driving rain to Aunt Betty's Café. The wipers flashed back and forth fast, but the pelting rain obscured the blacktop. Glad when they finally stopped outside the diner, Jenna jumped out and dashed inside. Susie was in her office and Jenna slipped behind the counter with Kane on her heels. She explained what had happened. "We believe it's Leona. Do you have her details?"

"Yes." The color had drained from Susie's face. "Leona Brinley. Her shift finished around two." She swallowed hard. "Just before, Ty came in for lunch. He spoke to her and left before she finished her shift. He was asking me about men who looked like him that came by."

A jolt went through Jenna. "Carter? He left around two?"

"Yeah, I guess." Susie made notes and handed the sheet of paper to Jenna. "That's her details and her next of kin contact number. Do you want me to call Leona? Then we'll know for sure if it's not her?"

"Go ahead." Kane leaned against the wall, water pooling from his slicker.

"It goes to voicemail." Susie swallowed hard and put the phone down. "Are we in danger?"

"You should inform everyone who works here to be careful and move around in twos if possible." Kane blew out a long breath. "This killer doesn't need a reason."

FORTY-THREE

TUESDAY

After a sleepless night, Jenna woke at five when Kane rolled out of bed to tend the horses. Their life had changed in the last twenty-four hours. She tried to keep her mind on the cases but the fear that something bad would happen to Tauri nagged at her. She'd checked the doors and windows and the sleeping child countless times overnight and the previous day had called Nanny Raya at the kindergarten every few hours to check on their safety. Her safe haven had been invaded and nothing would ever be the same. She watched Kane dressing in the dark and sat up. "I want to help you with the horses but I'm too scared to leave Tauri alone."

"The rain has cleared." Kane peered out the window. "I'll turn them out into the corral for the day. It won't take me long to muck out. I'll groom them tonight, when we can all be together in the barn." He sat on the bed and cupped her face. "Wolfe has experts working on an advanced warning system and others to create a removable deterrent." He smiled at her. "Something to prevent choppers landing in our yard but something we can remove when we want one to land. He's suggested a net that can be mechanically rolled up to allow landing. No chopper pilot would risk being caught up in a net."

Impressed, Jenna nodded. "Like a swimming pool cover but in the air?"

"I guess." He kissed her and held her close. "We'll take every precaution against anyone hurting us again. I'm not leaving your side, and Tauri will be in safe hands at all times. We just have a few more days before the trial. Once I testify, hurting me or my family won't gain them anything. When this is done, they'll know what happened to Mateo and that I'll kill without a second thought anyone of them who comes close. I'm the threat, Jenna. The tables have turned."

Nodding, Jenna slid out of bed. "I know you'll protect us, Dave, but living like this is like being in jail."

"The threat is always going to be there, Jenna." Kane met her gaze. "We both knew that going into this marriage. I admit I made a mistake offering to do the arms deal for the FBI. For one crazy moment, I let my guard down to help a friend. Trust is everything to me, and Carter has been as close to me as Wolfe for some time now. If he's dirty, I'll never trust anyone again."

Dismayed, Jenna turned to look at him. "As in working for the cartel?"

"Yeah." Kane rolled his shoulders. "Okay, Jo gave us a good explanation, but it still doesn't sit right with me. I'm seeing a sudden change of character. He goes missing for days on end— what's that all about? Then he resembles the suspect in four murders. I don't know what to think anymore."

"If he's a psychopath, he's the best I've ever seen." Jenna shook her head. "We know him. All his bravado is a front. I honestly believe he never gets involved with women, as in a girl-friend, because he doesn't want to get hurt. That means he cares. He's always been there for us and Jo. I just won't believe he killed those women." She looked at him. "He loves Tauri. I refuse to believe he'd deliberately hurt anyone."

"I'll be watching him." Kane headed for the door.

Jenna had set the table and had the coffee brewing by the time Kane finished his chores. As he took a shower, her phone chimed. It was Agent Katz. "Sheriff Alton."

"I've had a ton of problems with the recent CCTV footage." Katz sucked in a deep breath. *"Wolfe informed me last night about the fourth murder and I accessed what CCTV footage I could find. I've never had any problems downloading CCTV footage before, but this time it was slow. Maybe it was the weather, but unfortunately, all the footage I've found with the victims shows without a doubt Agent Ty Carter was with them. I have a film of him getting into the last victim's pickup on Main yesterday afternoon a little after two. There's no doubt it's him. I have uploaded all the files for you. See for yourself."*

Swallowing the bile creeping up the back of her throat, Jenna gripped the back of the chair, trying to think. "Are these the times he admits to speaking to the victims?"

"No, these are the times he denies speaking to the victims. I centered my investigation on those specific times as you have witnesses." Beth drummed her fingernails on the desk. *"This isn't something I enjoyed doing, Sheriff. I like Carter and believed him to be a solid agent. I hope there is a logical explanation, but right now, this proves beyond doubt he lied in his statement."*

Shocked by the implications, Jenna white-knuckled the back of the chair. "Okay. Thank you for your assistance, Agent Katz. We'll be in touch." She disconnected and sat staring into space.

"Is something wrong?" Kane walked into the kitchen with Tauri. "You look like you've seen a ghost."

Forcing a smile, Jenna gave Tauri a hug and then stood to pour the coffee and a glass of milk. "I'll explain later." She moved her eyes toward Tauri and back to Kane. "It's just a work thing." She sat at the table as Kane went about making breakfast in his usual swift and efficient way. She looked at Tauri. "Did you enjoy having Nanny Raya at kindergarten yesterday?"

"Yes, she told stories and taught us a dance." Tauri smiled. "She said she would come back and we'd do painting today."

"That sounds neat." Kane smiled at him over one shoulder. "Over the holidays Uncle Shane is coming by to help me rebuild my motorcycle. Do you want to help?"

"Yes." Tauri frowned at him. "You mustn't break it again. It makes mommy scared."

Realizing the mention of the Harley had touched a raw memory, Jenna went to explain but Kane flashed her a look. She blinked and sipped her coffee. They'd spoken to a counselor about their son and discussed ways to help him feel safe again by providing a stable and predictable environment. When a problem arose, they needed to talk about his feelings, listen without judgment, and validate their emotions. Encouraging him to participate in art or something else he enjoyed was important too.

"Tauri, what happened wasn't my or Mommy's fault." Kane crouched in front of him. "Those bad people can't hurt us again. In a little while, I'm going to court to make sure they're locked in jail forever."

"Yes, Atohi told me that you and Mommy put bad men in jail." Tauri hugged Kane around the neck. "You saved us from the bad men, Daddy, but I'm scared they'll come back."

"They won't." Kane looked at Jenna over Tauri's shoulder, his eyes filled with concern. "I promise." He hugged him close. "I've shown you the safe room. If ever at any time you feel scared, you can go in there and lock the door. No one can get inside." He held him away, and smiled at him. "You won't need the safe room but it's there to make us all feel better. We are mighty warriors. They will never hurt us or Mommy again."

"Okay." Tauri smiled at him and climbed into his seat. He took a long drink of his milk leaving a white moustache. "Are we having pancakes today? I love pancakes."

FORTY-FOUR

At the office, Jenna called everyone in to view the footage Agent Katz had provided. They all stared in disbelief as Carter's face was clearly visible on the screen. She looked at Kane. "Call him and see if he'll come in voluntarily."

"You at the cabin?" Kane put his phone on speaker.

"Nope just walked out of Aunt Betty's. What's up?" Carter sounded the same as usual.

"Drop by the office. I have something to show you." Kane disconnected and looked at Jenna. "He doesn't sound too worried."

Five minutes later Carter walked into the office and smiled around a toothpick, Zorro at his heels.

"Please tell me you have a solid suspect." Carter looked at Jenna and dropped his toothpick into the garbage.

Shaking her head, Jenna stared at him, unable to believe he was capable of murder. "I've already read you your rights. We have evidence implicating you in the murders of four women. Do you want me to call a lawyer?"

"What evidence?" Carter sat down and shook his head. "I

haven't killed anyone. This is crazy talk. Show me what you've got. You owe me that at least."

Jenna turned around her computer screen and played the clips, the dates prominent on the screen. "You can't deny that's you."

"Oh, yes I do." Carter shook his head. "The last one, supposedly of me climbing into the pickup." He pulled a thumb drive from his inside pocket and slid it across the table. "Kalo has copies of these as well. I took them through the library window at two yesterday afternoon. I figured someone was setting me up and when I saw that jerk who looks just like me climbing into the pickup, I took photos. I can't be in the pickup and taking photos as well, can I? Something stinks here and it ain't me."

Jenna stared at the images, all date and time stamped. "Well, okay, but what about the others?" She scrolled through CCTV footage. "That's you in the general store."

"No, it can't be because I wasn't in town the day this was taken." Carter shook his head. "I had to go back to the office, if you recall, to get files for the director." He pointed to the next footage. "Or here." He looked at Jenna. "What's missing, Jenna?"

Concerned, Jenna stared once more at each set of footage. She lifted her gaze to him. "Zorro."

"You saying someone put your face in this footage?" Kane stared at him. "How could they do that before Agent Katz collected it?"

"Call Kalo and ask him." Carter shrugged. "He'll know."

Jenna made a video call and Kalo picked up. She explained the situation. "Agent Katz did mention she had trouble accessing the image files. Maybe someone tampered with them but they all look genuine to us."

"This is the problem. It's easy to tamper with video footage, but looping it back into the system without creating a stagger

means this guy has a high level of expertise. Usually, we can tell if footage has been tampered with, but I can see from the files they are extensive. It might take some time to examine all of them." Kalo's brow creased into a frown. *"Just a minute and I'll take a look."* He looked at his screen array and nodded. *"This is good. I'm thinking deepfake technology. As in using AI to change the face on an image or footage. It's becoming easier and easier to use now. It's even available on phones."*

Understanding the concept as she'd seen deepfake technology on TV, Jenna nodded. "Yeah, I know about it, but how do we tell the difference between fake and the real thing?"

"Some things aren't quite right. For instance, speech may be delayed but not often." Kalo's gaze drifted from the screen and then back to her. *"I'll have to dig deep and see if I can locate the original footage. Agent Katz will need to be aware, so I'll contact her. Between us we'll be able to trace the source files, but it will take time."*

"Just do it before I'm charged with murder." Carter leaned forward in his chair. "Ask Jo to come here as well. Get her a ride ASAP. I need her."

"Okay, I'm on it." Kalo disconnected.

"Here take this." Carter removed his weapon and handed it to Kane. "Stick to procedure. Lock me up if you like but I'm not going anywhere. I want to find this killer and clear my name."

Nodding, Jenna looked at him. "None of us believe you're capable of murder, Ty. I'm sure if you were in my position, you'd want answers too. It certainly looks like someone is framing you."

"From the evidence, I'd agree." Kane gave Carter a long look. "You must understand that being part of a team, we must have absolute trust in each other." He narrowed his gaze. "The problem for me is that I've seen the enemy infiltrate a team, live, fight, laugh, and cry together for years—and then murder everyone in their beds." He placed Carter's pistol on the desk.

"My suspicion keeps me alive." He met his gaze. "I'm sure you understand, being a SEAL and all."

"I do and I can understand why y'all believe I'm implicated in the murders." Carter tossed a toothpick into his mouth and moved it across his lips. "That sure looks like me in the footage, but if you figure I've been undercover for the last five years to bring down a deputy sheriff for heaven knows what, you're batshit crazy." He shook his head and then raised one eyebrow. "Your name was never mentioned, not at any meeting and not on any paperwork."

"So I've heard." Kane shrugged. "The story is, one of Mateo's men took my photograph and passed it through the prison system until they got a name. It sounds too good to be true, but time will tell, won't it? My travel arrangements to get to the trial are the problem. If I get hit before or on the way to the trial, we'll all know it came from your team."

Feeling the tension rising, Jenna looked from one to the other. "Then we'll make our own arrangements." She gave Kane a knowing look. "We'll take it out of their hands and use our resources to get to California. That way only we know the plans."

"Yeah, that sounds like a good idea." Kane smiled at her. "I'll make a few calls."

The phone rang, as if on cue. It was Wolfe. Jenna flicked a glance at Kane and raised one eyebrow. "Hey, Shane, what do you have for me?"

"A positive ID on Leona Brinley." Wolfe's footsteps echoed on tile. *"It's the same cause of death as the other victims. We're scouring the vehicle for trace evidence but have found nothing significant."*

Jenna glanced at the others. "I have you on speaker. Dave will call you later, but can you use your contacts to arrange for us to travel to California for the trial? Dave isn't trusting the FBI to watch his back."

"I'll call him tonight. We'll work out something." He chuckled. *"I haven't been to California for a long time. I might come with you. He'll need someone to watch his back."*

"I'd like that." Kane smiled. "We'll get to see the ocean." He glanced at Jenna. "Speak to you later." The line went dead as Wolfe disconnected.

Clearing her throat, Jenna tapped her pen on the desk. "Let's get this meeting back on track." She looked at Rio. "What do you know about the latest deepfake developments? They're moving ahead so fast. I'm aware of the new proposed legislations to protect people but I know this is something you follow."

"It's all over." Rio shrugged. "Most times, celebrities are used to endorse products or schemes on social media. It's all fake. Fake news stories. I mean, now they can take a dead celebrity and make a movie that is an exact replica of the real person. AI is boundless and dangerous. We won't know if what we are seeing is real anymore. If this is what happened to Carter, it's entry-level manipulation. If you want a more detailed analysis, I can give it to you."

Surprised that technology had moved so fast, Jenna shook her head. "No, thanks. That's fine. Now what?"

"We need to assume one of our two suspects is the Casanova Killer." Kane raised an eyebrow. "I suggest we split up and go and find them."

Jenna nodded. "We'll bring them in for questioning." She swung her gaze to Carter. "You're coming with us."

"Yes, ma'am." Carter tipped his hat and stood.

FORTY-FIVE

Piper Rio enjoyed working at the sheriff's department. She liked people and came into contact with all walks of lives during her time there. Maggie had left her in charge of the counter for a time and explained how to take payments for fines and take down details from anyone calling in on the hotline about the CCTV footage collection. Something big was brewing in the office. Everyone had been holed up in Jenna's office for over an hour. As they spilled down the stairs, she waved Rio over. "What's happening?"

"We're bringing in suspects for questioning." Rio frowned. "I'm heading over to the Diamond Bar Ranch with Rowley. Make a note of where we're going in the daybook."

Nodding, Piper picked up a pen. "What about Jenna?"

"She'll be with Kane and Carter. They're going to stop by Living Things, the woodcarving store in town." Rio slapped the table. "Gotta go."

As she watched her brother follow Rowley out of the door, she made the notes in the daybook and looked up as Jenna stopped at the counter. "Maggie will be back in five minutes. No one has been by for ages."

"Okay." Jenna pulled on gloves. "We'll be busy once we get back. I want you to order a variety of things for lunch. Order what you'd like for yourself as well. Sandwiches, bagels, cinnamon rolls, any assorted pastries are good. Everyone eats when they can during investigations, so speak to Susie or Wendy and they'll know what we usually order, plus we'll be feeding three extra men." She turned as Kane came by with Carter and then looked back at her. "When it's ready, will you drop by and collect it? That's if Maggie is in the office."

Nodding, Piper smiled at her. "Not a problem. What time do you want me to have it here?"

"Between twelve and one, we should be through interviewing the suspects by then." Jenna pulled up the hood of her jacket and hurried after Kane.

After making a few notes and entering the team's whereabouts in the daybook just as Maggie had taught her, she wandered through the office and collected the cups on Rio's and Rowley's desks. She carried them to the kitchenette and washed them. As she returned, she noticed Rio's computer screen was active and couldn't resist peeking at what he'd been doing. She sat at his desk and wiggled the mouse. The screen lit up with a page of files. She had heard about the Casanova Killer on the news and looked all around before clicking on the file of the same name. More files covered the screen and the crime scene image files caught her attention. Butterflies fluttered in her stomach as she clicked and opened the files. Horrified at the images flooding the screen, she swallowed hard and, hands trembling, closed the files and hurried back to the counter. The killer of those poor women was in town. He could be anywhere. Was one of the suspects the teams were bringing in for questioning the killer? Would she come face-to-face with him today? The idea sent a wave of nausea through her as she slipped back behind the desk. The sheriff's office suddenly seemed very big and empty.

Needing to hear a friendly voice, Piper called Aunt Betty's Café and spoke to Wendy. After explaining what she needed, Wendy told her to drop by at twelve-thirty and the order would be ready. A few moments later, Maggie walked back into the office. Piper heaved a sigh of relief and smiled at her. "The sheriff is out but they'll all be back soon with suspects."

"Good, you've made a note in the daybook." Maggie dropped a book of raffle tickets on the counter and then rifled through the drawers and pulled out a cardboard cutout of a picture of the Her Broken Wings Foundation. She set this on the counter. "It's the Thanksgiving fundraiser raffle. This year they're holding an arts and crafts raffle at the townhall. Are you going?"

Piper shrugged. "I might. It depends on how much it costs to fix my truck." She chewed on her bottom lip. "Usually, I ask Kane to look at it, but he's been too busy of late. I know he'll be using all his downtime fixing his Harley."

"What's wrong with it?" Maggie frowned.

Rolling her eyes, Piper shrugged. "I have no idea. Sometimes it starts and other times it goes *click, click, click*. George at Miller's Garage said he can take a look today or maybe tomorrow."

She spent the next twenty minutes or so tidying the office. When it was quiet, Maggie just played on the computer. It was never the same. They had times when six or seven people would arrive and then no one for hours. With reluctance, she pulled out her tablet and sat down to study. The next moment, Jenna and Kane walked through the front door. Between them was a man who looked like Carter, but Carter and Zorro came in right behind them. Piper peered over her tablet, trying to get a better look at the suspect, but they all moved swiftly through the office and headed down to the interview rooms. She raised both eyebrows. *Now, it's getting interesting.*

FORTY-SIX

To gain the cooperation of both suspects, Kane had arranged for their vehicles to be driven to the office. The idea intended to lull both suspects into a false sense of security with both believing their time at the interview would be short. It might be, if they didn't spill the beans, but with no solid evidence against either man, they had no valid reason to hold them. At times, waiting for forensic evidence to be processed was enough cause but as Wolfe had found nothing at any of the crime scenes, they couldn't use that as an excuse.

Inside the interview room, Jenna sat at the table beside him, and Carter leaned casually against the door. Kane figured the three of them appeared threatening enough to make a criminal talk, but Chase Holden leaned back in his seat as if they'd just invited him over for a drink. His nonchalance was unnatural, as most people were anxious when facing law enforcement and he'd introduced Carter as FBI. Holden just looked from one to the other, almost eager to answer their questions. Kane pulled a fresh legal pad from the drawer and nodded to Jenna to start the recording. He stated the time and date and who was in the room. He looked at Holden and read him his rights. Holden refused a lawyer, but apart from that, he still gave no significant reaction to the severity of the situation. "We're investigating the murders of four women—"

"Four women?" Holden narrowed his gaze. "When the deputies spoke to me, they mentioned three women were missing, now they're dead? I know Dakota, Jennifer, and Johanna. How did they die?"

Glad he'd gotten a reaction, Kane scrutinized Holden's face. "The other woman was Leona Brinley." He made a few random notes. "Did you drop by the Triple Z Roadhouse at any time yesterday?"

"I drove past it a little after one and then a little after two." Holden shrugged. "I had a delivery out at Buffalo Ridge."

"Did you stop at the roadhouse?" Jenna leaned on the table staring at him.

"Nope, but I do know a woman named Leona." Holden moved around in his chair. It was the first time he'd looked uncomfortable. "She works at Aunt Betty's Café."

Kane nodded. "So you just happen to know all of the four women who were murdered in the last few days. That seems a little strange don't you agree?"

"Maybe, but I never hurt anyone." Holden blew out a long breath. "I like the quiet life, just me and my creations. I dropped out of the crazy lifestyle to get my head back on." He looked from one to the other. "I had a software development company. It made millions and I sold it and stayed on as a director. There was a problem in one of the security programs and they fired me. I was happy to leave and come here. All I wanted was open spaces after years in the concrete jungle."

"What do you know about deepfake technology?" Jenna twirled a pen in her fingers and smiled at him. "It's fascinating how they can manipulate images isn't it?"

"I know about it from what I've seen on TV." Holden

swiped at the end of his nose. "I haven't looked into it, as I said I want to leave that part of my life behind for a time."

Unconvinced, Kane ran questions through his mind. This man had admitted to knowing all the victims, had spoken to all of them, had IT knowledge, and could have, for all he knew, manipulated the CCTV footage to implicate Carter, but they had no proof he was involved in their murders. "What do you know about stun guns? Have you ever purchased one?"

"No." Holden narrowed his eyes. "If someone threatened me, I'd be more inclined to purchase a handgun. I wouldn't risk getting close enough to use a stun gun and giving someone the chance of sticking me with a blade."

"Do you own a handgun?" Jenna lifted her gaze to him.

"Yeah, and a rifle." Holden shrugged. "I go into the forest to collect fallen trees. It's not a place I'd risk going unarmed."

"Did you get a ride in a light-colored pickup yesterday around two?" Carter pushed off from the wall and, pressing his knuckles into the top of the desk, stared at Holden. "I figure I saw you climbing into Leona's pickup."

"Nope." Holden shook his head, "That must have been someone else. It wasn't me. After I got home from the delivery, I was in my shed working."

"Can anyone verify that?" Jenna lifted her chin and stared at him. "It would make things easier for you if you had a witness."

"Nope." Holden picked at his fingernails and a small frown creased his brow. "I didn't speak to anyone until about four-thirty, when I received a delivery of new chisels."

Unable to shake anything of interest from the suspect, Kane made a note of the time on his legal pad and stood. "That's all we have for you this time." He pulled open the door and handed him a set of keys. "Your ride is out front. Thanks for your cooperation."

"Sure." Holden tossed the keys in his hand. "I hope you find the killer. I liked those women." He headed for the front door.

Kane looked from Jenna to Carter. "He didn't so much as flinch."

"Maybe he's used to handling high pressure?" Jenna switched off the recording. "He did work in a stressful job."

"I don't trust him." Carter's eyes narrowed. "Who is next?"

Kane looked into the passageway and then back to Carter. "Rio and Rowley have just brought in Dallas Strauss. He's worked in gaming, as in creating games. He dropped out from burnout. He's wealthy and works as a ranch hand at the Diamond Bar Ranch. He resembles you too."

"Darn! Another cowboy who looks like me?" Carter shook his head. "And I figured I was one of a kind."

FORTY-SEVEN

"Nope." Dallas Strauss shook his head. "I can't say I spoke to Leona yesterday. I have noticed her and she's served me meals at Aunt Betty's once or twice, but I'm sure it was Susie who dropped by my table for a chat. I like to be friendly with the servers. You get more with honey than vinegar, right?" He wiggled his eyebrows at Jenna in an absurd attempt to be charming. It didn't work.

Keeping her face expressionless, Jenna met his gaze. "We have CCTV footage of you climbing into Leona's truck. Are you going to tell me that isn't true?"

"It wasn't me." Strauss frowned. "I didn't need a ride. I had my truck and if I'd gone with her, I figure my boss would have been asking me where I'd been all day. I was back at the ranch before three. Ask him. I dropped by his office with an invoice from the produce store."

Jenna made unnecessary notes—everything was being recorded—but when interviewing a suspect, making notes made them believe what they were saying was relevant. In fact, it was just a pause to give her time to rearrange her thoughts. She raised her eyes. "You used to design and develop video games, is that correct?"

"Yeah, I'm taking a break from that right now." Strauss shrugged. "I'm burned out."

Nodding, Jenna twirled her pen in her fingers. "Have you used deepfake technology in creating video games?"

"AI is a massive contributor to video games and one of the uses of deepfakes would be the avatars." He looked at Jenna. "Are you a gamer?"

"No." Jenna frowned. "The games have evolved very fast over the last few months. Can you give me a few more details?"

"Basically, when a gamer wants to assume a role as a character, his likeness is used. This is one use of deepfake technology. The AI program is able to substitute a likeness of the player for the character." Strauss shrugged. "I've been out of touch for a time and I'm not fully aware of the advances. It's moving very fast at the moment, and from what I've heard, the pitfalls ahead are great. It's gone way past gaming now."

"So you're saying, we can't trust what we're seeing." Kane leaned back in his seat.

"Unless it's with your own eyes." Strauss shrugged. "When you watch movies or shows when the old people are young again, that's a deepfake. It's all about competing algorithms. The two algorithms form a generative adversarial network, called GAN. This is used to create the fake."

Casting a look at Kane, Jenna leaned forward. "So how much skill would it take to change, say, CCTV footage?"

"It takes a degree in the technology, at least, and experience." Strauss rubbed his hands on his thighs. "Plus, the raw data. Unless they were hackers and could access the footage at high speed, change it and feed it back into the video stream without being noticed. I figure that would be illegal."

"Is that something you're capable of doing?" Kane stared at him his face emotionless.

"It's within my capabilities if I was working with my team." Strauss raised both eyebrows. "I don't have that technology in the bunkhouse out at the ranch. I don't even own a laptop. When I stepped away to rest my brain, it was absolute."

"Can you run down the timeline of yesterday?" Carter was eyeing Strauss with curiosity.

"I worked around the ranch as usual, left around twelve and went to the produce store." Strauss stared into space. "It was raining buckets and I parked under cover for them to load my truck with feed. I covered it with a tarp and headed out of town to speak to a rancher who'd had problems with one of our cutting horses. I checked out the horse, who didn't like to work in the rain." He chuckled. "Came back to town, dined at Aunt Betty's, and then went back to the ranch."

"Do you own a stun gun?" Kane raised one eyebrow and leaned forward.

"Nope." Strauss frowned. "There's cattle prods at the ranch."

"If you wanted to increase the amperage in a stun gun, how would you do it?" Kane's mouth twitched up at one corner. "I've always wanted to know."

"I know about gaming, not electrical engineering or whatever." Strauss met his gaze. "Why would you want to do that anyway? You planning on killing someone? The idea, if I'm not mistaken, is to stun someone with that device, not fry them alive."

Jenna switched off the recording. "Indeed. Thank you for your time. The information on deepfake was very enlightening."

"I'm just glad we have DNA to rely on." Kane pushed to his feet and used his card to open the door. He handed Strauss his keys. "Your vehicle is outside."

"Glad I could help." Strauss walked out of the door and headed down the passageway whistling.

Jenna looked from Kane to Carter. "Again, he could have committed the murders, right time, right place. He understood what happens if the amps on a stun gun are increased. Ask a dozen people and only a few would be aware of the consequences. The thing that concerns me is how the killer set up the ride with Leona."

"I spoke to her at the café and whoever climbed into her truck was wearing clothes like mine and sunglasses... in the rain." Carter shook his head slowly. "Leona was aware I'm an FBI agent. If I flagged her down and asked her for a ride for some stupid reason, it's likely she'd accept. She came across as flirty, so if she thought this guy was me, I doubt she would have taken much convincing."

The idea was feasible, and Jenna stood and gathered her things before turning to him. "Okay, say this doppelganger murdered her. How did he get back to town?"

"Leona worked the same shift every day." Kane leaned against the wall, one eyebrow cocked. "It would be an easy setup." He looked at Jenna. "He'd drive to the Triple Z Roadhouse, park his truck, and get a ride back to town. He has two options: most of the drivers would give a man a ride in the pouring rain, or he could take the bus. The bus comes through there around midday, that's easy enough to check. He'd likely planned to go and speak to Leona to make her familiar with him, but then Carter walked in and struck up a conversation." He shot Carter a look. "You wear the same brown jacket when you're not working. Both Holden and Strauss have similar jackets. All of you wear the same hats, throw on a pair of sunglasses and you'd all look similar to a casual acquaintance."

Chewing on her pen, Jenna thought for a beat. "Apart from the voice." She looked from one to the other. "Don't take this as anything but an observation, Carter, but you have a sexy drawl, and don't sound as if you were raised here. The other two are similar."

"Sexy drawl, huh?" Carter grinned at her. "I figure that's the nicest thing anyone has ever said to me."

"Don't let it go to your head." Kane opened the door and held it for the others to pass.

"Too late." Carter chuckled and sauntered along the passageway.

FORTY-EIGHT

Piper filled the coffee pots in Jenna's office and went downstairs to fill the one in the kitchenette used by Rio and Rowley. It was something Maggie always did for the team when they were working nonstop on a case. As she walked down the stairs, Jenna came from the interview rooms followed by the rest of the team. She smiled at her. "I filled the coffee pots and I'll head down to Aunt Betty's to collect the takeout now."

"Thank you. We all need a break." Jenna smiled at her. "I'm really happy you accepted the internship. Having you here in your spare time is like a breath of sunshine. We really appreciate your help."

It wasn't difficult to enjoy working with Jenna. The team were all like family. Piper smiled. "I didn't know I'd get paid as well. I just wanted to help out." She grinned. "Cade will be so jealous but he's working on his truck right now."

"It's what the mayor wants for our town. He encourages internships as he wants the locals to remain in town for work rather than take their talent out of state." Jenna waved a hand toward the stairs. "I need to get back to work. Catch you later."

Piper headed for her truck. For once it started okay and

she headed along Main. Luckily there was an angle parking spot right outside Aunt Betty's, but another vehicle coming in the opposite direction was slowing down looking for a space. She accelerated and barely made the spot without hitting the vehicles on either side. She jumped from her truck and looked into the black eyes of the driver of the other vehicle. Anger radiated from him and she could see his mouth move but didn't catch what he'd said. She took a step toward the sidewalk when his mouth turned down in a snarl and his window buzzed down. Before he could say anything, Piper giggled. "You snooze, you lose." She turned and hurried into Aunt Betty's.

She collected the sealed boxes, surprised at seeing evidence stickers all over them and frowned at Susie. "What's with the evidence stickers?"

"Some food was tampered with a time ago." Susie shrugged. "Kane likes to make sure the food gets to them without being poisoned along the way."

Piper nodded. "Oh, I see."

Her phone buzzed in her pocket. It was George from Miller's Garage. "Yeah, sure, I can drop it in at three, not a problem. Thanks for fitting it in for me."

Glad her truck could be seen early, she carried the box of takeout to her truck and climbed inside. Across the road, she noticed the angry man still glaring at her. She shrugged. He could have the parking spot now. It wasn't as if he'd waited long. She drove back to the office, delivered the box to Jenna, and went downstairs to the front counter. "Is it okay if I drop my truck into Miller's Garage at three? He said he'd look at it right away. I'll wait for him to fix it and then head home, if that's okay?"

"That's just fine." Maggie smiled at her. "You've been such a help for me. I needed some time to plan for Thanksgiving. We have the entire family dropping by this year."

The afternoon sped by and she left a little before three to drop her truck at Miller's Garage. "How long will it take?"

"That depends on what's wrong with it." George Miller smiled at her. "You should ask me for an estimate before I start working on it."

Nodding, Piper gave him her phone number. "I'll go and wait at the pizzeria. Can you call me when you know how much it will cost?"

"Okay." George nodded and gave her details to his daughter, who entered them onto the computer. "It will be an hour or so. There's one customer in front of you."

She wasn't overly concerned about the cost. The truck was in great condition. Kane and her brother Zac had worked on it last summer. Whatever was wrong was something minor and she had money. Her parents' insurance was more than enough to pay for college and then some. "Okay, thanks."

She waited at the pizzeria listening to the conversations around her. Knowing she'd be coming by, she hadn't eaten lunch and was starving. She paced herself, buying a slice of pizza and then waiting some time before getting another. A few of her friends dropped by and she chatted with them for a while. Time moved by fast, but it was starting to get dark and still no word from the garage. She decided to walk back and find out what had happened. As she stepped out onto the sidewalk a cold chill slid down her spine. Across Main, the angry man in the truck sat staring at her. The sight of him made the hairs on the back of her neck prickle, but what could he do to her? People still walked along Main and no one in Black Rock Falls just stood by if someone was in trouble. It wasn't that kind of town. Pushing away the disturbing feeling the man gave her, she lifted her chin and walked confidently along the sidewalk. If he was trying to spook her just because she took his parking spot, he needed to get a life.

A cold wind buffeted her all the way to Miller's Garage and

she pushed open the door to the office, glad to be inside. She looked at the girl on the counter. "No one called. Is my truck ready?"

"No, I'm sorry. I've been waiting for a callback on a part. As you wanted an estimate, I needed to be sure before ordering it, but the list price is two hundred, so it will be that plus labor." The woman smiled at her. "They said they'd call right back on the delivery time." She glanced at her watch. "I doubt they will now. They close at five. We have loaners here. Do you want one?"

Disappointed, Piper glanced out at the darkening sky. It was a long walk home but not far enough to take a loaner. In the morning, she could get a ride with Rio to the sheriff's office and by the end of the day, with luck, her truck would be ready, if not, she'd walk home. She looked at the woman. "I'll be fine and please tell George to go ahead and fix it if it's under five hundred dollars. If it's any more, give me a call."

"Sure." The woman smiled. "I'm sorry we couldn't get the part for you today."

Buttoning her coat against the ice-cold wind, Piper stepped out onto Main determined to walk home. She could go back to the office and wait for Zac to finish work, but he could be tied up for hours. She thought for a beat. Living in Black Rock Falls had its restrictions, and her brother could see serial killers on every corner and was constantly reminding her to stay safe. It drove her crazy. He'd likely scold her for walking home alone, but it wasn't as if he were her dad, and he needed to stop treating her like a child. Determined to prove how responsible she could be, she lifted her chin and headed down Main. She had nothing else to do, and as she walked, paused to browse store windows. She wanted to find something suitable to wear for the Thanksgiving dinner at Jenna's house. She loved the family atmosphere and seeing everyone so happy. The one thing Jenna excelled at was making people feel like they belonged. Most of the stores were closing and she quickened her step. As she glanced into a storefront window, she noticed the scary man's truck crawling along the road. *Is he following me?*

Piper swallowed hard when he pulled into a parking spot and climbed out. Now she could see him clearly. He resembled Carter, but it wasn't him. She'd met Carter many times and he was always at the celebrations at Jenna's house. He had a handsome face and remarkable green eyes. This man's black eyes seemed to cut right through her and gave her the creeps. The sheriff's office was close by, and she needed to walk past it to get home. If he was still following her, she'd go inside. She might want to prove a point to Zac, but being suicidal wasn't part of the equation and she quickened her pace. She slowed at the office to look behind her. Relief flooded over her. He wasn't there. She'd overreacted and could just imagine if she'd run into the office making a big fuss about nothing. Zac would never let her out alone again.

Just to be certain, Piper stood for a few moments searching the sidewalks to make sure the man wasn't anywhere in sight. Confident the perceived threat had passed, she moved on. Their house was opposite Stanton Forest. At first, they'd lived in a house owned by the sheriff's office, but as her brother had received a substantial inheritance, including insurance payouts and recently the proceeds from the sale of their parents' home, he'd purchased a big old ranch-style house, surrounded by acres of land. It had plenty of room for everyone, including their housekeeper, Mrs. Jacobs, who had been like a grandma since they'd arrived in Black Rock Falls. Inside they had five bedrooms and a study, plus a separate residence for their housekeeper.

The streetlights blinked on as dusk dropped over the landscape. It was strange how everything turned from green and gold to gray and black as night fell, as if night sucked all the life out of the scenery. As if set to a timetable, the mist oozed from the rivers, through the forest and drifted across the blacktop. It was only about a mile to go and Piper wished she'd taken the offer of a loaner. It didn't seem so far in her truck but on foot, Stanton stretched out before her endlessly.

Gritting her teeth and pushing freezing fingers deep into the pockets of her coat, she placed one foot in front of the other and ran as fast as possible between each streetlight, but they didn't go into the rural areas and a darkening expanse loomed ahead. At the end of the streetlights the ranch houses were set far apart. The sidewalk vanished and she moved onto the black-top. In the dusk, she could still make her way. Although the sun had set, it didn't get full dark for a time yet. Thirsty and wishing she'd taken a bottle of water with her, she put one foot in front of the other. A few vehicles went by, making her leap onto the road shoulder, but when they went by the night closed in around her. The forest creaked and groaned, owls hooted, and she wished she'd had the forethought to bring her bear spray with her. She'd left the cannister in her truck, along with her backpack. All she had with her was her phone. Tucked into the case was an ATM card and her driver's license.

When headlights swept over her as someone turned into a fire road behind her, she didn't turn to watch. Many people lived in cabins spread all over the forest and she just kept on walking. Not much farther now. Once around the next sweeping bend she'd see the lights of her home in the distance. Stanton stretched out, disappearing into darkness as it curved away from her, and she followed the yellow line, although in the deepening darkness it was hardly visible. If it got much darker, she'd use her phone to walk the last few yards.

The sound of footsteps came from behind her, the *tap, tap, tap* of the steel tip of a cowboy boot hitting the blacktop. Her heart missed a beat as she listened, sure she'd imagined the sound. It paused and then came again. Taking a deep breath, she stopped walking and turned to stare along the empty road. Was someone there? It was difficult to see if anyone was walking along the forest side of the road. The tall pines cast long shadows and would hide anyone from view. All a person had to do was stand still. She turned slowly and picked up her pace. Two seconds later the footsteps came again. Unease crept over her. Where had they come from? Maybe it was someone returning from a hunting trip? She turned again. The footsteps stopped. She hadn't imagined it, that was for sure, but all alone in this part of town, maybe someone was trying to scare her? If it was Cade, she'd kill him. If so, the trick was working just fine. She moved on and the footsteps started up again. She stopped and the footfalls faded. Whoever was doing this to her was giving her the creeps. *Is this some kind of sick joke?*

FORTY-NINE

Cold wind moved the trees and a swirl of fall leaves danced across the blacktop. Nerves shredded, Piper pushed on, her hands bunched into fists in her pockets and eyes moving from side to side searching for a stick or something she could use as a weapon. In that moment a wave of panic hit her, as she recalled Zac mentioning that the Casanova Killer resembled Carter. Had it been a joke? She'd only heard a snatch of the conversation as Zac and Rowley walked past the counter earlier in the day. Carter had been at the office and appeared to be his normal self, surely if the killer looked like him, someone would have mentioned it to her? Maybe not. Rio never discussed his work with her, but she'd overheard a conversation about the victims being found in their homes and not out in the forest. She increased her pace and could hardly hear the footsteps behind her for her heavy breathing. *What if it is the killer?*

She'd listened without too much interest when Zac had lectured her and Cade about the dangers in Black Rock Falls and what to do in a variety of situations. Being followed in the dark wasn't one of them but she remembered him telling her the first thing to do if being followed is to hide. She drifted from the blacktop as if oblivious to the footsteps and into the shadows of the trees lining Stanton. Tripping over dead vegetation, she stumbled between the rough trunks and crouched down. Pulling up her hood and unbuttoning her coat to shield the light from her phone, she called Rio. "Zac, I'm walking home and I believe someone is following me. He looks like Carter."

"Where are you?" Rio's calming voice soothed her nerves.

Piper kept her voice to a whisper. "I'm hiding in the forest. Close to the bend on Stanton before the house. I can't run that far. It's pointless calling Cade—his truck is in pieces—and Mrs. Jacobs won't be home for ages. She's at the quilting club."

"He'll be able to see your phone. Keep in the forest, but once you disconnect move your position. We'll be coming in Kane's truck. We'll go past you, and then once we've hit the bend, we'll drop out and come back." Rio was informing Jenna, and footsteps thundered over the tiled floor. *"We're on our way. We'll be there in a few minutes. Keep moving toward the house when you can. If not, hole up somewhere dark. Don't come out when you see us. Just whisper. We'll hear you."* A car door slammed shut and an engine roared into life. *"Disconnect now and move."*

Terrified, Piper pushed her phone into her pocket and, keeping low to the ground, crawled along an animal track between the trees. The pine needles lay thick over the ground and stuck painfully into the palms of her hands. Pinecones bruised her shins but she kept moving. Where could she hide? She scanned the darkness, finding nothing, but recalled seeing dense vegetation toward the edge of the road. It would give her cover. Trying to be as quiet as possible, she turned and headed in that direction and snuck under a bush. Panting, she searched all around for the man. From here, she could make out the blacktop but any vehicle that came by would likely pick her up in the headlights. Maybe if she pulled her hood over her face, she'd blend into the shadows.

The *tap, tap, tap* of footsteps sounded loud over the beating of her heart, and then the shadows moved and the cowboy emerged from the night. His head swung back and forth as he searched for her. Piper held her breath as he walked straight toward her, passing close by before heading back toward town. Was he leaving? No, he was retracing his steps to discover where she'd left the highway.

The light of his phone almost blinded her, as he moved it back and forth staring at the ground for her footprints. She ducked down and covered her face and then pushed her knuckles into her mouth to stop the sound of her heavy breathing. The lights of a vehicle coming fast lit up the highway and the man vanished into the forest. One thing she did recognize was the sound of Kane's truck, affectionately known as the Beast. It roared past and she had the sudden impulse to jump out and wave her arms at it. She swallowed hard. At the speed he was moving, she'd be dead and likely kill everyone in the vehicle. Trembling, she hunkered down and waited. Moving now would give away her hiding place. All she could do was wait and hope he didn't find her.

FIFTY

Heart in her throat, Jenna gripped the seat as Kane turned off the lights of the Beast and they drifted almost silently off the road and into the bushes. They all slipped from the truck. If this was the Casanova Killer, his threat was unknown. He could be carrying a pistol as well as a stun gun. She'd listened to Kane as they'd driven to the location. His suggestion that he and Carter take the side of the road they assumed Piper was hiding and Jenna and Rio spread out along the other side. Kane and Carter could move through a forest like cats. They'd all grabbed night-vision goggles as they left the office and hiding in the dark wouldn't be a problem. For once, they had the advantage—if they could get to Piper in time.

It surprised Jenna, how calm Rio had been. He'd given details and had the team moving before he disconnected from Piper and now, apart from a determined expression, he was fully in control of the situation as always. Kane had discussed with Carter about taking down the man using hand-to-hand combat. Like her, Kane wanted answers, and if this was their man, they needed to know what made him tick. The problem was, there were so many unusual people in Black Rock Falls.

This man might just be walking home or he could be anything from a stalker to a psychopath. Unfortunately, there was no way of telling until they apprehended him.

She moved closer to Rio as Kane gave hand signals to Carter and they vanished into the forest on the opposite side of the road. "We'll stick to the shadows. Try not to make a sound."

"Copy that." Rio followed close behind, scanning the blacktop and the forest as they approached the bend in the road.

A scream pierced the night and it shot through Jenna like a blade. She ran forward, weapon in her hand, and rounded the bend in the road.

"Get away from me, you creep." Piper burst from the forest and sprinted up the road.

Behind Piper, a man grabbed at her long hair and tugged. "You're not getting away from me."

Screaming, Piper turned and raked down the man's face with both hands and kicked him hard in the shins. She grabbed her hair and dragged it from his grasp and turned to run but hadn't gotten more than a few yards before she tripped and sprawled across the road.

The cowboy wiped at his streaming eyes and cursed at her.

"It could have been easy but now I'll make you pay." He pulled a knife from a sheath at his waist and moved closer.

Watching in horror as Piper tried to crawl away from her attacker, Jenna ran, weapon aimed at the man, but she had no hope of hitting him. The next second, Kane and Carter burst out of the trees. Kane went high and Carter low and they tackled the man to the blacktop, hitting with such force they slid halfway across the road. Terror gripped her as Kane and Carter fought a man fueled with adrenaline and hellbent on murder. It was as if they were trying to tackle a grizzly. The knife in the man's hand glinted in the moonlight and Jenna stopped running to aim her weapon at the sprawling mass of bodies.

"Don't shoot." Rio was beside her. "Give them space."

Stomach squeezing, Jenna could only stand by and watch as Carter wrapped himself around the man's kicking legs. Above him, Kane had both hands locked on the hand with the knife. They rolled in a stream of cursing, their captive bucking and trying to headbutt Kane in the face. Kane avoided the attempts, the man's head hitting Kane's shoulder as he slammed the man's hand down hard on the blacktop repeatedly until the knife came loose and spun away landing at Jenna's feet. The man wasn't finished yet, even pinned under two bodies he rolled and arched his back, trying to bite Kane. Carter had the man's legs in a death grip and he wasn't going anywhere. Running closer and pointing her weapon at the man's head, Jenna raised her voice. "Enough, you're done."

The man roared in anger, head bobbing and teeth flashing like a rabid dog. The next moment Kane reared up, drew back his fist, and punched him hard in the face. The man's head bounced off the blacktop and he lay still.

"This guy is as strong as a bull and as wild as a bobcat." Kane sat on the blacktop rubbing his knuckles and shaking his head.

"It's the killing frenzy. It makes them strong." Carter released his grip on the man's legs and stood, offering Kane his hand.

"It's called hysterical strength. Happens when people's lives are threatened usually. They receive a huge shot of adrenaline and can perform superhuman acts of strength." Rio shrugged as if being a human encyclopedia was normal. "Just sayin'." He wrapped his arms around Piper and whispered to her.

"Somehow, I knew you'd have the answer." Carter went to pick up his hat from the road and returned grinning. "I wish I had your instant recall."

The threat neutralized, Jenna turned her attention to Piper. She holstered her weapon and walked to her, removing her night-vision goggles. "Are you hurt, Piper?"

"She's fine. Just frightened is all." Rio rubbed his sister's back and rocked her like a baby.

"That's him, isn't it?" Piper lifted her face from Rio's chest and stepped away. "The Casanova Killer?"

Frowning and keeping her distance, Jenna turned to look at the prone man. Right now he was just a dark inert mass on the blacktop. "I guess we'll find out soon enough." She searched her pockets for a flashlight and turned to Kane. "Where are your goggles?"

"In the bushes. We'll need to locate them before we leave." Kane stared down at the man. He stood feet apart with one hand resting on his weapon. "Who is this clown? Can you aim your flashlight on him?" He pulled examination gloves from his pocket and snapped them on. "I'll pat him down."

Moving closer with caution, Jenna aimed the beam at the man's face. A red welt had formed under one eye and bruising was evident where Kane had hit him. Scratches down his cheeks made it difficult to identify him in the dim light. His eyes were rolled back in his head, but she could see his chest rising and falling. She took another step toward him and ran the flashlight over him, fully expecting him to rise up and grab her by the throat. He was dressed like a Carter clone, same hat and jacket, and the blond hair was almost the same but not so much the face. This man had a short fat nose, but Carter's was long and straight and he always had a tan. This guy's face was sheet white under the bruising. She looked at Kane. "You sure he's out cold?"

"I'm sure." Kane met her gaze. "He's not going anywhere anytime soon."

Jenna moved the beam back to the man's face and bent to stare a little closer at him and then looked at Kane. "I recognize him. The suspects all look alike but I'm certain that's Dallas Strauss, the ranch hand. Well, I wonder what turned him into a killer?"

"Well, Dallas Strauss, it's all over for you now." Kane pulled a stun gun from Strauss' jacket pocket and held it up to Carter. "Get a photo of this... Wait a minute. He has a Glock in a shoulder holster." He checked him all over and then rolled him over and cuffed him.

Jenna held open an evidence bag and Kane tossed in the weapons and Strauss' wallet and keys. "We caught him in the act, although following someone along the highway seems a little strange."

"Maybe Piper triggered him?" Kane shrugged and straightened his hat.

"I'll go and look for the goggles." Carter used his phone light to search the bushes, coming back with both sets a few minutes later.

"He's going to be out for a while." Kane waved to Rio. "Help me get him off the road and I'll go get my truck. We wouldn't want him squashed by an eighteen-wheeler, duty of care and all."

"It sure would save a long, drawn-out court case." Carter shrugged. "Can we put it to a vote?"

Jenna glared at him. "Absolutely not." Following Kane and Rio to the edge of the forest, she bent to check Strauss' pulse. "He seems okay. You hit him real hard. You could have killed him."

"Nah." Kane smiled at her. "I know how much you and Jo want to get inside these guys' heads. Although, if he'd bitten me, things might have gotten nasty."

Jenna looked at Piper, the girl was hugging her chest, her face ashen. She turned back to Kane. "Where are we going to put him? We can't transport him with Piper."

"I'll ride in the bed with him." Carter shrugged. "If he wakes up, I might just hit him again." He shook his head. "The trouble this jerk has caused me, he'd deserve it. Humph... he doesn't look anything like me. Some people need their eyes tested."

Jenna smiled at him. "I never had any doubt. I mean Thanksgiving and all the holidays wouldn't be the same without you, Ty."

"Yeah, sorry for giving you such a hard time." Kane bent to secure Strauss' ankles. "Walk with me. He's not going anywhere."

"While you're doing that, I'll call Wolfe and bring him up to speed." Jenna pulled out her phone. "I'll ask him to meet us at the office. We'll need swabs from Piper and Strauss."

"That man was in town today." Piper indicated to Strauss and moved to Rio's side. "He's been following me all day, but he was driving a truck. He didn't walk from town. He just suddenly showed up behind me." She pointed toward town. "I heard footsteps back there about five hundred yards or so. I didn't hear a vehicle, so he must have parked off road close by and then followed me."

"Did he say anything to you in town?" Rio put his arm around her. "Did he threaten you or anything? When did you first see him?"

"No, he didn't say a word until just before." Piper explained her encounter with Strauss. "So, I guess I did provoke him. Although, I don't figure he'd heard what I said and he didn't buzz his window down until after. His eyes were like black bottomless pits. At first, he seemed to be there every time I turned around, but then when I headed to your office, he vanished and then showed up here." She took in her brother's worried expression and shrugged. "If he'd been following me when I got to the office, I'd have told you, but he'd gone by then and I figured it was okay."

"If ever anyone is following you, I want you to call me right away." Rio stared down at her. "Don't wait. You came so close to dying tonight I don't want you to ever take a chance like that again."

"I won't and next time I'll take the loaner." Piper blew out a long sigh. "I didn't realize it would take so long to walk home."

At her feet Strauss moaned and his eyes flicked open. Jenna pushed her phone back into her pocket and drew her M18 pistol and aimed it at his face. "Your day isn't going so well, Mr. Strauss. Don't give me an excuse to make it a whole lot worse."

FIFTY-ONE

Wolfe arrived at the sheriff's office with Emily and went straight to Jenna's office. Inside, Piper sat on a chair, sipping hot chocolate awkwardly with plastic bags over each hand. Beside her, Rio was working on a report on his laptop. Keeping his tone casual, he smiled at Piper. "Hey, I hear you had a close call tonight?"

"Yeah, but I'm fine." Piper frowned. "I'm not sure why I can't just go home."

Wolfe nodded. "Ah, that's because I need to take a few swabs and check under your fingernails for skin samples. That's why they bagged your hands. Criminals are slippery and will use any excuse to get away, so we use forensics to assist the DA make a case against them. He attacked you and you fought back. You have three solid witnesses, but we won't use Zac as a witness as he's your brother." He glanced at Emily. "You check the nails and I'll do the preliminary."

"Okay." Emily placed a forensic kit on Jenna's desk and went to work collecting skin samples from under Piper's nails.

Wolfe rested one hip on the edge of the desk, keeping the situation as casual as possible. Piper had suffered a serious shock, and he didn't want to add to the problem. "First of all, are you hurt? Did you suffer any injuries?"

"He pulled my hair." Piper frowned and held out her hand for Emily to check her nails.

Wolfe examined her head and found significant bruising. "I'll need to take a few pictures of your scalp. Em, if you've finished, come here and hold open the hair for me please." He took a camera from his bag and took some close-up shots.

"There's a scratch on her neck, Dad." Emily lifted Piper's hair. "Get a shot of that as well. I'll swab it for DNA traces."

Wolfe looked Piper over again. "You fell onto the blacktop. Did you hurt any part of you? Do you have any bruises?"

"My hands are grazed but that's all." Piper looked at him, her eyes pleading. "I just want to go home."

He nodded. "Okay, I'll take some shots of them as well." He took the shots. "We're nearly done, but before you go home I want you to go to the showers and remove all your outer clothing, place everything in an evidence bag. Emily has a sweatshirt and pants you can wear home. I want Emily to check you don't have any other injuries. We need all the evidence we can find to put your attacker in jail."

"Why all the forensics?" Rio stood staring at him. "She wasn't raped. This is going a little too far. She's exhausted and in shock."

Swinging his attention to Rio, Wolfe smiled. "It's better to have more than less evidence to present in court. So far Piper is the only woman to have survived an attack by this man. I mean to make sure her testimony will be backed by the best forensic evidence available." He indicated toward the passageway. "I'm going down to the cells to take swabs from the accused. In cases with law enforcement as witnesses, it's better to have solid evidence a crime occurred than offer any chance for a lawyer to put doubt into a jury's mind. Everything I'm doing here backs up the witnesses' reports."

He patted Piper on the arm. "We'll see you at Thanksgiving. If you have any headaches or problems, come and see me and I'll run a few tests, but I believe the bruising on your scalp is superficial."

"Okay, thanks." Piper stood and followed Emily to the showers.

Waiting until Piper was out of earshot, Wolfe turned to Rio. "When she's done, take her home and stay with her. She's very calm and the shock of what happened might hit her suddenly. Watch her closely and call me if you need any advice."

"Copy that." Rio nodded his expression serious.

Wolfe headed down to the cells. If Piper's skin was under Strauss' nails and her DNA was present in the scratches on his face, the evidence would be solid. He nodded to himself. Up to now, he'd found nothing to tie Strauss to the killings. Now he had his stun gun and he would bet a dollar to a dime that Strauss never cleaned it between victims.

FIFTY-TWO

After calling Sam Cross, the local defense attorney for Strauss, Jenna went into the interview room with Kane and Carter to discuss their questions for the suspect. Through the open door, she heard footsteps and looked up to see Jo Wells, with a laptop tucked under one arm. "Jo, great to see you."

"I have crucial evidence in the case, exonerating Carter." Jo glanced at Carter. "Oh, I'm glad to see you're on this side of the desk. I figured when Maggie said you were all down here that you were being questioned in relation to the murders."

"No, we caught a guy who looks just like me." Carter smiled around a toothpick, stood, and pulled out a chair for her. "We're just discussing tactics while we're waiting for his lawyer."

"Oh, Sam Cross is here." Jo indicated behind her. "Rowley took him down to the cells."

Jenna leaned back in her chair and looked at Jo. "What evidence do you have?"

"Oh it's incredible and thanks to the fast work of Kalo and Agent Katz—they worked on these media files together—we have the original and altered footage. Here, I'll show you."

Excited, but wary, Jenna held up a hand. "Before we see

this footage give me more information. This is putting the cart before the horse."

"Right." Jo pulled out a notebook. "I have the basics. Agent Katz is writing a full report and has emailed a request to the judge here in town for a search warrant for all computer equipment at the Diamond Bar Ranch. She traced the IP address and found it in seconds." She scanned her notes. "As Kalo believed, deepfake technology was used to alter the footage. The government has many programs to detect deepfakes and he used one to prove Carter's innocence. The person who altered the footage is very proficient. He was able to download the footage and replace it without leaving hardly a trace. As Agent Katz is incredible at cybercrime and so is Kalo, between them they managed to backtrack the files to the perpetrator's hard drive, extract it, and compare it." She grinned. "They hacked the hacker. All this is how Kalo explained it, but a full report will be ready ASAP."

Astonished, Jenna nodded. "I don't quite understand the mechanics of deepfakes, but I have seen the results. It's incredible, but when this type of thing happens, it's terrifying as well."

"Yeah, being falsely accused of murder sure takes some getting used to." Carter removed his hat and ran his fingers around the rim. He winked at Jo. "I knew you and Kalo would come through for me."

"Can we look at the footage?" Kane drummed his fingers on the table. "We'll need to interview Strauss soon. It's getting late and I'd like him out of our hair and cooling his heels in County so we can collect Tauri. He's had a bad week and us being late only makes things worse for him."

Understanding his concern, Jenna squeezed his arm. "I called him before we came down here. I told him we were just next door and would be by after dinner to collect him. He's fine. He gets to watch TV and eat hot dogs."

"Here you go, watch this. You won't believe it." Jo turned her laptop toward them and started a video file.

Two video files ran side by side, one original and one using deepfake. It was without doubt Strauss in the original footage. The altered files showed Carter, and no matter how many times Jenna replayed the files would she have ever believed they were fake. "Oh, that is incredible."

"The problem I see is if Strauss can do this so easily"— Kane's face was like stone—"how long before more criminals learn how to do it? From my understanding it's available software and more and more programs are coming onto the market daily. Unless local law enforcement agencies have access to this new fake-media-detecting technology real fast, video evidence won't be admissible in court before too long."

"Kalo told me there are a ton of detectors available now." Jo looked at Kane. "But you're correct, many small towns won't be aware of the massive step forward in technology." She shook her head. "AI is amazing but I can see many problems ahead. It's moving so fast no one knows what the future will bring. Let's hope it's beneficial."

Jenna looked up as Rowley knocked on the door. She smiled at him. "Can we interview the prisoner?"

"Yeah, Sam Cross says he's ready to talk." Rowley moved his attention to Kane. "Strauss is angry. Sam interviewed him outside the cell. He'll need to be restrained or someone is going to get hurt."

"Not a problem." Kane and Carter stood in unison. "We'll go and get him." He looked at Jenna. "Maybe you and Jo should wait outside until we get him secured."

Jenna nodded and stepped outside, followed by Jo. Rowley wasn't exaggerating when he said Strauss was angry. Shackled hand and foot, Kane had a good hold of him as Carter secured him to the desk. When Sam Cross motioned to Jenna that he wanted to speak to her, she went to his side. She couldn't quite recall when she'd seen the laidback lawyer looking so disturbed. "Is everything okay?"

"He's admitted to killing the women and wants to tell his story." Cross gave her a long searching look. "He'll be pleading guilty to the four counts of murder you're looking to charge him with, and I figure he was hoping someone would stop him. How sound of mind he is, is for the courts to decide, but I'll be asking for an evaluation when we get to court for sentencing."

Jenna nodded. "Did he give you the impression this had been going on for a time before he came to Black Rock Falls?"

"You know I can't discuss my client's thoughts with you, Jenna." Cross hunched his shoulders as if carrying a great weight. "As a sheriff I suggest you do what you normally do to follow up in a homicide."

Raising one eyebrow, Jenna met his gaze. "Yes, I'll follow normal procedure and notify all states. I can't believe he confessed. It sure makes our work easier."

Surprised as Strauss looked anything but cooperative, Jenna indicated toward Jo. "You know Agent Wells. She'd like to get as much information from him as possible. Interviewing psychopaths is her specialty and any information to add to her behavioral research will help us understand what makes them tick."

"I don't figure anyone will understand them or how their minds work." Cross folded his arms across his chest and then shook his head. "I've never met one the same as another, but if she wants to probe his mind, go right ahead. I wouldn't mind finding out why he killed women either."

Waving Jo toward the door, Jenna smiled at her. "He's admitted killing the four women in Black Rock Falls, but I figure this murder spree goes back a little further. He's way too slick to be just starting off on his life of crime. You see what you can get out of him. Rowley already got a signed confession from him."

"Okay, I'll see what I can do." Jo walked past her and into the room.

Flanked by Kane and Carter, with Sam Cross sitting beside Strauss, Jenna relaxed and went through the usual procedure of setting up a recorded interview. She'd already read Strauss his rights in a previous interview. "This is Special Agent Jo Wells. She is a behavioral analyst and author of a number of books on the subject of criminal psychopathic behavior. Are you willing to speak to her?"

"I want to kill both of you right now." Strauss glared at them with black empty eyes. "My lawyer said talking would make things easier for me when I'm sentenced. I know I'm going to jail. Now I know the girl I tried to murder is the sister of a deputy, I've got no chance of walking, have I?"

Unfazed by his anger, Jenna met his gaze. "No, I'm afraid you picked the wrong woman this time."

"What makes you feel like killing, Mr. Strauss?" Jo leaned forward in her chair and tipped her head to one side as if examining him.

"Arrogant women like you and her." Strauss glared at Jenna.

"So this need to kill has been around for a time?" Jo's expression was passive. "When did it start?"

"Right around the time my mom took me to a cop station and left me there. I was six." Strauss spat on the table and glared at them. "Do you know how that feels? No, you don't, do you?"

"That must have been terrifying for a young boy." Jo frowned. "What about your dad? Was he in the picture?"

"Nope." Strauss shrugged. "It got worse from then on."

"Tell me what happened." Jo leaned back in her chair. "It must have been difficult for you."

"It wasn't any different from most kids of the same age and in the same position. Nobody cared. We were just problems to be dealt with. I figure they would have had us euthanized like unwanted pets if it was possible." Strauss lifted one shoulder in a half shrug. "Mine is the usual story I guess you've heard over and over again. I was tossed around in the system for years and when I got out my life changed. I found I could communicate with computers and was very successful at college. My job paid me a fortune from day one. I met other gaming nerds and after hearing their experiences, I figured my resentment toward women was normal. Then I met a girl and my life seemed to be going okay. We got engaged but then she threatened to leave me for another man. I got angry and hit her and she left, but I hunted her down and murdered her." He smiled. "If I couldn't have her, then no one else could. I know all women are like my mom. I give them a chance, act nice, but it takes only one wrong word and I'll murder them. It was messy at first but I got better as I went along." He paused for a beat as if savoring a memory. "I made millions creating games. My money made it easy to hide the murders." He leaned forward, his chains clinking, and stared at Jo. "Do you know you can hire people to clean up a murder scene? Dispose of bodies? It just takes money."

"Do you remember the names of the women you killed?" Jo glanced at Jenna and back to Strauss.

"Yeah, they are all on my computer." Strauss chuckled. "In a code you'll never break."

Jenna needed information. "The stun gun. Did you change the amperage to make it lethal?"

"Nope." Strauss smiled. "I purchased it on the dark web. Did you know you can find anything you like on there and anyone you need?"

The angry man had turned docile and was trying to use his charm. The idea made Jenna's stomach roll. She needed to end this interview. She had a confession and Jo had his reasons for killing. It was time to send Dallas Strauss off to County to await his court hearing. "So I hear." She glanced at Jo, who gave her a nod. "Thank you for being so honest with us. That's all we need for now. My deputy will take your statement and once that's signed you'll be on your way to County. Mr. Cross will advise you what happens next, then my deputies will take you back to the cells."

"Better hope I don't escape, Sheriff." Strauss chuckled and his black eyes bore into her. "I know where you live."

FIFTY-THREE
ONE WEEK LATER

Snow had fallen by the time they arrived home from Eduardo Souza's trial in LA, and the ranch and the surrounding landscape resembled a Christmas card. As the Beast swung into the driveway, Jenna could hear Duke barking. When they arrived at the garage, Duke was tearing around in circles, with Zorro on his heels, looking splendid in a red coat. They climbed from the truck and met Rowley as he walked from the barn. "We're home safe and well." She smiled at him.

"Everything is fine here." Rowley nodded to Kane. "Horses are tended and Jo is in the kitchen cooking supper. I'm guessing you'll all be wanting an early night?"

"Yeah, I'm beat." Carter bent to rub Zorro all over. "I see leaving food in the feeder worked just fine for you." He looked at Kane. "That was a great idea. He knows it's okay to eat from the feeder."

"I told you he was fine." Rowley chuckled. "Although, I had to wait unto he went into the ranch house with Jo before I refilled his food and water. He wouldn't let me in the cottage the first time. That day Jo refilled it."

"I appreciate you watching him for me. He usually prefers

to starve himself to death if I go anywhere without him." Carter hauled his bags from the back of the truck. "I'll drop my things in the cottage and be right back." He headed off, leaving a trail of footprints in the snow with Zorro bounding along beside him.

"Duke is dancing." Tauri rubbed the dog's ears and laughed when Duke licked his cheek.

"He's happy we're home." Kane grinned at the dog's happy dance and patted Tauri on the back. "It's freezing out here. Why don't you head inside and tell Jo we're home? We'll be right along."

"How did the trial go?" Rowley, suddenly serious, looked from one to the other.

"I gave my evidence and the prosecutor says it's a slam dunk." Kane frowned. "We didn't stick around for the jury to make a decision. We wanted to get home. It's safer knowing the people around you. In California, we had federal marshals guarding us during the trial. My time there was two days but I was one of the last witnesses. The lawyers did their summing up and then it went to the jury."

Jenna frowned. "We thought it would drag on forever. Every day I figured someone would crash through the door and try to murder us in our sleep. Nothing happened, no death threats. It's way too quiet. I feel like I'm waiting for the other shoe to drop."

"Carter and Styles are sure they've arrested the major players." Kane pushed his hands into his pockets. "There's no one taking over the cartel from the reports, and all their bank accounts were frozen, all deemed as assets from crime, so they'll never get their hands on the money."

"The trial was on the news and they said the star witness had flown in from overseas." Rowley pulled on his ear. "They said, after an attempt on your life, you took your family to an undisclosed location in France."

Nodding, Jenna looked at Rowley. "No one hereabouts

knows about Dave's involvement in the trial. The men who attacked him are dead. The story of him moving overseas was deliberately leaked to hopefully prevent any living relatives of the cartel searching for him. He was well protected going to court. I wouldn't have recognized him."

"How did they do that?" Rowley raised both eyebrows. "Dave's a little hard to miss."

Jenna laughed. "Smart thinking. They got a skinny, tall federal marshal wearing a baseball cap and hiding his face to pretend to be Dave."

"I went in as one of the four federal marshals guarding the witness. I was wearing a hat and sunglasses. No one gave me a second glance; all the attention was on the skinny guy." Kane grinned. "That was Wolfe's idea and it worked out just fine."

Rubbing her arms, Jenna looked at Rowley. "Come inside, it's freezing out here. I'll make hot chocolate, or coffee if you'd prefer."

"Thanks, but I'll be getting home before the snow gets any deeper." Rowley touched his hat. "We'll drop by over Thanksgiving."

"Thanks for watching the ranch and Jo while we were away. I appreciate it." Kane slapped him on the back. "I owe you one."

"Catch you later." Rowley ambled to his truck with a wave.

Inside the ranch house, Jenna shed her jacket and boots and inhaled the delicious aroma of cooking. The heat from the fire in the family room seeped into her chilled body like a warm hug. It was so good to be home. Footsteps sounded on the polished wooden floors as Tauri and Jo's daughter, Jaime, came running through the house. "Hey, Jaime, good to see you again."

"I've been riding Anna's pony." Jaime grinned at Jenna, showing a missing front tooth.

"I'm getting a horse after the melt." Tauri smiled. "Uncle

Atohi is giving me one. Help me think of a good name." He turned and they went back into the family room.

"He's happy to be home." Kane hung Duke's coat on a peg in the mudroom and dried the dog's legs before straightening. "Now I smell of dog. I'll go and wash up for supper."

Jenna pushed her feet into her slippers and went to the kitchen. She liked Jo and they'd become very close over the years they'd worked together. "Hey."

"There you are." Jo took down cups and poured three cups of coffee. "I had a call from Styles. He's still hanging around the courthouse. He figures the jury will reach a verdict soon. They asked the judge a question and send out a request about five minutes ago."

Jenna frowned. "That will be a fast decision."

"I don't know, it's been eight hours." Jo poured coffee into cups. "I've seen them reach a guilty verdict in four hours. The evidence is compelling and it's not just Dave's testimony. His was the icing on the cake, backed up with all the surveillance footage of the arms deal. They had footage of Eduardo Souza shooting an unarmed man as well. The charges against him are as long as my arm. He won't walk this time." She smiled. "I watched the footage of Dave walking into court. Where was he? I couldn't make him out. All I saw was a hunched guy with a newspaper covering his face."

"I was in the security detail." Kane walked into the room.

Jenna sat down at the table pulling a cup of coffee toward her. "Jo thinks the verdict will come down soon."

"Yeah, they'll all want to be home for Thanksgiving." Kane peered into the pots on the stove and sniffed. "I'm sure he'll be found guilty and it will be wrapped up apart from sentencing tomorrow, for sure."

* * *

The following morning, Jenna woke early and sat up wondering if she'd overslept. She stared at the light peeking through the drapes and climbed from the bed to look outside. Frost covered the window in an intricate icy design. She shivered and rubbed a small hole in the ice to peer out at the thick coating of snow that had fallen overnight. It was the day before Thanksgiving, and she had twenty-four hours to arrange everything for her guests. She had Jo to help her this year and Kane would cook as usual. She slipped on her slippers and robe and padded out to the kitchen, stopping along the way to increase the thermostat on the heating. She filled the coffee pot and stood by the phone making a list of things to do. As usual, Kane had ordered everything they needed, and the turkey would be delivered this morning. The pantry was filled to overflowing, Jo would make her famous pumpkin pies, but maybe Kane needed her to prepare the side dishes.

She counted the guests and made a note. She needed to get chairs from the basement. They always ate in the kitchen. The house did have a dining room but the kitchen was huge and very cozy. The table in there extended and would fit everyone and after dinner it was a great place for her, Jo, Norrell, and Wolfe's girls to sit and chat while the men watched football. This year Atohi Blackhawk had agreed to join them, but Nanny Raya had gone to visit her relatives. She leaned on the counter as the smell of freshly brewed coffee filled the room and looked at the calendar hanging on the wall. Time went by so fast and her birthday was after Christmas. Another year had flown by but next year couldn't come fast enough. There were exciting times ahead. Life with Tauri had changed everything and now they made firm plans for vacations. Her little boy's life was going to be as normal as possible for a child with parents in law enforcement.

When Kane's arms came around her, infusing her body

with warmth, she leaned into him. "I had planned on taking coffee into you for a change."

"I came out to make sure you were okay." Kane pressed a kiss on her cheek. "You've been gone for a time."

Happy and contented, Jenna smiled. "I'm fine. I was making a list of things to do for tomorrow."

"It's a little after five." Kane rested his chin on her shoulder. "Come back to bed. I have everything organized. It's been a stressful couple of weeks and tomorrow you'll have a houseful of guests. Why don't you put your feet up for the rest of the day or play with the kids?"

Giggling, Jenna turned in his arms and cupped his face. "You'll do anything to keep me out of the kitchen, won't you?" She kissed him and then turned back to the counter. "Go back to bed. I'm making the coffee."

"Yes, ma'am."

The day moved along swiftly, and Jenna spent her time filling the drinks refrigerator and getting wine from the cellar. Kane's wine cellar was growing by the year and he was very specific about what he wanted on the table for Thanksgiving. She had a ton of beer as well. With the guys watching football, she'd make sure they had plenty of snacks as well. When Kane's phone rang a little after one, she walked into the kitchen hoping it wasn't a problem. Having to go into the office over Thanksgiving would be a disaster and the team needed a break. She walked into the kitchen and stared at him.

"Okay, thanks for letting me know." Kane disconnected and smiled at Jenna. "That was Styles. The jury found Eduardo Souza guilty on all counts. Sentencing is set for the new year."

Punching the air, Jenna grinned at Jo. "With the confession and the amount of DNA trace evidence found on the stun gun, plus the names of the victims Kalo was able to collect from Strauss' files, hidden among the files on the ranch's computer, we have two criminals off the streets this month. That's a good result if I say so myself."

"It is indeed." Kane went back to stuffing the turkey. "Let's hope we can keep crime-free until after the melt. It will be good to grab some downtime over Christmas."

A cold shiver raised the hairs on the back of Jenna's neck. "There you go again, tempting fate."

EPILOGUE

THANKSGIVING

Thanksgiving was an all-out family affair. Jenna's guests started arriving at noon, and everyone carried a plate of some delicious dish. They had a light lunch together, chatting about everything and nothing, while from the kitchen the fabulous aromas of food cooking drifted along the passageway. Jenna's eyes almost popped out of her head at the sight of so many pumpkin pies and cherry pies along the counter. She looked at Jo. "Will we eat that many pies?"

"Count heads, I figure we have fifteen people and they'll all want pie." Jo waved a hand at the cherry pies. "Those were an afterthought. Just something different for a change. Everything else is traditional. Dave made honey-glazed carrots. I couldn't resist taking a bite and I'm not going home without the recipe." She laughed. "How did you manage to marry such an incredible cook? He makes everything from scratch."

Proud, Jenna's cheeks heated. "Well, he told me he had to learn how to cook or starve when he moved in with me. Well, he realized cooking isn't something I do well. I do a mean burned toast." She laughed. "This is why I'm usually delegated to peeling potatoes or making salads. I can, however clean the house and stack the dishwasher and I'm excellent at laundry."

"It's time to set the table." Kane walked into the kitchen with Tauri and Duke on his heels. "Tauri wants to help, and Duke wants any leftovers before we've eaten." He grinned at Jenna. "I'll spread the tablecloths. The meal is ready and everyone is starving."

The table set and the dishes spread evenly along its length, Kane placed the turkey on the table to the applause of everyone seated. Beside her, Kane took his seat and offered his hands to Jenna on one side and Wolfe on the other. Jenna smiled at him and nodded. She held Tauri's hand and he giggled.

"We thank you, Lord, for this meal you have provided and for the company of our family and friends." Kane looked at Jenna. "You go first."

Jenna looked around the table and her eyes misted. "I'm thankful to have all of you in my life and for having Tauri in our lives."

"I'm thankful for my mommy and daddy and Uncle Atohi and everyone." Tauri grinned.

They went around the table, each person giving thanks. It was a very special moment. It came to Norrell's turn.

"I'm thankful for meeting Shane and finding a new family, who I love and cherish." Norrell leaned against Wolfe and smiled.

"I'm thankful that Norrell has agreed to marry me." Wolfe grinned broadly and lifted their joined hands to display Norrell's engagement ring. "We're thinking maybe June next year."

Heart bursting with joy, Jenna grinned at them. "Congratulations, it's about time."

"Yes, it is." Emily giggled. "We've all been keeping our fingers crossed."

"Okay, Dave." Wolfe smiled at Kane. "Your turn. Please don't tell us you're thankful for buying a new motorcycle."

"Nope." Kane turned to look at Jenna, his eyes moist with unshed tears. "I am so very thankful. Last year Tauri arrived in our lives. To have a wonderful, unexpected gift of a son is mind-blowing. They say miracles happen at the most unexpected times, but two in the space of a year? How is this possible?"

"Two?" Carter leaned forward. "You holding out on us, Dave?"

"Yeah, we have been, but only for a short time." Kane smiled at Jenna and squeezed her hand. "I'm thankful because my beautiful Jenna is pregnant."

A LETTER FROM D.K. HOOD

Dear Reader,

Thank you so much for choosing my novel and coming with me on another adventure with Kane and Alton in *Eyes Tight Shut*.

If you'd like to keep up to date with all my latest releases, just sign up at the website link below. I will never share your email address or spam you, and you can unsubscribe at any time.

www.bookouture.com/dk-hood

What an exciting time ahead for Jenna and Dave! What will the future bring? Black Rock Falls—beautiful one day, Serial Killer Central the next. Is anyone safe? Time will tell when I take you once again on another roller-coaster thrill ride into the unknown in book twenty-three.

If you enjoyed *Eyes Tight Shut*, I would be very grateful if you could leave a review and recommend my book to your friends and family. I really enjoy hearing from readers, so feel free to ask me questions at any time. You can get in touch on my Facebook page or Twitter/X or through my website.

Thank you so much for your support.

D.K. Hood

KEEP IN TOUCH WITH D.K. HOOD

www.dkhood.com

 facebook.com/dkhoodauthor
x.com/DKHood_Author

ACKNOWLEDGMENTS

Many thanks to my editor, Helen Jenner, for her patience and professionalism. I value your guidance and friendship.

To the incredible narrator of my books, Patricia Rodrigues, who brings my characters to life and adds the extra thrill to every page. I can't thank you enough.

To my copy editor, Ian Hodder, for his knowledge and guidance.

Special mention to my proofreader, Claire Rushbrook, who makes sure every copy is perfect.

To Noelle Holten, who always goes the extra mile to promote my books. Thank you so much.

To #TeamBookouture, who are listed at the end of this book. I couldn't have written this series without your support.

To my Facebook friends: Donna Clark, Mandy White, Trudy Newman, Sue Plant, and Brian Rhoads. Many thanks for joining me in Black Rock Falls.

PUBLISHING TEAM

Turning a manuscript into a book requires the efforts of many people. The publishing team at Bookouture would like to acknowledge everyone who contributed to this publication.

Audio
Alba Proko
Sinead O'Connor
Melissa Tran

Commercial
Lauren Morrissette
Hannah Richmond
Imogen Allport

Cover design
Blacksheep

Data and analysis
Mark Alder
Mohamed Bussuri

Editorial
Helen Jenner
Ria Clare